The Illustrated Man

Books by Ray Bradbury

NOVELS

The Martian Chronicles

Fahrenheit 451

Dandelion Wine

Something Wicked This Way Comes

Death Is a Lonely Business

A Graveyard for Lunatics

Green Shadows, White Whale

Ahmed and the Oblivion Machines:
  A Fable

Let's All Kill Constance

Farewell Summer

SHORT STORY COLLECTIONS

Dark Carnival

The Illustrated Man

The Golden Apples of the Sun

The October Country

A Medicine for Melancholy

R Is for Rocket

The Machineries of Joy

The Autumn People

The Vintage Bradbury

S Is for Space

Twice 22

I Sing the Body Electric!

Long After Midnight

The Small Assassin

The Mummies of Guanajuato

Beyond 1984: Remembrance of Things
  Future

This Attic Where the Meadow Greens

The Ghosts of Forever

The Last Circus and the Electrocution

The Stories of Ray Bradbury

The Complete Poems of Ray Bradbury

The Love Affair

Dinosaur Tales

A Memory of Murder

The Climate of Palettes

Classic Stories, Volume One

Classic Stories, Volume Two

Yestermorrow

Quicker Than the Eye

Driving Blind

Ray Bradbury Collected Short Stories

One More for the Road

Bradbury Stories

The Cat's Pajamas

A Sound of Thunder and Other Stories

The Dragon Who Ate His Tail

Now and Forever

Summer Morning, Summer Night

We'll Always Have Paris

A Pleasure to Burn

NONFICTION

The Essence of Creative Writing

Zen in the Art of Writing

The God in Science Fiction

Journey to Far Metaphor

Bradbury Speaks

The
Illustrated Man

_____

Ray Bradbury

HARPER**PERENNIAL** MODERN**CLASSICS**

NEW YORK • LONDON • TORONTO • SYDNEY • NEW DELHI • AUCKLAND

To Henry Kuttner
with my grateful thanks
for his help and encouragement
on this book

HARPER**PERENNIAL** ⬤ MODERN**CLASSICS**

First published in hardcover by Avon Books in 1999, reprinted in hardcover by William Morrow in 2001.

Page 276 constitutes an extension of this copyright page.

First Harper Perennial Modern Classics edition published 2011.

Designed by Kellan Peck

Library of Congress Catalog Card Number: 97-93228

ISBN 978-0-06-207997-8 (pbk.)

15   RRD   10

Dancing, So As Not to Be Dead

An Introduction by
Ray Bradbury

My waiter friend, Laurent, working at the Brasserie Champs du Mars near the Eiffel Tower, one night while serving me *Une Grande Beer*, explained his life.

"I work from ten to twelve hours, sometimes fourteen," he says, "and then at midnight I go dancing, dancing, dancing until four or five in the morning and go to bed and sleep until ten and then up, up and to work by eleven and another ten or twelve or sometimes fifteen hours of work."

"How can you do that?" I ask.

"Easily," he says. "To be asleep is to be dead. It is like death. So we dance, we dance so as not to be dead. We do not want that."

"How old are you?" I ask, at last.

"Twenty-three," he says.

"Ah," I say and take his elbow gently. "Ah. Twenty-three, is it?"

"Twenty-three," he says, smiling. "And *you?*"

"Seventy-six," I say. "And I do not want to be dead, either. But I am not twenty-three. How can I answer? What do *I* do?"

"Yes," says Laurent, still smiling and innocent, "what do *you* do at three in the morning?"

"Write," I say, at last.

"Write!" Laurent says, astonished. *"Write?"*

"So as not to be dead," I say. "Like you."

"Me?"

"Yes," I say, smiling now, myself. "At three in the morning, I write, I write, I write!"

"You are very lucky," says Laurent. "You are very young."

"So far," I say, and finish my beer and go up to my typewriter to finish a story.

What then is my choreography to outwit Death?

In story after story, *The Illustrated Man* hid metaphors aching to explode.

In most cases I don't even know the metaphors lay waiting to be printed off my retina.

We theorize about what goes on in the brain, but it is mostly undiscovered country. A writer's work is to coax the stuff out and see how it plays. Surprise, as I have often said, is everything.

Take "Kaleidoscope," for instance. I decided one morning forty-six years ago to explode a rocket and toss my astronauts out into a wilderness of Space to see what would happen. The result was a story that was reprinted in countless anthologies and appeared and reappeared in high school and college auditoriums. Students across country performed the story in class, to teach me once again that theater doesn't need sets, lights, costumes, or sound. Just actors in school or in someone's garage or storefront speaking the lines and sensing the passion.

Shakespeare's bare stage still stays as prime example. Watching the kids act the dark territory of "Kaleidoscope"

on a bright summer afternoon in San Fernando Valley decided me to write and stage my own version. How do you
cram a million miles of interplanetary flight onto a stage forty
feet wide and twenty deep before an audience of ninety-nine?
You just *do* it. And when the last human meteor fires down
the sky, there's not a dry eye in the house. All Space, Time,
and the heartbeats of seven men are trapped in the words
which, when spoken, set them free.

What if is the operative term for many of these stories.

What if you landed on a far world the day after Christ
had just left to go elsewhere? Or what if He were still there,
waiting? Hence, "The Man."

What if you could create a world within a room, that
forty years later would be dubbed the first Virtual Reality,
and introduced a family to that room where it's walls might
operate on their psyches and deliver forth nightmares? I built
the room on my typewriter and let my family prowl. By noon
the lions had leaped off the walls and my children were
having tea at the *finale*.

What if a man could order a Marionette Robot that was
his exact clone? What would happen if he left it with his
wife while he went out nights? "Marionettes, Inc."

What if all your favorite childhood authors hid out on
Mars because their books were being burned on Earth? "The
Exiles." The start of more fires I would light with books three
years later: *Fahrenheit 451*.

What if the Colored people (that's what they were called
when I wrote "The Other Foot" in 1949) arrived on Mars
first, put down roots, built towns, and prepared to welcome
the Whites when they arrived? What would happen next? I
wrote the story to find out. Then, I couldn't find an American
magazine that would buy the story. It was long before the

Civil Rights movement, the Cold War was starting up, and the House UnAmerican Committee was holding hearings headed by Parnell Thomas (Joseph McCarthy arrived later). In such an atmosphere no editor wanted to land on Mars with my dark immigrants. I finally gave "The Other Foot" to *New Story*, a Paris-based magazine edited by Martha Foley's son, David.

And again, *What if* you had an acre of junk in your backyard? Would you be tempted to weld it together and take a journey to the Moon? There was just such a junkyard forty feet behind my house in Tucson, Arizona, when I was twelve. There I made lunar trips on late afternoons and then ran to a locomotive elephants' graveyard two blocks away where I climbed up in abandoned steam engines to whistle-stop my way to Kankakee, Oswego, and far Rockaway. Between the junkyard rocket and the long-lost locomotives, I was never home. Thus, "The Rocket."

The *What ifs* ricocheted around in my head.

In other words, the left side of my brain, if there *is* a left side, proposed. The right side of my brain, if there *is* a right side, disposed.

No use proposing on the left if there is no one home on the right. I was lucky in my genetics. God, the Cosmos, the Life Force, what ever fits, gave me the right side as ball-catcher for anything the stuff from left field pitched over the plate. One half, the left, seems obvious. The other half, the right, stays mysterious, daring you to fetch it out in the light.

The seance, which is to say the typewriter, computer, pen, pencil, and paper are there to catch the ghosts before they thin out in midair.

Cut the comedy, my father would grouch. What do you mean in plain English?

What I'm trying to say is that the creative process is much like the old-fashioned way of taking photos with a huge camera and you horsing around under a black cloth seeking pictures in the dark. The subjects might not have stood still. There might have been too much light. Or not enough. One can only fumble, but fumble quickly, hoping for a developed snap.

These then are developed snaps, roused at dawn, posed at breakfast, and finalized by noon. All with no *finales* at 10:00 A.M., all with happy or unhappy endings just after lunch or with weak coffee and strong brandy at four.

Taking a chance on love, as one old song put it.

Or in the words of Mel Brooks' Twelve Chairs song:

> *"Hope for the best,*
> *Expect the worst,*
> *You could be Tolstoy*
> *Or Fannie Hurst."*

I hoped for H. G. Wells or to share company with Jules Verne. When I worked out a living space between the two I was ecstatic.

I end as I began. With my Parisian waiter friend, Laurent, dancing all night, dancing, dancing.

My tunes and numbers are here. They have filled my years, the years when I refused to die. And in order to do that I wrote, I wrote, I wrote, at noon or 3:00 A.M.

So as not to be dead.

Contents

Prologue:
The Illustrated Man

*I*t was a warm afternoon in early September when I first met the Illustrated Man. Walking along an asphalt road, I was on the final leg of a two weeks' walking tour of Wisconsin. Late in the afternoon I stopped, ate some pork, beans, and a doughnut, and was preparing to stretch out and read when the Illustrated Man walked over the hill and stood for a moment against the sky.

I didn't know he was Illustrated then. I only knew that he was tall, once well muscled, but now, for some reason, going to fat. I recall that his arms were long, and the hands thick, but that his face was like a child's, set upon a massive body.

He seemed only to sense my presence, for he didn't look directly at me when he spoke his first words:

"Do you know where I can find a job?"

"I'm afraid not," I said.

"I haven't had a job that's lasted in forty years," he said.

Though it was a hot late afternoon, he wore his wool shirt buttoned tight about his neck. His sleeves were rolled and buttoned down over his thick wrists. Perspiration was streaming from his face, yet he made no move to open his shirt.

"Well," he said at last, "this is as good a place as any to spend the night. Do you mind company?"

"I have some extra food you'd be welcome to," I said.

He sat down heavily, grunting. "You'll be sorry you asked me to stay," he said. "Everyone always is. That's why I'm walking. Here it is, early September, the cream of the Labor Day carnival season. I should be making money hand over fist at any small town side show celebration, but here I am with no prospects."

He took off an immense shoe and peered at it closely. "I usually keep a job about ten days. Then something happens and they fire me. By now every carnival in America won't touch me with a ten-foot pole."

"What seems to be the trouble?" I asked.

For answer, he unbuttoned his tight collar, slowly. With his eyes shut, he put a slow hand to the task of unbuttoning his shirt all the way down. He slipped his fingers in to feel his chest. "Funny," he said, eyes still shut. "You can't feel them but they're there. I always hope that someday I'll look and they'll be gone. I walk in the sun for hours on the hottest days, baking, and hope that my sweat'll wash them off, the sun'll cook them off, but at sundown they're still there." He turned his head slightly toward me and exposed his chest. "Are they still there now?"

After a long while I exhaled. "Yes," I said. "They're still there."

The Illustrations.

"Another reason I keep my collar buttoned up," he said, opening his eyes, "is the children. They follow me along country roads. Everyone wants to see the pictures, and yet nobody wants to see them."

He took his shirt off and wadded it in his hands. He was covered with Illustrations from the blue tattooed ring about his neck to his belt line.

"It keeps right on going," he said, guessing my thought. "All of me is Illustrated. Look." He opened his hand. On his palm was a rose, freshly cut, with drops of crystal water among the soft pink petals. I put my hand out to touch it, but it was only an Illustration.

As for the rest of him, I cannot say how I sat and stared, for he was a riot of rockets and fountains and people, in such intricate detail and color that you could hear the voices murmuring small and muted, from the crowds that inhabited his body. When his flesh twitched, the tiny mouths flickered, the tiny green-and-gold eyes winked, the tiny pink hands gestured. There were yellow meadows and blue rivers and mountains and stars and suns and planets spread in a Milky Way across his chest. The people themselves were in twenty or more odd groups upon his arms, shoulders, back, sides, and wrists, as well as on the flat of his stomach. You found them in forests of hair, lurking among a constellation of freckles, or peering from armpit caverns, diamond eyes aglitter. Each seemed intent upon his own activity; each was a separate gallery portrait.

"Why, they're beautiful!" I said.

How can I explain about his Illustrations? If El Greco had painted miniatures in his prime, no bigger than your hand, infinitely detailed, with all his sulphurous color, elongation, and anatomy, perhaps he might have used this man's body for his art. The colors burned in three dimensions. They were windows looking in upon fiery reality. Here, gathered on one wall, were all the finest scenes in the universe; the man was a walking treasure gallery. This wasn't the work of a cheap carnival tattoo man with three colors and whisky on his breath. This was the accomplishment of a living genius, vibrant, clear, and beautiful.

"Oh, yes," said the Illustrated Man. "I'm so proud of my Illustrations that I'd like to burn them off. I've tried sandpaper, acid, a knife . . ."

The sun was setting. The moon was already up in the East.

"For, you see," said the Illustrated Man, "these Illustrations predict the future."

I said nothing.

"It's all right in sunlight," he went on. "I could keep a carnival day job. But at night—the pictures move. The pictures change."

I must have smiled. "How long have you been Illustrated?"

"In 1900, when I was twenty years old and working a carnival,

I broke my leg. It laid me up; I had to do something to keep my hand in, so I decided to get tattooed."

"But who tattooed you? What happened to the artist?"

"She went back to the future," he said. "I mean it. She was an old woman in a little house in the middle of Wisconsin here somewhere not far from this place. A little old witch who looked a thousand years old one moment and twenty years old the next, but she said she could travel in time. I laughed. Now, I know better."

"How did you happen to meet her?"

He told me. He had seen her painted sign by the road: SKIN ILLUSTRATION! Illustration instead of tattoo! Artistic! So he had sat all night while her magic needles stung him wasp stings and delicate bee stings. By morning he looked like a man who had fallen into a twenty-color print press and been squeezed out, all bright and picturesque.

"I've hunted every summer for fifty years," he said, putting his hands out on the air. "When I find that witch I'm going to kill her."

The sun was gone. Now the first stars were shining and the moon had brightened the fields of grass and wheat. Still the Illustrated Man's pictures glowed like charcoals in the half light, like scattered rubies and emeralds, with Rouault colors and Picasso colors and the long, pressed-out El Greco bodies.

"So people fire me when my pictures move. They don't like it when violent things happen in my Illustrations. Each Illustration is a little story. If you watch them, in a few minutes they tell you a tale. In three hours of looking you could see eighteen or twenty stories acted right on my body, you could hear voices and think thoughts. It's all here, just waiting for you to look. But most of all, there's a special spot on my body." He bared his back. "See?" There's no special design on my right shoulder blade, just a jumble."

"Yes."

"When I've been around a person long enough, that spot clouds

over and fills in. If I'm with a woman, her picture comes there on my
back, in an hour, and shows her whole life—how she'll live, how she'll
die, what she'll look like when she's sixty. And if it's a man, an hour
later his picture's here on my back. It shows him falling off a cliff, or
dying under a train. So I'm fired again."

All the time he had been talking his hands had wandered over the
Illustrations, as if to adjust their frames, to brush away dust—the
motions of a connoisseur, an art patron. Now he lay back, long and
full in the moonlight. It was a warm night. There was no breeze and
the air was stifling. We both had our shirts off.

"And you've never found the old woman?"

"Never."

"And you think she came from the future?"

"How else could she know these stories she painted on me?"

He shut his eyes tiredly. His voice grew fainter. "Sometimes at
night I can feel them, the pictures, like ants, crawling on my skin. Then
I know they're doing what they have to do. I never look at them any
more. I just try to rest. I don't sleep much. Don't you look at them
either, I warn you. Turn the other way when you sleep."

I lay back a few feet from him. He didn't seem violent, and the
pictures were beautiful. Otherwise I might have been tempted to get out
and away from such babbling. But the Illustrations . . . I let my eyes
fill up on them. Any person would go a little mad with such things
upon his body.

The night was serene. I could hear the Illustrated Man's breathing
in the moonlight. Crickets were stirring gently in the distant ravines. I
lay with my body sidewise so I could watch the Illustrations. Perhaps
half an hour passed. Whether the Illustrated Man slept I could not tell,
but suddenly I heard him whisper, "They're moving, aren't they?"

I waited a minute.

Then I said, "Yes."

The pictures were moving, each in its turn, each for a brief minute or two. There in the moonlight, with the tiny tinkling thoughts and the distant sea voices, it seemed, each little drama was enacted. Whether it took an hour or three hours for the dramas to finish, it would be hard to say. I only know that I lay fascinated and did not move while the stars wheeled in the sky.

Eighteen Illustrations, eighteen tales. I counted them one by one.

Primarily my eyes focused upon a scene, a large house with two people in it. I saw a flight of vultures on a blazing flesh sky, I saw yellow lions, and I heard voices.

The first Illustration quivered and came to life. . . .

The Veldt

"George, I wish you'd look at the nursery."
          "What's wrong with it?"
"I don't know."
"Well, then."
"I just want you to look at it, is all, or call a psychologist in to look at it."
"What would a psychologist want with a nursery?"
"You know very well what he'd want." His wife paused in the middle of the kitchen and watched the stove busy humming to itself, making supper for four.
"It's just that the nursery is different now than it was."
"All right, let's have a look."
They walked down the hall of their soundproofed, Happy-life Home, which had cost them thirty thousand dollars installed, this house which clothed and fed and rocked them to sleep and played and sang and was good to them. Their approach sensitized a switch somewhere and the nursery light flicked on when they came within ten feet of it. Similarly, behind them, in the halls, lights went on and off as they left them behind, with a soft automaticity.

"Well," said George Hadley.

They stood on the thatched floor of the nursery. It was forty feet across by forty feet long and thirty feet high; it had cost half again as much as the rest of the house. "But nothing's too good for our children," George had said.

The nursery was silent. It was empty as a jungle glade at hot high noon. The walls were blank and two dimensional. Now, as George and Lydia Hadley stood in the center of the room, the walls began to purr and recede into crystalline distance, it seemed, and presently an African veldt appeared, in three dimensions, on all sides, in colors reproduced to the final pebble and bit of straw. The ceiling above them became a deep sky with a hot yellow sun.

George Hadley felt the perspiration start on his brow.

"Let's get out of this sun," he said. "This is a little too real. But I don't see anything wrong."

"Wait a moment, you'll see," said his wife.

Now the hidden odorophonics were beginning to blow a wind of odor at the two people in the middle of the baked veldtland. The hot straw smell of lion grass, the cool green smell of the hidden water hole, the great rusty smell of animals, the smell of dust like a red paprika in the hot air. And now the sounds: the thump of distant antelope feet on grassy sod, the papery rustling of vultures. A shadow passed through the sky. The shadow flickered on George Hadley's upturned, sweating face.

"Filthy creatures," he heard his wife say.

"The vultures."

"You see, there are the lions, far over, that way. Now they're on their way to the water hole. They've just been eating," said Lydia. "I don't know what."

"Some animal." George Hadley put his hand up to shield

off the burning light from his squinted eyes. "A zebra or a baby giraffe, maybe."

"Are you sure?" His wife sounded peculiarly tense.

"No, it's a little late to be *sure*," he said, amused. "Nothing over there I can see but cleaned bone, and the vultures dropping for what's left."

"Did you hear that scream?" she asked.

"No."

"About a minute ago?"

"Sorry, no."

The lions were coming. And again George Hadley was filled with admiration for the mechanical genius who had conceived this room. A miracle of efficiency selling for an absurdly low price. Every home should have one. Oh, occasionally they frightened you with their clinical accuracy, they startled you, gave you a twinge, but most of the time what fun for everyone, not only your own son and daughter, but for yourself when you felt like a quick jaunt to a foreign land, a quick change of scenery. Well, here it was!

And here were the lions now, fifteen feet away, so real, so feverishly and startlingly real that you could feel the prickling fur on your hand, and your mouth was stuffed with the dusty upholstery smell of their heated pelts, and the yellow of them was in your eyes like the yellow of an exquisite French tapestry, the yellows of lions and summer grass, and the sound of the matted lion lungs exhaling on the silent noontide, and the smell of meat from the panting, dripping mouths.

The lions stood looking at George and Lydia Hadley with terrible green-yellow eyes.

"Watch out!" screamed Lydia.

The lions came running at them.

Lydia bolted and ran. Instinctively, George sprang after her. Outside in the hall, with the door slammed, he was laughing and she was crying, and they both stood appalled at the other's reaction.

"George!"

"Lydia! Oh, my dear poor sweet Lydia!"

"They almost got us!"

"Walls, Lydia, remember; crystal walls, that's all they are. Oh, they look real, I must admit—Africa in your parlor—but it's all dimensional superactionary, supersensitive color film and mental tape film behind glass screens. It's all odorophonics and sonics, Lydia. Here's my handkerchief."

"I'm afraid." She came to him and put her body against him and cried steadily. "Did you see? Did you feel? It's too real."

"Now, Lydia . . ."

"You've got to tell Wendy and Peter not to read any more on Africa."

"Of course—of course." He patted her.

"Promise?"

"Sure."

"And lock the nursery for a few days until I get my nerves settled."

"You know how difficult Peter is about that. When I punished him a month ago by locking the nursery for even a few hours—the tantrum he threw! And Wendy too. They *live* for the nursery."

"It's got to be locked, that's all there is to it."

"All right." Reluctantly he locked the huge door. "You've been working too hard. You need a rest."

"I don't know—I don't know," she said, blowing her nose, sitting down in a chair that immediately began to rock and comfort her. "Maybe I don't have enough to do. Maybe I have time to think too much. Why don't we shut the whole house off for a few days and take a vacation?"

"You mean you want to fry my eggs for me?"

"Yes." She nodded.

"And darn my socks?"

"Yes." A frantic, watery-eyed nodding.

"And sweep the house?"

"Yes, yes—oh, yes!"

"But I thought that's why we bought this house, so we wouldn't have to do anything?"

"That's just it. I feel like I don't belong here. The house is wife and mother now and nursemaid. Can I compete with an African veldt? Can I give a bath and scrub the children as efficiently or quickly as the automatic scrub bath can? I cannot. And it isn't just me. It's you. You've been awfully nervous lately."

"I suppose I have been smoking too much."

"You look as if you didn't know what to do with yourself in this house, either. You smoke a little more every morning and drink a little more every afternoon and need a little more sedative every night. You're beginning to feel unnecessary too."

"Am I?" He paused and tried to feel into himself to see what was really there.

"Oh, George!" She looked beyond him, at the nursery door. "Those lions can't get out of there, can they?"

He looked at the door and saw it tremble as if something had jumped against it from the other side.

"Of course not," he said.

*   *   *

At dinner they ate alone, for Wendy and Peter were at a special plastic carnival across town and had televised home to say they'd be late, to go ahead eating. So George Hadley, bemused, sat watching the dining-room table produce warm dishes of food from its mechanical interior.

"We forgot the ketchup," he said.

"Sorry," said a small voice within the table, and ketchup appeared.

As for the nursery, thought George Hadley, it won't hurt for the children to be locked out of it awhile. Too much of anything isn't good for anyone. And it was clearly indicated that the children had been spending a little too much time on Africa. That *sun.* He could feel it on his neck, still, like a hot paw. And the *lions.* And the smell of blood. Remarkable how the nursery caught the telepathic emanations of the children's minds and created life to fill their every desire. The children thought lions, and there were lions. The children thought zebras, and there were zebras. Sun—sun. Giraffes—giraffes. Death and death.

That *last.* He chewed tastelessly on the meat that the table had cut for him. Death thoughts. They were awfully young, Wendy and Peter, for death thoughts. Or, no, you were never too young, really. Long before you knew what death was you were wishing it on someone else. When you were two years old you were shooting people with cap pistols.

But this—the long, hot African veldt—the awful death in the jaws of a lion. And repeated again and again.

"Where are you going?"

He didn't answer Lydia. Preoccupied, he let the lights glow softly on ahead of him, extinguish behind him as he padded to the nursery door. He listened against it. Far away, a lion roared.

He unlocked the door and opened it. Just before he stepped inside, he heard a faraway scream. And then another roar from the lions, which subsided quickly.

He stepped into Africa. How many times in the last year had he opened this door and found Wonderland, Alice, the Mock Turtle, or Aladdin and his Magical Lamp, or Jack Pumpkinhead of Oz, or Dr. Doolittle, or the cow jumping over a very real-appearing moon—all the delightful contraptions of a make-believe world. How often had he seen Pegasus flying in the sky ceiling, or seen fountains of red fireworks, or heard angel voices singing. But now, this yellow hot Africa, this bake oven with murder in the heat. Perhaps Lydia was right. Perhaps they needed a little vacation from the fantasy which was growing a bit too real for ten-year-old children. It was all right to exercise one's mind with gymnastic fantasies, but when the lively child mind settled on one pattern . . . ? It seemed that, at a distance, for the past month, he had heard lions roaring, and smelled their strong odor seeping as far away as his study door. But, being busy, he had paid it no attention.

George Hadley stood on the African grassland alone. The lions looked up from their feeding, watching him. The only flaw to the illusion was the open door through which he could see his wife, far down the dark hall, like a framed picture, eating her dinner abstractedly.

"Go away," he said to the lions.

They did not go.

He knew the principle of the room exactly. You sent out your thoughts. Whatever you thought would appear.

"Let's have Aladdin and his lamp," he snapped.

The veldtland remained; the lions remained.

"Come on, room! I demand Aladdin!" he said.

Nothing happened. The lions mumbled in their baked pelts.

"Aladdin!"

He went back to dinner. "The fool room's out of order," he said. "It won't respond."

"Or—"

"Or what?"

"Or it *can't* respond." said Lydia, "because the children have thought about Africa and lions and killing so many days that the room's in a rut."

"Could be."

"Or Peter's set it to remain that way."

"*Set* it?"

"He may have got into the machinery and fixed something."

"Peter doesn't know machinery."

"He's a wise one for ten. That I.Q. of his—"

"Nevertheless—"

"Hello, Mom. Hello, Dad."

The Hadleys turned. Wendy and Peter were coming in the front door, cheeks like peppermint candy, eyes like bright blue agate marbles, a smell of ozone on their jumpers from their trip in the helicopter.

"You're just in time for supper," said both parents.

"We're full of strawberry ice cream and hot dogs," said the children, holding hands. "But we'll sit and watch."

"Yes, come tell us about the nursery," said George Hadley.

The brother and sister blinked at him and then at each other. "Nursery?"

"All about Africa and everything," said the father with false joviality.

"I don't understand," said Peter.

"Your mother and I were just traveling through Africa with rod and reel; Tom Swift and his Electric Lion," said George Hadley.

"There's no Africa in the nursery," said Peter simply.

"Oh, come now, Peter. We know better."

"I don't remember any Africa," said Peter to Wendy. "Do you?"

"No."

"Run see and come tell."

She obeyed.

"Wendy, come back here!" said George Hadley, but she was gone. The house lights followed her like a flock of fireflies. Too late, he realized he had forgotten to lock the nursery door after his last inspection.

"Wendy'll look and come tell us," said Peter.

"She doesn't have to tell *me*. I've seen it."

"I'm sure you're mistaken, Father."

"I'm not, Peter. Come along now."

But Wendy was back. "It's not Africa," she said breathlessly.

"We'll see about this," said George Hadley, and they all walked down the hall together and opened the nursery door.

There was a green, lovely forest, a lovely river, a purple mountain, high voices singing, and Rima, lovely and mysterious, lurking in the trees with colorful flights of butterflies, like animated bouquets, lingering in her long hair. The African veldtland was gone. The lions were gone. Only Rima was here now, singing a song so beautiful that it brought tears to your eyes.

George Hadley looked in at the changed scene. "Go to bed," he said to the children.

They opened their mouths.

"You heard me," he said.

They went off to the air closet, where a wind sucked them like brown leaves up the flue to their slumber rooms.

George Hadley walked through the singing glade and picked up something that lay in the corner near where the lions had been. He walked slowly back to his wife.

"What is that?" she asked.

"An old wallet of mine," he said.

He showed it to her. The smell of hot grass was on it and the smell of a lion. There were drops of saliva on it, it had been chewed, and there were blood smears on both sides.

He closed the nursery door and locked it, tight.

In the middle of the night he was still awake and he knew his wife was awake. "Do you think Wendy changed it?" she said at last, in the dark room.

"Of course."

"Made it from a veldt into a forest and put Rima there instead of lions?"

"Yes."

"Why?"

"I don't know. But it's staying locked until I find out."

"How did your wallet get there?"

"I don't know anything," he said, "except that I'm beginning to be sorry we bought that room for the children. If children are neurotic at all, a room like that—"

"It's supposed to help them work off their neuroses in a healthful way."

"I'm starting to wonder." He stared at the ceiling.

"We've given the children everything they ever wanted. Is this our reward—secrecy, disobedience?"

"Who was it said, 'Children are carpets, they should be stepped on occasionally'? We've never lifted a hand. They're insufferable—let's admit it. They come and go when they like; they treat us as if *we* were offspring. They're spoiled and we're spoiled."

"They've been acting funny ever since you forbade them to take the rocket to New York a few months ago."

"They're not old enough to do that alone, I explained."

"Nevertheless, I've noticed they've been decidedly cool toward us since."

"I think I'll have David McClean come tomorrow morning to have a look at Africa."

"But it's not Africa now, it's Green Mansions country and Rima."

"I have a feeling it'll be Africa again before then."

A moment later they heard the screams.

Two screams. Two people screaming from downstairs. And then a roar of lions.

"Wendy and Peter aren't in their rooms," said his wife.

He lay in his bed with his beating heart. "No," he said. "They've broken into the nursery."

"Those screams—they sound familiar."

"Do they?"

"Yes, awfully."

And, although their beds tried very hard, the two adults couldn't be rocked to sleep for another hour. A smell of cats was in the night air.

"Father?" said Peter.

"Yes."

Peter looked at his shoes. He never looked at his father anymore, nor at his mother. "You aren't going to lock up the nursery for good, are you?"

"That all depends."

"On what?" snapped Peter.

"On you and your sister. If you intersperse this Africa with a little variety—oh, Sweden perhaps, or Denmark or China—"

"I thought we were free to play as we wished."

"You are, within reasonable bounds."

"What's wrong with Africa, Father?"

"Oh, so now you admit you have been conjuring up Africa, do you?"

"I wouldn't want the nursery locked up," said Peter coldly. "Ever."

"Matter of fact, we're thinking of turning the whole house off for about a month. Live sort of a carefree one-for-all existence."

"That sounds dreadful! Would I have to tie my own shoes instead of letting the shoe tier do it? And brush my own teeth and comb my hair and give myself a bath?"

"It would be fun for a change, don't you think?"

"No, it would be horrid. I didn't like it when you took out the picture painter last month."

"That's because I wanted you to learn to paint all by yourself, son."

"I don't want to do anything but look and listen and smell; what else *is* there to do?"

"All right, go play in Africa."

"Will you shut off the house sometime soon?"

"We're considering it."

"I don't think you'd better consider it any more, Father."

"I won't have any threats from my son!"

"Very well." And Peter strolled off to the nursery.

"Am I on time?" said David McClean.

"Breakfast?" asked George Hadley.

"Thanks, had some. What's the trouble?"

"David, you're a psychologist."

"I should hope so."

"Well, then, have a look at our nursery. You saw it a year ago when you dropped by; did you notice anything peculiar about it then?"

"Can't say I did; the usual violences, a tendency toward a slight paranoia here or there, usual in children because they feel persecuted by parents constantly, but, oh, really nothing."

They walked down the hall. "I locked the nursery up," explained the father, "and the children broke back into it during the night. I let them stay so they could form the patterns for you to see."

There was a terrible screaming from the nursery.

"There it is," said George Hadley. "See what you make of it."

They walked in on the children without rapping.

The screams had faded. The lions were feeding.

"Run outside a moment, children," said George Hadley. "No, don't change the mental combination. Leave the walls as they are. Get!"

With the children gone, the two men stood studying the lions clustered at a distance, eating with great relish whatever it was they had caught.

"I wish I knew what it was," said George Hadley. "Sometimes I can almost see. Do you think if I brought high-powered binoculars here and—"

David McClean laughed dryly. "Hardly." He turned to study all four walls. "How long has this been going on?"

"A little over a month."

"It certainly doesn't *feel* good."

"I want facts, not feelings."

"My dear George, a psychologist never saw a fact in his life. He only hears about feelings; vague things. This doesn't feel good, I tell you. Trust my hunches and my instincts. I have a nose for something bad. This is very bad. My advice to you is to have the whole damn room torn down and your children brought to me every day during the next year for treatment."

"Is it that bad?"

"I'm afraid so. One of the original uses of these nurseries was so that we could study the patterns left on the walls by the child's mind, study at our leisure, and help the child. In this case, however, the room has become a channel toward—destructive thoughts, instead of a release away from them."

"Didn't you sense this before?"

"I sensed only that you had spoiled your children more than most. And now you're letting them down in some way. What way?"

"I wouldn't let them go to New York."

"What else?"

"I've taken a few machines from the house and threatened them, a month ago, with closing up the nursery unless they did their homework. I did close it for a few days to show I meant business."

"Ah, ha!"

"Does that mean anything?"

"Everything. Where before they had a Santa Claus now they have a Scrooge. Children prefer Santa. You've let this room and this house replace you and your wife in your children's affections. This room is their mother and father, far more important in their lives than their real parents. And now you come along and want to shut it off. No wonder there's hatred here. You can feel it coming out of the sky. Feel that sun. George, you'll have to change your life. Like too many others, you've built it around creature comforts. Why, you'd starve tomorrow if something went wrong in your kitchen. You wouldn't know how to tap an egg. Nevertheless, turn everything off. Start new. It'll take time. But we'll make good children out of bad in a year, wait and see."

"But won't the shock be too much for the children, shutting the room up abruptly, for good?"

"I don't want them going any deeper into this, that's all."

The lions were finished with their red feast.

The lions were standing on the edge of the clearing watching the two men.

"Now *I'm* feeling persecuted," said McClean. "Let's get out of here. I never have cared for these damned rooms. Make me nervous."

"The lions look real, don't they?" said George Hadley. "I don't suppose there's any way—"

"What?"

"—that they could *become* real?"

"Not that I know."

"Some flaw in the machinery, a tampering or something?"

"No."

They went to the door.

"I don't imagine the room will like being turned off," said the father.

"Nothing ever likes to die—even a room."

"I wonder if it hates me for wanting to switch it off?"

"Paranoia is thick around here today," said David McClean. "You can follow it like a spoor. Hello." He bent and picked up a bloody scarf. "This yours?"

"No." George Hadley's face was rigid. "It belongs to Lydia."

They went to the fuse box together and threw the switch that killed the nursery.

The two children were in hysterics. They screamed and pranced and threw things. They yelled and sobbed and swore and jumped at the furniture.

"You can't do that to the nursery, you can't!"

"Now, children."

The children flung themselves onto a couch, weeping.

"George," said Lydia Hadley, "turn on the nursery, just for a few moments. You can't be so abrupt."

"No."

"You can't be so cruel."

"Lydia, it's off, and it stays off. And the whole damn house dies as of here and now. The more I see of the mess we've put ourselves in, the more it sickens me. We've been contemplating our mechanical, electronic navels for too long. My God, how we need a breath of honest air!"

And he marched about the house turning off the voice clocks, the stoves, the heaters, the shoe shiners, the shoe lacers, the body scrubbers and swabbers and massagers, and every other machine he could put his hand to.

The house was full of dead bodies, it seemed. It felt like

a mechanical cemetery. So silent. None of the humming hidden energy of machines waiting to function at the tap of a button.

"Don't let them do it!" wailed Peter at the ceiling, as if he was talking to the house, the nursery. "Don't let Father kill everything." He turned to his father. "Oh, I hate you!"

"Insults won't get you anywhere."

"I wish you were dead!"

"We were, for a long while. Now we're going to really start living. Instead of being handled and massaged, we're going to *live*."

Wendy was still crying and Peter joined her again. "Just a moment, just one moment, just another moment of nursery," they wailed.

"Oh, George," said the wife, "it can't hurt."

"All right—all right, if they'll only just shut up. One minute, mind you, and then off forever."

"Daddy, Daddy, Daddy!" sang the children, smiling with wet faces.

"And then we're going on a vacation. David McClean is coming back in half an hour to help us move out and get to the airport. I'm going to dress. You turn the nursery on for a minute, Lydia, just a minute, mind you."

And the three of them went babbling off while he let himself be vacuumed upstairs through the air flue and set about dressing himself. A minute later Lydia appeared.

"I'll be glad when we get away," she sighed.

"Did you leave them in the nursery?"

"I wanted to dress too. Oh, that horrid Africa. What can they see in it?"

"Well, in five minutes we'll be on our way to Iowa. Lord,

how did we ever get in this house? What prompted us to buy a nightmare?"

"Pride, money, foolishness."

"I think we'd better get downstairs before those kids get engrossed with those damned beasts again."

Just then they heard the children calling, "Daddy, Mommy, come quick—quick!"

They went downstairs in the air flue and ran down the hall. The children were nowhere in sight. "Wendy? Peter!"

They ran into the nursery. The veldtland was empty save for the lions waiting, looking at them. "Peter, Wendy?"

The door slammed.

"Wendy, Peter!"

George Hadley and his wife whirled and ran back to the door.

"Open the door!" cried George Hadley, trying the knob. "Why, they've locked it from the outside! Peter!" He beat at the door. "Open up!"

He heard Peter's voice outside, against the door.

"Don't let them switch off the nursery and the house," he was saying.

Mr. and Mrs. George Hadley beat at the door. "Now, don't be ridiculous, children. It's time to go. Mr. McClean'll be here in a minute and . . ."

And then they heard the sounds.

The lions on three sides of them, in the yellow veldt grass, padding through the dry straw, rumbling and roaring in their throats.

The lions.

Mr. Hadley looked at his wife and they turned and looked back at the beasts edging slowly forward, crouching, tails stiff.

Mr. and Mrs. Hadley screamed.

And suddenly they realized why those other screams had sounded familiar.

"Well, here I am," said David McClean in the nursery doorway. "Oh, hello." He stared at the two children seated in the center of the open glade eating a little picnic lunch. Beyond them was the water hole and the yellow veldtland; above was the hot sun. He began to perspire. "Where are your father and mother?"

The children looked up and smiled. "Oh, they'll be here directly."

"Good, we must get going." At a distance Mr. McClean saw the lions fighting and clawing and then quieting down to feed in silence under the shady trees.

He squinted at the lions with his hand up to his eyes.

Now the lions were done feeding. They moved to the water hole to drink.

A shadow flickered over Mr. McClean's hot face. Many shadows flickered. The vultures were dropping down the blazing sky.

"A cup of tea?" asked Wendy in the silence.

The Illustrated Man shifted in his sleep. He turned, and each time he turned another picture came to view, coloring his back, his arm, his wrist. He flung a hand over the dry night grass. The fingers uncurled and there upon his palm another Illustration stirred to life. He twisted, and on his chest was an empty space of stars and blackness, deep, deep, and something moving among those stars, something falling in the blackness, falling while I watched. . . .

Kaleidoscope

The first concussion cut the rocket up the side with a giant can opener. The men were thrown into space like a dozen wriggling silverfish. They were scattered into a dark sea; and the ship, in a million pieces, went on, a meteor swarm seeking a lost sun.

"Barkley, Barkley, where are you?"

The sound of voices calling like lost children on a cold night.

"Woode, Woode!"

"Captain!"

"Hollis, Hollis, this is Stone."

"Stone, this is Hollis. Where are you?"

"I don't know. How can I? Which way is up? I'm falling. Good God, I'm falling."

They fell. They fell as pebbles fall down wells. They were scattered as jackstones are scattered from a gigantic throw. And now instead of men there were only voices— all kinds of voices, disembodied and impassioned, in varying degrees of terror and resignation.

"We're going away from each other."

This was true. Hollis, swinging head over heels, knew this was true. He knew it with a vague acceptance. They were parting to go their separate ways, and nothing could bring them back. They were wearing their sealed-tight space suits with the glass tubes over their pale faces, but they hadn't had time to lock on their force units. With them they could be small lifeboats in space, saving themselves, saving others, collecting together, finding each other until they were an island of men with some plan. But without the force units snapped to their shoulders they were meteors, senseless, each going to a separate and irrevocable fate.

A period of perhaps ten minutes elapsed while the first terror died and a metallic calm took its place. Space began to weave its strange voices in and out, on a great dark loom, crossing, recrossing, making a final pattern.

"Stone to Hollis. How long can we talk by phone?"

"It depends on how fast you're going your way and I'm going mine."

"An hour, I make it."

"That should do it," said Hollis, abstracted and quiet.

"What happened?" said Hollis a minute later.

"The rocket blew up, that's all. Rockets do blow up."

"Which way are you going?"

"It looks like I'll hit the moon."

"It's Earth for me. Back to old Mother Earth at ten thousand miles per hour. I'll burn like a match." Hollis thought of it with a queer abstraction of mind. He seemed to be removed from his body, watching it fall down and down through space, as objective as he had been in regard to the first falling snowflakes of a winter season long gone.

*　　*　　*

The others were silent, thinking of the destiny that had brought them to this, falling, falling, and nothing they could do to change it. Even the captain was quiet, for there was no command or plan he knew that could put things back together again.

"Oh, it's a long way down. Oh, it's a long way down, a long, long, long way down," said a voice. "I don't want to die, I don't want to die, it's a long way down."

"Who's that?"

"I don't know."

"Stimson, I think. Stimson, is that you?"

"It's a long, long way and I don't like it. Oh, God, I don't like it."

"Stimson, this is Hollis. Stimson, you hear me?"

A pause while they fell separate from one another.

"Stimson?"

"Yes." He replied at last.

"Stimson, take it easy; we're all in the same fix."

"I don't want to be here. I want to be somewhere else."

"There's a chance we'll be found."

"I must be, I must be," said Stimson. "I don't believe this; I don't believe any of this is happening."

"It's a bad dream," said someone.

"Shut up!" said Hollis.

"Come and make me," said the voice. It was Applegate. He laughed easily, with a similar objectivity. "Come and shut me up."

Hollis for the first time felt the impossibility of his position. A great anger filled him, for he wanted more than anything at this moment to be able to do something to Applegate. He had wanted for many years to do something and now it was too late. Applegate was only a telephonic voice.

Falling, falling, falling . . .

Now, as if they had discovered the horror, two of the men began to scream. In a nightmare Hollis saw one of them float by, very near, screaming and screaming.

"Stop it!" The man was almost at his fingertips, screaming insanely. He would never stop. He would go on screaming for a million miles, as long as he was in radio range, disturbing all of them, making it impossible for them to talk to one another.

Hollis reached out. It was best this way. He made the extra effort and touched the man. He grasped the man's ankle and pulled himself up along the body until he reached the head. The man screamed and clawed frantically, like a drowning swimmer. The screaming filled the universe.

One way or the other, thought Hollis. The moon or Earth or meteors will kill him, so why not now?

He smashed the man's glass mask with his iron fist. The screaming stopped. He pushed off from the body and let it spin away on its own course, falling.

Falling, falling down space Hollis and the rest of them went in the long, endless dropping and whirling of silence.

"Hollis, you still there?"

Hollis did not speak, but felt the rush of heat in his face.

"This is Applegate again."

"All right, Applegate."

"Let's talk. We haven't anything else to do."

The captain cut in. "That's enough of that. We've got to figure a way out of this."

"Captain, why don't you shut up?" said Applegate.

"What!"

"You heard me, Captain. Don't pull your rank on me, you're ten thousand miles away by now, and let's not kid ourselves. As Stimson puts it, it's a long way down."

"See here, Applegate!"

"Can it. This is a mutiny of one. I haven't a damn thing to lose. Your ship was a bad ship and you were a bad captain and I hope you break when you hit the Moon."

"I'm ordering you to stop!"

"Go on, order me again." Applegate smiled across ten thousand miles. The captain was silent. Applegate continued. "Where were we, Hollis? Oh yes, I remember. I hate you too. But you know that. You've know it for a long time."

Hollis clenched his fists, helplessly.

"I want to tell you something," said Applegate. "Make you happy. I was the one who blackballed you with the Rocket Company five years ago."

A meteor flashed by. Hollis looked down and his left hand was gone. Blood spurted. Suddenly there was no air in his suit. He had enough air in his lungs to move his right hand over and twist a knob at his left elbow, tightening the joint and sealing the leak. It had happened so quickly that he was not surprised. Nothing surprised him anymore. The air in the suit came back to normal in an instant now that the leak was sealed. And the blood that had flowed so swiftly was pressured as he fastened the knob yet tighter, until it made a tourniquet.

All of this took place in a terrible silence on his part. And the other men chatted. That one man, Lespere, went on and on with his talk about his wife on Mars, his wife on Venus, his wife on Jupiter, his money, his wondrous times, his drunkenness, his gambling, his happiness. On and on, while they all fell. Lespere reminisced on the past, happy, while he fell to his death.

It was so very odd. Space, thousands of miles of space, and these voices vibrating in the center of it. No one visible at all, and only the radio waves quivering and trying to quicken other men into emotion.

"Are you angry, Hollis?"

"No." And he was not. The abstraction has returned and he was a thing of dull concrete, forever falling nowhere.

"You wanted to get to the top all your life, Hollis. You always wondered what happened. I put the black mark on you just before I was tossed out myself."

"That isn't important," said Hollis. And it was not. It was gone. When life is over it is like a flicker of bright film, an instant on the screen, all of its prejudices and passions condensed and illumined for an instant on space, and before you could cry out, "There was a happy day, there a bad one, there an evil face, there a good one," the film burned to a cinder, the screen went dark.

From this outer edge of his life, looking back, there was only one remorse, and that was only that he wished to go on living. Did all dying people feel this way, as if they had never lived? Did life seem that short, indeed, over and done before you took a breath? Did it seem this abrupt and impossible to everyone, or only to himself, here, now, with a few hours left to him for thought and deliberation?

One of the other men, Lespere, was talking. "Well, I had me a good time: I had a wife on Mars, Venus, and Jupiter. Each of them had money and treated me swell. I got drunk and once I gambled away twenty thousand dollars."

But you're here now, thought Hollis. I didn't have any

of those things. When I was living I was jealous of you, Lespere; when I had another day ahead of me I envied you your women and your good times. Women frightened me and I went into space, always wanting them and jealous of you for having them, and money, and as much happiness as you could have in your own wild way. But now, falling here, with everything over, I'm not jealous of you anymore, because it's over for you as it is for me, and right now it's like it never was. Hollis craned his face forward and shouted into the telephone.

"It's all over, Lespere!"

Silence.

"It's just as if it never was, Lespere!"

"Who's that?" Lespere's faltering voice.

"This is Hollis."

He was being mean. He felt the meanness, the senseless meanness of dying. Applegate had hurt him; now he wanted to hurt another. Applegate and space had both wounded him.

"You're out here, Lespere. It's all over. It's just as if it had never happened, isn't it?"

"No."

"When anything's over, it's just like it never happened. Where's your life any better than mine, now? Now is what counts. Is it any better? Is it?"

"Yes, it's better!"

"How!"

"Because I got my thoughts, I remember!" cried Lespere, far away, indignant, holding his memories to his chest with both hands.

And he was right. With a feeling of cold water rushing through his head and body, Hollis knew he was right. There were differences between memories and dreams. He had only dreams of things he had wanted to do, while Lespere had memories of things done and accomplished. And this knowledge began to pull Hollis apart, with a slow, quivering precision.

"What good does it do you?" he cried to Lespere. "Now?" When a thing's over it's not good anymore. You're no better off than me."

"I'm resting easy," said Lespere. "I've had my turn. I'm not getting mean at the end, like you."

"Mean?" Hollis turned the word on his tongue. He had never been mean, as long as he could remember, in his life. He had never dared to be mean. He must have saved it all of these years for such a time as this. "Mean." He rolled the word into the back of his mind. He felt tears start into his eyes and roll down his face. Someone must have heard his gasping voice.

"Take it easy, Hollis."

It was, of course, ridiculous. Only a minute before he had been giving advice to others, to Stimson; he had felt a braveness which he had thought to be the genuine thing, and now he knew that it had been nothing but shock and the objectivity possible in shock. Now he was trying to pack a lifetime of suppressed emotion into an interval of minutes.

"I know how you feel, Hollis," said Lespere, now twenty thousand miles away, his voice fading. "I don't take it personally."

But aren't we equal? he wondered. Lespere and I? Here, now? If a thing's over, it's done, and what good is it? You die anyway. But he knew he was rationalizing, for it was like trying to tell the difference between a live man and a corpse. There was a spark in one, and not in the other—an aura, a mysterious element.

So it was with Lespere and himself; Lespere had lived a good full life, and it made him a different man now, and he, Hollis, had been as good as dead for many years. They came to death by separate paths and, in all likelihood, if there were kinds of death, their kinds would be as different as night from day. The quality of death, like that of life, must be of an infinite variety, and if one has already died once, then what was there to look for in dying for good and all, as he was now?

It was a second later that he discovered his right foot was cut sheer away. It almost made him laugh. The air was gone from his suit again. He bent quickly, and there was blood, and the meteor had taken flesh and suit away to the ankle. Oh, death in space was most humorous. It cut you away, piece by piece, like a black and invisible butcher. He tightened the valve at the knee, his head whirling into pain, fighting to remain aware, and with the valve tightened, the blood retained, the air kept, he straightened up and went on falling, falling, for that was all there was left to do.

"Hollis?"

Hollis nodded sleepily, tired of waiting for death.

"This is Applegate again," said the voice.

"Yes."

"I've had time to think. I listened to you. This isn't good. It makes us bad. This is a bad way to die. It brings all the bile out. You listening, Hollis?"

"Yes."

"I lied. A minute ago. I lied. I didn't blackball you. I don't know why I said that. Guess I wanted to hurt you. You seemed the one to hurt. We've always fought. Guess I'm getting old fast and repenting fast. I guess listening to you be mean made me ashamed. Whatever the reason, I want you to know I was an idiot too. There's not an ounce of truth in what I said. To hell with you."

Hollis felt his heart begin to work again. It seemed as if it hadn't worked for five minutes, but now all of his limbs began to take color and warmth. The shock was over, and the successive shocks of anger and terror and loneliness were passing. He felt like a man emerging from a cold shower in the morning, ready for breakfast and a new day.

"Thanks, Applegate."

"Don't mention it. Up your nose, you bastard."

"Hey," said Stone.

"What?" Hollis called across space; for Stone, of all of them, was a good friend.

"I've got myself into a meteor swarm, some little asteroids."

"Meteors?"

"I think it's the Myrmidone cluster that goes out past Mars and in toward Earth once every five years. I'm right in the middle. It's like a big kaleidoscope. You get all kinds of colors and shapes and sizes. God, it's beautiful, all that metal."

Silence.

"I'm going with them," said Stone. "They're taking me off with them. I'll be damned." He laughed.

Hollis looked to see, but saw nothing. There were only the great diamonds and sapphires and emerald mists and velvet inks of space, with God's voice mingling among the crystal fires. There was a kind of wonder and imagination in the thought of Stone going off in the meteor swarm, out past Mars for years and coming in toward Earth every five years, passing in and out of the planet's ken for the next million centuries, Stone and the Myrmidone cluster eternal and unending, shifting and shaping like the kaleidoscope colors when you were a child and held the long tube to the sun and gave it a twirl.

"So long, Hollis." Stone's voice, very faint now. "So long."

"Good luck," shouted Hollis across thirty thousand miles.

"Don't be funny," said Stone, and was gone.

The stars closed in.

Now all the voices were fading, each on his own trajectory, some to Mars, others into farthest space. And Hollis himself . . . He looked down. He, of all the others, was going back to Earth alone.

"So long."

"Take it easy."

"So long, Hollis." That was Applegate.

The many good-bys. The short farewells. And now the great loose brain was disintegrating. The components of the brain which had worked so beautifully and efficiently in the skull case of the rocket ship firing through space were dying one by one; the meaning of their life together was falling apart. And as a body dies when the brain ceases functioning, so the spirit of the ship and their long time together and what they meant to one another was dying. Applegate was now no more than a finger blown from the parent body, no longer to be despised and worked against. The brain was exploded, and the senseless, useless fragments of it were far scattered. The voices faded and now all of space was silent. Hollis was alone, falling.

They were all alone. Their voices had died like echoes of the words of God spoken and vibrating in the starred deep. There went the captain to the Moon; there Stone with the meteor swarm; there Stimson; there Applegate toward

Pluto, there Smith and Turner and Underwood and all the rest, the shards of the kaleidoscope that had formed a thinking pattern for so long, hurled apart.

And I? thought Hollis. What can I do? Is there anything I can do now to make up for a terrible and empty life? If only I could do one good thing to make up for the meanness I collected all these years and didn't even know was in me! But there's no one here but myself, and how can you do good all alone? You can't. Tomorrow night I'll hit Earth's atmosphere.

I'll burn, he thought, and be scattered in ashes all over the continental lands. I'll be put to use. Just a little bit, but ashes are ashes and they'll add to the land.

He fell swiftly, like a bullet, like a pebble, like an iron weight, objective, objective all of the time now, not sad or happy or anything, but only wishing he could do a good thing now that everything was gone, a good thing for just himself to know about.

When I hit the atmosphere, I'll burn like a meteor.

"I wonder," he said, "if anyone'll see me?"

The small boy on the country road looked up and screamed. "Look, Mom, look! A falling star!"

The blazing white star fell down the sky of dusk in Illinois.

"Make a wish," said his mother. "Make a wish."

The Illustrated Man turned in the moonlight. He turned again . . . and again . . . and again. . . .

The Other Foot

When they heard the news they came out of the restaurants and cafés and hotels and looked at the sky. They lifted their dark hands over their upturned white eyes. Their mouths hung wide. In the hot noon for thousands of miles there were little towns where the dark people stood with their shadows under them, looking up.

In her kitchen Hattie Johnson covered the boiling soup, wiped her thin fingers on a cloth, and walked carefully to the back porch.

"Come on, Ma! Hey, Ma, come on—you'll miss it!"

"Hey, Mom!"

Three little Negro boys danced around in the dusty yard, yelling. Now and then they looked at the house frantically.

"I'm coming," said Hattie, and opened the screen door. "Where you hear this rumor?"

"Up at Jones's, Ma. They say a rocket's coming, first one in twenty years, with a white man in it!"

"What's a white man? I never seen one."

"You'll find out," said Hattie. "Yes indeed, you'll find out."

"Tell us about one, Ma. Tell like you did."

Hattie frowned. "Well, it's been a long time. I was a little girl, you see. That was back in 1965."

"Tell us about a white man, Mom!"

She came and stood in the yard, looking up at the blue clear Martian sky with the thin white Martian clouds, and in the distance the Martian hills broiling in the heat. She said at last, "Well, first of all, they got white hands."

"White hands!" The boys joked, slapping each other.

"And they got white arms."

"White arms!" hooted the boys.

"And white faces."

"White faces! *Really?*"

"White like *this*, Mom?" The smallest threw dust on his face, sneezing. "This way?"

"Whiter than that," she said gravely, and turned to the sky again. There was a troubled thing in her eyes, as if she was looking for a thundershower up high, and not seeing it made her worry. "Maybe you better go inside."

"Oh, Mom!" They stared at her in disbelief. "We got to watch, we just got to. Nothing's going to happen, is it?"

"I don't know. I got a feeling, is all."

"We just want to see the ship and maybe run down to the port and see that white man. What's he like, huh, Mom?"

"I don't know. I just don't know," she mused, shaking her head.

"Tell us some more!"

"Well, the white people live on Earth, which is where we all come from, twenty years ago. We just up and walked away and came to Mars and set down and built towns and here we are. Now we're Martians instead of Earth people. And no white men've come up here in all that time. That's the story."

"Why didn't they come up, Mom?"

"Well, 'cause. Right after we got up here, Earth got in an atom war. They blew each other up terribly. They forgot us. When they finished fighting, after years, they didn't have any rockets. Took them until recently to build more. So here they come now, twenty years later, to visit." She gazed at her children numbly and then began to walk. "You wait here. I'm going down the line to Elizabeth Brown's house. You promise to stay?"

"We don't want to but we will."

"All right, then." And she ran off down the road.

At the Browns' she arrived in time to see everybody packed into the family car. "Hey there, Hattie! Come on along!"

"Where you going?" she said, breathlessly running up.

"To see the white man!"

"That's right," said Mr. Brown seriously. He waved at his load. "These children never saw one, and *I* almost forgot."

"What you going to do with that white man?" asked Hattie.

"Do?" said everyone. "Why—just *look* at him, is all."

"You sure?"

"What else can we do?"

"I don't know," said Hattie. "I just thought there might be trouble."

"What kind of trouble?"

"You *know*," said Hattie vaguely, embarrassed. "You ain't going to lynch him?"

"Lynch him?" Everyone laughed. Mr. Brown slapped his

knee. "Why, bless you, child, no! We're going to shake his hand. Ain't we, everyone?"

"Sure, sure!"

Another car drove up from another direction and Hattie gave a cry. "Willie!"

"What you doing 'way down here? Where're the kids?" shouted her husband angrily. He glared at the others. "You going down like a bunch of fools to see that man come in?"

"That appears to be just right," agreed Mr. Brown, nodding and smiling.

"Well, take your guns along," said Willie. "I'm on my way home for mine right now!"

"Willie!"

"You get in this car, Hattie." He held the door open firmly, looking at her until she obeyed. Without another word to the others he roared the car down the dusty road.

"Willie, not so fast!"

"Not so fast, huh? We'll see about that." He watched the road tear under the car. "What right they got coming up here this late? Why don't they leave us in peace? Why didn't they blow themselves up on that old world and let us be?"

"Willie, that ain't no Christian way to talk."

"I'm not feeling Christian," he said savagely, gripping the wheel. "I'm just feeling mean. After all them years of doing what they did to our folks—my mom and dad, and your mom and dad—You remember? You remember how they hung my father on Knockwood Hill and shot my mother? You remember? Or you got a memory that's short like the others?"

"I remember," she said.

"You remember Dr. Phillips and Mr. Burton and their big houses, and my mother's washing shack, and Dad working when he was old, and the thanks he got was being hung by Dr. Phillips and Mr. Burton. Well," said Willie, "the shoe's on the other foot now. We'll see who gets laws passed against him, who gets lynched, who rides the back of streetcars, who gets segregated in shows. We'll just wait and see."

"Oh, Willie, you're talking trouble."

"Everybody's talking. Everybody's thought on this day, thinking it'd never be. Thinking, What kind of day would it be if the white man ever came up here to Mars? But here's the day, and we can't run away."

"Ain't you going to let the white people live up here?"

"Sure." He smiled, but it was a wide, mean smile, and his eyes were mad. "They can come up and live and work here; why, certainly. All they got to do to deserve it is live in their own small part of town, the slums, and shine our shoes for us, and mop up our trash, and sit in the last row in the balcony. That's all we ask. And once a week we hang one or two of them. Simple."

"You don't sound human, and I don't like it."

"You'll have to get used to it," he said. He braked the car to a stop before the house and jumped out. "Find my guns and some rope. We'll do this right."

"Oh, Willie," she wailed, and just sat there in the car while he ran up the steps and slammed the front door.

She went along. She didn't want to go along, but he rattled around in the attic, cursing like a crazy man until he found four guns. She saw the brutal metal of them glittering in the black attic, and she couldn't see him at all, he was so dark; she heard only his swearing, and at last his long legs came climbing down from the attic in a shower of dust, and he stacked up bunches of brass shells and blew out the gun chambers and clicked shells into them, his face stern and heavy and folded in upon the gnawing bitterness there. "Leave us alone," he kept muttering, his hands flying away from him suddenly, uncontrolled. "Leave us blame alone, why don't they?"

"Willie, Willie."

"You too—you too." And he gave her the same look, and a pressure of his hatred touched her mind.

Outside the window the boys gabbled to each other. "White as milk, she said. White as milk."

"White as this old flower, you see?"

"White as a stone, like chalk you write with."

Willie plunged out of the house. "You children come inside, I'm locking you up. You ain't seeing no white man, you ain't talking about them, you ain't doing nothing. Come on now."

"But, Daddy—"

He shoved them through the door and went and fetched a bucket of paint and a stencil and from the garage a long thick hairy rope coil into which he fashioned a hangman's knot, very carefully watching the sky while his hands felt their way at their task.

And then they were in the car, leaving bolls of dust behind them down the road. "Slow up, Willie."

"This is no slowing-up time," he said. "This is a hurrying time, and I'm hurrying."

All along the road people were looking up in the sky, or climbing in their cars, or riding in cars, and guns were sticking up out of some cars like telescopes sighting all the evils of a world coming to an end.

She looked at the guns. "You been talking," she accused her husband.

"That's what I been doing," he grunted, nodding. He

watched the road, fiercely. "I stopped at every house and I told them what to do, to get their guns, to get paint, to bring rope and be ready. And here we all are, the welcoming committee, to give them the key to the city. Yes, sir!"

She pressed her thin dark hands together to push away the terror growing in her now, and she felt the car bucket and lurch around other cars. She heard the voices yelling, Hey, Willie, look! and hands holding up ropes and guns as they rushed by! and mouths smiling at them in the swift rushing.

"Here we are," said Willie, and braked the car into dusty halting and silence. He kicked the door open with a big foot and, laden with weapons, stepped out, lugging them across the airport meadow.

"Have you *thought*, Willie?"

"That's all I done for twenty years. I was sixteen when I left Earth, and I was glad to leave," he said. "There wasn't anything there for me or you or anybody like us. I've never been sorry I left. We've had peace here, the first time we ever drew a solid breath. Now, come on."

He pushed through the dark crowd which came to meet him.

"Willie, Willie, what we gonna do?" they said.

"Here's a gun," he said. "Here's a gun. Here's another." He passed them out with savage jabs of his arms. "Here's a pistol. Here's a shotgun."

The people were so close together it looked like one dark body with a thousand arms reaching out to take the weapons. "Willie, Willie."

His wife stood tall and silent by him, her fluted lips pressed shut, and her large eyes wet and tragic. "Bring the paint," he said to her. And she lugged a gallon can of yellow paint across the field to where, at that moment, a trolley car was pulling up, with a fresh-painted sign on its front, To THE WHITE MAN'S LANDING, full of talking people who got off and ran across the meadow, stumbling, looking up. Women with picnic boxes, men with straw hats, in shirt sleeves. The streetcar stood humming and empty. Willie climbed up, set the paint cans down, opened them, stirred the paint, tested a brush, drew forth a stencil, and climbed up on a seat.

"Hey, there!" The conductor came around behind him, his coin changer jangling. "What you think you're doing? Get down off there!"

"You see what I'm doing. Keep your shirt on."

And Willie began the stenciling in yellow paint. He dabbed on an *F* and an *O* and an *R* with terrible pride in his work. And when he finished it the conductor squinted up and read the fresh glinting yellow words: FOR WHITES: REAR SECTION. He read it again. FOR WHITES. He blinked. REAR SECTION. The conductor looked at Willie and began to smile.

"Does that suit you?" asked Willie, stepping down.

Said the conductor, "That suits me just fine, sir."

Hattie was looking at the sign from outside, and holding her hands over her breasts.

Willie returned to the crowd, which was growing now, taking size from every auto that groaned to a halt, and every new trolley car which squealed around the bend from the nearby town.

Willie climbed up on a packing box. "Let's have a delegation to paint every streetcar in the next hour. Volunteers?"

Hands leapt up.

"Get going!"

They went.

"Let's have a delegation to fix theater seats, roped off, the last two rows for whites."

More hands.

"Go on!"

They ran off.

Willie peered around, bubbled with perspiration, panting with exertion, proud of his energy, his hands on his wife's shoulder who stood under him looking at the ground with her downcast eyes. "Let's see now," he declared. "Oh yes. We got to pass a law this afternoon; no intermarriages!"

"That's right," said a lot of people.

"All shoeshine boys quit their jobs today."

"Quittin' right now!" Some men threw down the rags they carried, in their excitement, all across town.

"Got to pass a minimum wage law, don't we?"

"Sure!"

"Pay them white folks at least ten cents an hour."

"That's right!"

The mayor of the town hurried up. "Now look here, Willie Johnson. Get down off that box!"

"Mayor, I can't be made to do nothing like that."

"You're making a mob, Willie Johnson."

"That's the idea."

"The same thing you always hated when you were a kid. You're no better than some of those white men you yell about!"

"This is the other shoe, Mayor, and the other foot," said Willie, not even looking at the mayor, looking at the faces beneath him, some of them smiling, some of them doubtful, others bewildered, some of them reluctant and drawing away, fearful.

"You'll be sorry," said the mayor.

"We'll have an election and get a new mayor," said Willie. And he glanced off at the town where up and down the street signs were being hung, fresh-painted: LIMITED CLIENTELE *Right to serve customer revokable at any time.* He grinned and slapped his hands. Lord! And streetcars were being halted and sections being painted white in back, to suggest their future inhabitants. And theaters were being invaded and roped off by chuckling men, while their wives stood wondering on the curbs and children were spanked into houses to be hid away from this awful time.

"Are we all ready?" called Willie Johnson, the rope in his hands with the noose tied and neat.

"Ready!" shouted half the crowd. The other half murmured and moved like figures in a nightmare in which they wished no participation.

"Here it comes!" called a small boy.

Like marionette heads on a single string, the heads of the crowd turned upward.

Across the sky, very high and beautiful, a rocket burned on a sweep of orange fire. It circled and came down, causing all to gasp. It landed, setting the meadow afire here and there; the fire burned out, the rocket lay a moment in quiet, and then, as the silent crowd watched, a great door in the side of the vessel whispered out a breath of oxygen, the door slid back and an old man stepped out.

"A white man, a white man, a white man . . ." The words traveled back in the expectant crowd, the children speaking in each other's ears, whispering, butting each other, the words moving in ripples to where the crowd stopped and the streetcars stood in the windy sunlight, the smell of paint coming out their opened windows. The whispering wore itself away and it was gone.

No one moved.

The white man was tall and straight, but a deep weariness was in his face. He had not shaved this day, and his eyes were as old as the eyes of a man can be and still be alive. His eyes were colorless, almost white and sightless with things he had seen in the passing years. He was as thin as a winter bush. His hands trembled and he had to lean against the portway of the ship as he looked out over the crowd.

He put out a hand and half smiled, but drew his hand back.

No one moved.

He looked down into their faces, and perhaps he saw but did not see the guns and the ropes, and perhaps he smelled the paint. No one ever asked him. He began to talk. He started very quietly and slowly, expecting no interruptions, and receiving none, and his voice was very tired and old and pale.

"It doesn't matter who I am," he said. "I'd be just a name to you, anyhow. I don't know your names, either. That'll come later." He paused, closed his eyes for a moment, and then continued:

"Twenty years ago you left Earth. That's a long, long time. It's more like twenty centuries, so much has happened. After you left, the War came." He nodded slowly. "Yes, the *big* one. The Third One. It went on for a long time. Until last year. We bombed all of the cities of the world. We destroyed New York and London and Moscow and Paris and Shanghai and Bombay and Alexandria. We ruined it all. And when we finished with the big cities we went to the little cities and atom-bombed and burned them."

Now he began to name cities and places, and streets. And as he named them, a murmur rose up in his audience.

"We destroyed Natchez . . ."

A murmur.

"And Columbus, Georgia . . ."

Another murmur.

"We burned New Orleans . . ."

A sigh.

"And Atlanta . . ."

Still another.

"And there was nothing left of Greenwater, Alabama."

Willie Johnson jerked his head and his mouth opened. Hattie saw this gesture, and the recognition coming into his dark eyes.

"Nothing was left," said the old man in the port, speaking slowly. "Cotton fields, burned."

Oh, said everyone.

"Cotton mills bombed out—"

"Oh."

"And the factories, radioactive; everything radioactive. All the roads and the farms and the foods, radioactive. Everything." He named more names of towns and villages.

"Tampa."

"That's my town," someone whispered.

"Fulton."

"That's mine," someone else said.

"Memphis."

"Memphis. Did they burn *Memphis?*" A shocked query.

"Memphis, blown up."

"*Fourth* Street in Memphis?"

"All of it," said the old man.

It was stirring them now. After twenty years it was rushing back. The towns and the places, the trees and the brick buildings, the signs and the churches and the familiar stores,

all of it was coming to the surface among the gathered people. Each name touched memory, and there was no one present without a thought of another day. They were all old
enough for that, save the children.

"Laredo."

"I remember Laredo."

"New York City."

"I had a store in Harlem."

"Harlem, bombed out."

The ominous words. The familiar, remembered places.
The struggle to imagine all of those places in ruins.

Willie Johnson murmured the words, "Greenwater, Alabama. That's where I was born. I remember."

Gone. All of it gone. The man said so.

The man continued, "So we destroyed everything and
ruined everything, like the fools that we were and the fools
that we are. We killed millions. I don't think there are more
than five hundred thousand people left in the world, all kinds
and types. And out of all the wreckage we salvaged enough
metal to build this one rocket, and we came to Mars in it
this month to seek your help."

He hesitated and looked down among the faces to see
what could be found there, but he was uncertain.

Hattie Johnson felt her husband's arm tense, saw his
fingers grip the rope.

"We've been fools," said the old man quietly. "We've
brought the Earth and civilization down about our heads.
None of the cities are worth saving—they'll be radioactive
for a century. Earth is over and done with. Its age is through.
You have rockets here which you haven't tried to use to
return to Earth in twenty years. Now I've come to ask you
to use them. To come to Earth, to pick up the survivors and

bring them back to Mars. To help us go on at this time. We've been stupid. Before God we admit our stupidity and our evilness. All the Chinese and the Indians and the Russians and the British and the Americans. We're asking to be taken in. Your Martian soil has lain fallow for numberless centuries; there's room for everyone; it's good soil—I've seen your fields from above. We'll come and work it *for* you. Yes, we'll even do that. We deserve anything you want to do to us, but don't shut us out. We can't force you to act now. If you want I'll get into my ship and go back and that will be all there is to it. We won't bother you again. But we'll come here and we'll work for you and do the things you did for us—clean your houses, cook your meals, shine your shoes, and humble ourselves in the sight of God for the things we have done over the centuries to ourselves, to others, to you."

He was finished.

There was a silence of silences. A silence you could hold in your hand and a silence that came down like a pressure of a distant storm over the crowd. Their long arms hung like dark pendulums in the sunlight, and their eyes were upon the old man and he did not move now, but waited.

Willie Johnson held the rope in his hands. Those around him watched to see what he might do. His wife Hattie waited, clutching his arm.

She wanted to get at the hate of them all, to pry at it and work at it until she found a little chink, and then pull out a pebble or a stone or a brick and then a part of the wall, and, once started, the whole edifice might roar down and be done away with. It was teetering now. But which was the keystone, and how to get at it? How to touch them and get a thing started in all of them to make a ruin of their hate?

She looked at Willie there in the strong silence and the

only thing she knew about the situation was him and his life
and what had happened to him, and suddenly he was the
keystone; suddenly she knew that if he could be pried loose,
then the thing in all of them might be loosened and torn
away.

"Mister—" She stepped forward. She didn't even know
the first words to say. The crowd stared at her back; she felt
them staring. "Mister—"

The man turned to her with a tired smile.

"Mister," she said, "do you know Knockwood Hill in
Greenwater, Alabama?"

The old man spoke over his shoulder to someone within
the ship. A moment later a photographic map was handed
out and the man held it, waiting.

"You know the big oak on top of that hill, mister?"

The big oak. The place where Willie's father was shot
and hung and found swinging in the morning wind.

"Yes."

"Is that still there?" asked Hattie.

"It's gone," said the old man. "Blown up. The hill's all
gone, and the oak tree too. You see?" He touched the
photograph.

"Let me see that," said Willie, jerking forward and looking at the map.

Hattie blinked at the white man, heart pounding.

"Tell me about Greenwater," she said quickly.

"What do you want to know?"

"About Dr. Phillips. Is he still alive?"

A moment in which the information was found in a
clicking machine within the rocket . . .

"Killed in the war."

"And his son?"

"Dead."

"What about their house?"

"Burned. Like all the other houses."

"What about that other big tree on Knockwood Hill?"

"All the trees went—burned."

"*That* tree went, you're sure?" said Willie.

"Yes."

Willie's body loosened somewhat.

"And what about that Mr. Burton's house and Mr. Burton?"

"No houses at all left, no people."

"You know Mrs. Johnson's washing shack, my mother's place?"

The place where she was shot.

"That's gone too. Everything's gone. Here are the pictures, you can see for yourself."

The pictures were there to be held and looked at and thought about. The rocket was full of pictures and answers to questions. Any town, any building, any place.

Willie stood with the rope in his hands.

He was remembering Earth, the green Earth and the green town where he was born and raised, and he was thinking now of that town, gone to pieces, to ruin, blown up and scattered, all of the landmarks with it, all of the supposed or certain evil scattered with it, all of the hard men gone, the stables, the ironsmiths, the curio shops, the soda founts, the gin mills, the river bridges, the lynching trees, the buckshot-covered hills, the roads, the cows, the mimosas, and his own house as well as those big-pillared houses down near the long river, those white mortuaries where the women as delicate as moths fluttered in the autumn light, distant, far away. Those houses where the cold men rocked, with glasses of drink in their hands, guns leaned against the porch newels, sniffing the autumn airs and considering death. Gone, all gone; gone and never coming back. Now, for certain, all of that civilization ripped into confetti and strewn at their feet. Nothing, nothing of it left to hate—not an empty brass gun shell, or a twisted hemp, or a tree, or even a hill of it to hate. Nothing but some alien people in a rocket, people who might shine his shoes and ride in the back of trolleys or sit far up in midnight theaters . . .

"You won't have to do that," said Willie Johnson.

His wife glanced at his big hands.

His fingers were opening.

The rope, released, fell and coiled upon itself along the ground.

They ran through the streets of their town and tore down the new signs so quickly made, and painted out the fresh yellow signs on streetcars, and they cut down the ropes in the theater balconies, and unloaded their guns and stacked their ropes away.

"A new start for everyone," said Hattie, on the way home in their car.

"Yes," said Willie at last. "The Lord's let us come through, a few here and a few there. And what happens next is up to all of us. The time for being fools is over. We got to be something else except fools. I knew that when he talked. I knew then that now the white man's as lonely as we've always been. He's got no home now, just like we didn't have one for so long. Now everything's even. We can start all over again, on the same level."

He stopped the car and sat in it, not moving, while Hattie went to let the children out. They ran down to see their father. "You see the white man? You see him?" they cried.

"Yes, sir," said Willie, sitting behind the wheel, rubbing his face with his slow fingers. "Seems like for the first time today I really seen the white man—I really seen him clear."

The Highway

The cooling afternoon rain had come over the valley, touching the corn in the tilled mountain fields, tapping on the dry grass roof of the hut. In the rainy darkness the woman ground corn between cakes of lava rock, working steadily. In the wet lightlessness, somewhere, a baby cried.

Hernando stood waiting for the rain to cease so he might take the wooden plow into the field again. Below, the river boiled brown and thickened in its course. The concrete highway, another river, did not flow at all; it lay shining, empty. A car had not come along it in an hour. This was, in itself, of unusual interest. Over the years there had not been an hour when a car had not pulled up, someone shouting, "Hey there, can we take your picture?" Someone with a box that clicked, and a coin in his hand. If he walked slowly across the field without his hat, sometimes they called, "Oh, we want you with your hat on!" And they waved their hands, rich with gold things that told time, or identified them, or did nothing at all but winked like spider's eyes in the sun. So he would turn and go back to get his hat.

His wife spoke. "Something is wrong, Hernando?"

"*Sí*. The road. Something big has happened. Something big to make the road so empty this way."

He walked from the hut slowly and easily, the rain washing over the twined shoes of grass and thick tire rubber he wore. He remembered very well the incident of this pair of shoes. The tire had come into the hut with violence one night, exploding the chickens and the pots apart! It had come alone, rolling swiftly. The car, off which it had come, had rushed on, as far as the curve, and hung a moment, headlights reflected, before plunging into the river. The car was still there. One might see it on a good day, when the river ran slow and the mud cleared. Deep under, its metal shining, long and low and very rich, lay the car. But then the mud came in again and you saw nothing.

The following day he had carved the shoe soles from the tire rubber.

He reached the highway now, and stood upon it, listening to the small sounds it made in the rain.

Then, suddenly, as if at a signal, the cars came. Hundreds of them, miles of them, rushing and rushing as he stood, by and by him. The big long black cars heading north toward the United States, roaring, taking the curves at too great a speed. With a ceaseless blowing and honking. And there was something about the faces of the people packed into the cars, something which dropped him into a deep silence. He stood back to let the cars roar on. He counted them until he tired. Five hundred, a thousand cars passed, and there was something in the faces of all of them. But they moved too swiftly for him to tell what this thing was.

Finally the silence and emptiness returned. The swift

long low convertible cars were gone. He heard the last horn fade.

The road was empty again.

It had been like a funeral cortege. But a wild one, racing, hair out, screaming to some ceremony ever northward. Why? He could only shake his head and rub his fingers softly, at his sides.

Now, all alone, a final car. There was something very, very final about it. Down the mountain road in the thin cool rain, fuming up great clouds of steam, came an old Ford. It was traveling as swiftly as it might. He expected it to break apart any instant. When this ancient Ford saw Hernando it pulled up, caked with mud and rusted, the radiator bubbling angrily.

"May we have some water, please, señor!"

A young man, perhaps twenty-one, was driving. He wore a yellow sweater, an open-collared white shirt and gray pants. In the topless car the rain fell upon him and five young women packed so they could not move in the interior. They were all very pretty and they were keeping the rain from themselves and the driver with old newspapers. But the rain got through to them, soaking their bright dresses, soaking the young man. His hair was plastered with rain. But they did not seem to care. None complained, and this was unusual. Always before they complained, of rain, of heat, of time, of cold, of distance.

Hernando nodded. "I'll bring you water."

"Oh, please hurry!" one of the girls cried. She sounded very high and afraid. There was no impatience in her, only an asking out of fear. For the first time Hernando ran when a tourist asked, always before he had walked slower at such requests.

He returned with a hub lid full of water. This, too, had been a gift from the highway. One afternoon it had sailed like a flung coin into his field, round and glittering. The car to which it belonged had slid on, oblivious to the fact that it had lost a silver eye. Until now, he and his wife had used it for washing and cooking; it made a fine bowl.

As he poured the water into the boiling radiator, Hernando looked up at their stricken faces. "Oh, thank you, thank you," said one of the girls. "You don't know what this means."

Hernando smiled. "So much traffic in this hour. It all goes one way. North."

He did not mean to say anything to hurt them. But when he looked up again there all of them sat, in the rain, and they were crying. They were crying very hard. And the young man was trying to stop them by laying his hands on their shoulders and shaking them gently, one at a time, but they held their papers over their heads and their mouths moved and their eyes were shut and their faces changed color and they cried, some loud, some soft.

Hernando stood with the half-empty lid in his fingers. "I did not mean to say anything, señor," he apologized.

"That's all right," said the driver.

"What is wrong, señor?"

"Haven't you heard?" replied the young man, turning, holding tightly to the wheel with one hand, leaning forward. "It's happened."

This was bad. The others, at this, cried still harder, holding onto each other, forgetting the newspapers, letting the rain fall and mingle with their tears.

Hernando stiffened. He put the rest of the water into the radiator. He looked at the sky, which was black with storm. He looked at the river rushing. He felt the asphalt under his shoes.

He came to the side of the car. The young man took his hand and gave him a peso. "No." Hernando gave it back. "It is my pleasure."

"Thank you, you're so kind," said one of the girls, still sobbing. "Oh, Mama, Papa. Oh, I want to be home, I want to be home. Oh, Mama, Dad." And others held her.

"I did not hear, señor," said Hernando quietly.

"The war!" shouted the young man as if no one could hear. "It's come, the atom war, the end of the world!"

"Señor, señor," said Hernando.

"Thank you, thank you for your help. Good-by," said the young man.

"Good-by," they all said in the rain, not seeing him.

He stood while the car engaged its gears and rattled off down, fading away, through the valley. Finally it was gone, with the young women in it, the last car, the newspapers held and fluttered over their heads.

Hernando did not move for a long time. The rain ran very cold down his cheeks and along his fingers and into the woven garment on his legs. He held his breath, waiting, tight and tensed.

He watched the highway, but it did not move again. He doubted that it would move much for a very long time.

The rain stopped. The sky broke through the clouds. In ten minutes the storm was gone, like a bad breath. A sweet wind blew the smell of the jungle up to him. He could hear the river moving gently and easily on its way. The jungle was very green; everything was fresh. He walked down through the field to his house and picked up his plow. With his hands on it he looked at the sky beginning to burn hot with the sun.

His wife called out from her work. "What happened, Hernando?"

"It is nothing," he replied.

He set the plow in the furrow, he called sharply to his burro, "Burrrrrrr-o!" And they walked together through the rich field, under the clearing sky, on their tilled land by the deep river.

"What do they mean, 'the world'?" he said.

The Man

Captain Hart stood in the door of the rocket. "Why don't they come?" he said.

"Who knows?" said Martin, his lieutenant. "Do I know, Captain?"

"What kind of a place is this, anyway?" The captain lighted a cigar. He tossed the match out into the glittering meadow. The grass started to burn.

Martin moved to stamp it out with his boot.

"No," ordered Captain Hart, "let it burn. Maybe they'll come see what's happening then, the ignorant fools."

Martin shrugged and withdrew his foot from the spreading fire.

Captain Hart examined his watch. "An hour ago we landed here, and does the welcoming committee rush out with a brass band to shake our hands? No indeed! Here we ride millions of miles through space and the fine citizens of some silly town on some unknown planet ignore us!" He snorted, tapping his watch. "Well, I'll just give them five more minutes, and then—"

"And then what?" asked Martin, ever so politely, watching the captain's jowls shake.

"We'll fly over their damned city again and scare hell out of them." His voice grew quieter. "Do you think, Martin, maybe they didn't see us land?"

"They saw us. They looked up as we flew over."

"Then why aren't they running across the field? Are they hiding? Are they yellow?"

Martin shook his head. "No. Take these binoculars, sir. See for yourself. Everybody's walking around. They're not frightened. They—well, they just don't seem to care."

Captain Hart placed the binoculars to his tired eyes. Martin looked up and had time to observe the lines and the grooves of irritation, tiredness, nervousness there. Hart looked a million years old; he never slept, he ate little, and drove himself on, on. Now his mouth moved, aged and drear, but sharp, under the held binoculars.

"Really, Martin, I don't know why we bother. We build rockets, we go to all the trouble of crossing space, searching for them, and this is what we get. Neglect. Look at those idiots wander about in there. Don't they realize how big this is? The first space flight to touch their provincial land. How many times does that happen? Are they that blasé?"

Martin didn't know.

Captain Hart gave him back the binoculars wearily. "Why do we do it, Martin? This space travel, I mean. Always on the go. Always searching. Our insides always tight, never any rest."

"Maybe we're looking for peace and quiet. Certainly there's none on Earth," said Martin.

"No, there's not, is there?" Captain Hart was thoughtful, the fire damped down. "Not since Darwin, eh? Not since everything went by the board, everything we used to believe in, eh? Divine power and all that. And so you think maybe that's why we're going out to the stars, eh, Martin? Looking for our lost souls, is that it? Trying to get away from our evil planet to a good one?"

"Perhaps, sir. Certainly we're looking for something."

Captain Hart cleared his throat and tightened back into sharpness. "Well, right now we're looking for the mayor of that city there. Run in, tell them who we are, the first rocket expedition to Planet Forty-three in Star System Three. Captain Hart sends his salutations and desires to meet the mayor. On the double!"

"Yes, sir." Martin walked slowly across the meadow.

"Hurry!" snapped the captain.

"Yes, sir!" Martin trotted away. Then he walked again, smiling to himself.

The captain had smoked two cigars before Martin returned.

Martin stopped and looked up into the door of the rocket, swaying, seemingly unable to focus his eyes or think.

"Well?" snapped Hart. "What happened? Are they coming to welcome us?"

"No." Martin had to lean dizzily against the ship.

"Why not?"

"It's not important," said Martin. "Give me a cigarette, please, Captain." His fingers groped blindly at the rising pack, for he was looking at the golden city and blinking. He lighted one and smoked quietly for a long time.

"Say something!" cried the captain. "Aren't they interested in our rocket?"

Martin said, "What? Oh. The rocket?" He inspected his

cigarette. "No, they're not interested. Seems we came at an inopportune time."

"Inopportune time!"

Martin was patient. "Captain, listen. Something big happened yesterday in that city. It's so big, so important that we're second-rate—second fiddle. I've got to sit down." He lost his balance and sat heavily, gasping for air.

The captain chewed his cigar angrily. "What happened?"

Martin lifted his head, smoke from the burning cigarette in his fingers, blowing in the wind. "Sir, yesterday, in that city, a remarkable man appeared—good, intelligent, compassionate, and infinitely wise!"

The captain glared at his lieutenant. "What's that to do with us?"

"It's hard to explain. But he was a man for whom they'd waited a long time—a million years maybe. And yesterday he walked into their city. That's why today, sir, our rocket landing means nothing."

The captain sat down violently. "Who was it? Not Ashley? He didn't arrive in his rocket before us and steal my glory, did he?" He seized Martin's arm. His face was pale and dismayed.

"Not Ashley, sir."

"Then it was Burton! I knew it. Burton stole in ahead of us and ruined my landing! You can't trust anyone anymore."

"Not Burton, either, sir," said Martin quietly.

The captain was incredulous. "There were only three rockets. We were in the lead. This man who got here ahead of us? What was his name!"

"He didn't have a name. He doesn't need one. It would be different on every planet, sir."

The captain stared at his lieutenant with hard, cynical eyes.

"Well, what did he do that was so wonderful that no-body even looks at our ship?"

"For one thing," said Martin steadily, "he healed the sick and comforted the poor. He fought hypocrisy and dirty poli-tics and sat among the people, talking, through the day."

"Is that so wonderful?"

"Yes, Captain."

"I don't get this." The captain confronted Martin, peered into his face and eyes. "You been drinking, eh?" He was suspicious. He backed away. "I don't understand."

Martin looked at the city. "Captain, if you don't under-stand, there's no way of telling you."

The captain followed his gaze. The city was quiet and beautiful and a great peace lay over it. The captain stepped forward, taking his cigar from his lips. He squinted first at Martin, then at the golden spires of the buildings.

"You don't mean—you *can't* mean— That man you're talking about couldn't be—"

Martin nodded. "That's what I mean, sir."

The captain stood silently, not moving. He drew him-self up.

"I don't believe it," he said at last.

At high noon Captain Hart walked briskly into the city, accompanied by Lieutenant Martin and an assistant who was carrying some electrical equipment. Every once in a while the captain laughed loudly, put his hands on his hips and shook his head.

The mayor of the town confronted him. Martin set up a tripod, screwed a box onto it, and switched on the batteries.

"Are you the mayor?" The captain jabbed a finger out.

"I am," said the mayor.

The delicate apparatus stood between them, controlled and adjusted by Martin and the assistant. Instantaneous translations from any language were made by the box. The words sounded crisply on the mild air of the city.

"About this occurrence yesterday," said the captain. "It occurred?"

"It did."

"You have witnesses?"

"We have."

"May we talk to them?"

"Talk to any of us," said the mayor. "We are all witnesses."

In an aside to Martin the captain said, "Mass hallucination." To the mayor, "What did this man—this stranger—look like?"

"That would be hard to say," said the mayor, smiling a little.

"Why would it?"

"Opinions might differ slightly."

"I'd like your opinion, sir, anyway," said the captain. "Record this," he snapped to Martin over his shoulder. The lieutenant pressed the button of a hand recorder.

"Well," said the mayor of the city, "he was a very gentle and kind man. He was of a great and knowing intelligence."

"Yes—yes, I know, I know." The captain waved his fingers. "Generalizations. I want something specific. What did he look like?"

"I don't believe that is important," replied the mayor.

"It's very important," said the captain sternly. "I want a description of this fellow. If I can't get it from you, I'll get it from others." To Martin, "I'm sure it must have been Burton, pulling one of his practical jokes."

Martin would not look him in the face. Martin was coldly silent.

The captain snapped his fingers. "There was something or other—a healing?"

"Many healings," said the mayor.

"May I see one?"

"You may," said the mayor. "My son." He nodded at a small boy who stepped forward. "He was afflicted with a withered arm. Now, look upon it."

At this the captain laughed tolerantly. "Yes, yes. This isn't even circumstantial evidence, you know. I didn't see the boy's withered arm. I see only his arm whole and well. That's no proof. What proof have you that the boy's arm was withered yesterday and today is well?"

"My word is my proof," said the mayor simply.

"My dear man!" cried the captain. "You don't expect me to go on hearsay, do you? Oh, no!"

"I'm sorry," said the mayor, looking upon the captain with what appeared to be curiosity and pity.

"Do you have any pictures of the boy before today?" asked the captain.

After a moment a large oil portrait was carried forth, showing the son with a withered arm.

"My dear fellow!" The captain waved it away. "Anybody can paint a picture. Paintings lie. I want a photograph of the boy."

There was no photograph. Photography was not a known art in their society.

"Well," sighed the captain, face twitching, "let me talk to a few other citizens. We're getting nowhere." He pointed at a woman. "You." She hesitated. "Yes, you; come here," ordered the captain. "Tell me about this *wonderful* man you saw yesterday."

The woman looked steadily at the captain. "He walked among us and was very fine and good."

"What color were his eyes?"

"The color of the sun, the color of the sea, the color of a flower, the color of the mountains, the color of the night."

"That'll do." The captain threw up his hands. "See, Martin? Absolutely nothing. Some charlatan wanders through whispering sweet nothings in their ears and—"

"Please, stop it," said Martin.

The captain stepped back. "What?"

"You heard what I said," said Martin. "I like these people. I believe what they say. You're entitled to your opinion, but keep it to yourself, sir."

"You can't talk to me this way," shouted the captain.

"I've had enough of your highhandedness," replied Martin. "Leave these people alone. They've got something good and decent, and you come and foul up the nest and sneer at it. Well, I've talked to them too. I've gone through the city and seen their faces, and they've got something you'll never have—a little simple faith, and they'll move mountains with it. You, you're boiled because someone stole your act, got here ahead and made you unimportant."

"I'll give you five seconds to finish," remarked the captain. "I understand. You've been under a strain, Martin. Months of traveling in space, nostalgia, loneliness. And now, with this thing happening, I sympathize, Martin. I overlook your petty insubordination."

"I don't overlook your petty tyranny," replied Martin. "I'm stepping out. I'm staying here."

"You can't do that!"

"Can't I? Try and stop me. This is what I came looking for. I didn't know it, but this is it. This is for me. Take your filth somewhere else and foul up other nests with your doubt and your—scientific method!" He looked swiftly about. "These people have had an experience, and you can't seem to get it through your head that it's really happened and we were lucky enough to almost arrive in time to be in on it.

"People on Earth have talked about this man for twenty centuries after he walked through the old world. We've all wanted to see him and hear him, and never had the chance. And now, today, we just missed seeing him by a few hours."

Captain Hart looked at Martin's cheeks. "You're crying like a baby. Stop it."

"I don't care."

"Well, I do. In front of these natives we're to keep up a front. You're overwrought. As I said, I forgive you."

"I don't want your forgiveness."

"You idiot. Can't you see this is one of Burton's tricks, to fool these people, to bilk them, to establish his oil and mineral concerns under a religious guise! You fool, Martin. You absolute fool! You should know Earthmen by now. They'll do anything—blaspheme, lie, cheat, steal, kill, to get their ends. Anything is fine if it works; the true pragmatist, that's Burton. You know him!"

The captain scoffed heavily. "Come off it, Martin, admit it; this is the sort of scaly thing Burton might carry off, polish up these citizens and pluck them when they're ripe."

"No," said Martin, thinking of it.

The captain put his hands up. "That's Burton. That's him. That's his dirt, that's his criminal way. I have to admire the old dragon. Flaming in here in a blaze and a halo and a soft word and a loving touch, with a medicated salve here and a healing ray there. That's Burton all right!"

"No." Martin's voice was dazed. He covered his eyes. "No, I won't believe it."

"You don't want to believe." Captain Hart kept at it. "Admit it now. Admit it. It's just the thing Burton would do. Stop daydreaming, Martin. Wake up! It's morning. This is a real world and we're real, dirty people—Burton the dirtiest of us all!"

Martin turned away.

"There, there, Martin," said Hart, mechanically patting the man's back. "I understand. Quite a shock for you. I know. A rotten shame, and all that. That Burton is a rascal. You go take it easy. Let me handle this."

Martin walked off slowly toward the rocket.

Captain Hart watched him go. Then, taking a deep breath, he turned to the woman he had been questioning. "Well. Tell me some more about this man. As you were saying, madam?"

Later the officers of the rocket ship ate supper on card tables outside. The captain correlated his data to a silent Martin who sat red-eyed and brooding over his meal.

"Interviewed three dozen people, all of them full of the same milk and hogwash," said the captain. "It's Burton's work all right, I'm positive. He'll be spilling back in here tomorrow or next week to consolidate his miracles and beat us out in our contracts. I think I'll stick on and spoil it for him."

Martin glanced up sullenly. "I'll kill him," he said.

"Now, now, Martin! There, there, boy."

"I'll kill him—so help me, I will."

"We'll put an anchor on his wagon. You have to admit he's clever. Unethical but clever."

"He's dirty."

"You must promise not to do anything violent." Captain Hart checked his figures. "According to this, there were thirty miracles of healing performed, a blind man restored to vision, a leper cured. Oh, Burton's efficient, give him that."

A gong sounded. A moment later a man ran up. "Captain, sir. A report! Burton's ship is coming down. Also the Ashley ship, sir!"

"See!" Captain Hart beat the table. "Here come the jackals to the harvest! They can't wait to feed. Wait till I confront them. I'll make them cut me in on this feast—I will!"

Martin looked sick. He stared at the captain.

"Business, my dear boy, business," said the captain.

Everybody looked up. Two rockets swung down out of the sky.

When the rockets landed they almost crashed.

"What's wrong with those fools?" cried the captain, jumping up. The men ran across the meadowlands to the steaming ships. The captain arrived. The airlock door popped open on Burton's ship.

A man fell out into their arms.

"What's wrong?" cried Hart.

The man lay on the ground. They bent over him and he was burned, badly burned. His body was covered with wounds and scars and tissue that was inflamed and smoking. He looked up out of puffed eyes and his thick tongue moved in his split lips.

"What happened?" demanded the captain, kneeling down, shaking the man's arm.

"Sir, sir," whispered the dying man. "Forty-eight hours ago, back in Space Sector Seventy-nine DFS, off Planet One in this system, our ship, and Ashley's ship, ran into a cosmic storm, sir." Liquid ran gray from the man's nostrils. Blood trickled from his mouth. "Wiped out. All crew. Burton dead. Ashley died an hour ago. Only three survivals."

"Listen to me!" shouted Hart, bending over the bleeding man. "You didn't come to this planet before this very hour?"

Silence.

"Answer me!" cried Hart.

The dying man said, "No. Storm. Burton dead two days ago. This first landing on any world in six months."

"Are you sure?" shouted Hart, shaking violently, gripping the man in his hands. "Are you sure?"

"Sure, sure," mouthed the dying man.

"Burton died two days ago? You're positive?"

"Yes, yes," whispered the man. His head fell forward. The man was dead.

The captain knelt beside the silent body. The captain's face twitched, the muscles jerking involuntarily. The other members of the crew stood back of him looking down. Martin waited. The captain asked to be helped to his feet, finally, and this was done. They stood looking at the city. "That means—"

"That means?" said Martin.

"We're the only ones who've been here," whispered Captain Hart. "And that man—"

"What about that man, Captain?" asked Martin.

The captain's face twitched senselessly. He looked very old indeed, and gray. His eyes were glazed. He moved forward in the dry grass.

"Come along, Martin. Come along. Hold me up; for my sake, hold me. I'm afraid I'll fall. And hurry. We can't waste time—"

They moved, stumbling, toward the city, in the long dry grass, in the blowing wind.

*   *   *

Several hours later they were sitting in the mayor's auditorium. A thousand people had come and talked and gone. The captain had remained seated, his face haggard, listening, listening. There was so much light in the faces of those who came and testified and talked he could not bear to see them. And all the while his hands traveled, on his knees, together, on his belt, jerking and quivering.

When it was over, Captain Hart turned to the mayor and with strange eyes said:

"But you must know where he went?"

"He didn't say where he was going," replied the mayor.

"To one of the other nearby worlds?" demanded the captain.

"I don't know."

"You must know."

"Do you see him?" asked the mayor, indicating the crowd.

The captain looked. "No."

"Then he is probably gone," said the mayor.

"Probably, probably!" cried the captain weakly. "I've made a horrible mistake, and I want to see him now. Why, it just came to me, this is a most unusual thing in history. To be in on something like this. Why, the chances are one in billions we'd arrived at one certain planet among millions of planets the day after *he* came! You must know where he's gone!"

"Each finds him in his own way," replied the mayor gently.

"You're hiding him." The captain's face grew slowly ugly. Some of the old hardness returned in stages. He began to stand up.

"No," said the mayor.

"You know where he is then?" The captain's fingers twitched at the leather holster on his right side.

"I couldn't tell you where he is, exactly," said the mayor.

"I advise you to start talking," and the captain took out a small steel gun.

"There's no way," said the mayor, "to tell you anything."

"Liar!"

An expression of pity came into the mayor's face as he looked at Hart.

"You're very tired," he said. "You've traveled a long way and you belong to a tired people who've been without faith a long time, and you want to believe so much now that you're interfering with yourself. You'll only make it harder if you kill. You'll never find him that way."

"Where'd he go? He told you, you know. Come on, tell me!" The captain waved the gun.

The mayor shook his head.

"Tell me! Tell me!"

The gun cracked once, twice. The mayor fell, his arm wounded.

Martin leaped forward. "Captain!"

The gun flashed at Martin. "Don't interfere."

On the floor, holding his wounded arm, the mayor looked up. "Put down your gun. You're hurting yourself. You've never believed, and now that you think you believe, you hurt people because of it."

"I don't need you," said Hart, standing over him. "If I missed him by one day here, I'll go on to another world. And another and another. I'll miss him by half a day on the next planet, maybe, and a quarter of a day on the third planet, and two hours on the next, and an hour on the next, and half an hour on the next, and a minute on the next. But after that, one day I'll catch up with him! Do you hear that?" He was shouting now, leaning wearily over the man on the floor. He staggered with exhaustion. "Come along, Martin." He let the gun hang in his hand.

"No," said Martin. "I'm staying here."

"You're a fool. Stay if you like. But I'm going on, with the others, as far as I can go."

The mayor looked up at Martin. "I'll be all right. Leave me. Others will tend my wounds."

"I'll be back," said Martin. "I'll walk as far as the rocket."

They walked with vicious speed through the city. One could see with what effort the captain struggled to show all the old iron, to keep himself going. When he reached the rocket he slapped the side of it with a trembling hand. He holstered his gun. He looked at Martin.

"Well, Martin?"

Martin looked at him. "Well, Captain?"

The captain's eyes were on the sky. "Sure you won't— come with—with me, eh?"

"No, sir."

"It'll be a great adventure, by God. I know I'll find him."

"You are set on it now, aren't you, sir?" asked Martin.

The captain's face quivered and his eyes closed. "Yes."

"There's one thing I'd like to know."

"What?"

"Sir, when you find him—*if* you find him," asked Martin, "what will you ask of him?"

"Why—" The captain faltered, opening his eyes. His hands clenched and unclenched. He puzzled a moment and then broke into a strange smile. "Why, I'll ask him for a little—peace and quiet." He touched the rocket. "It's been a long time, a long, long time since—since I relaxed."

"Did you ever just try, Captain?"

"I don't understand," said Hart.

"Never mind. So long, Captain."

"Good-by, Mr. Martin."

The crew stood by the port. Out of their number only three were going on with Hart. Seven others were remaining behind, they said, with Martin.

Captain Hart surveyed them and uttered his verdict: "Fools!"

He, last of all, climbed into the airlock, gave a brisk salute, laughed sharply. The door slammed.

The rocket lifted into the sky on a pillar of fire.

Martin watched it go far away and vanish.

At the meadow's edge the mayor, supported by several men, beckoned.

"He's gone," said Martin, walking up.

"Yes, poor man, he's gone," said the mayor. "And he'll go on, planet after planet, seeking and seeking, and always and always he will be an hour late, or a half hour late, or ten minutes late, or a minute late. And finally he will miss out by only a few seconds. And when he has visited three hundred worlds and is seventy or eighty years old he will miss out by only a fraction of a second, and then a smaller fraction of a second. And he will go on and on, thinking to find that very thing which he left behind here, on this planet, in this city—"

Martin looked steadily at the mayor.

The mayor put out his hand. "Was there ever any doubt of it?" He beckoned to the others and turned. "Come along now. We mustn't keep him waiting."

They walked into the city.

The Long Rain

The rain continued. It was a hard rain, a perpetual rain, a sweating and steaming rain; it was a mizzle, a downpour, a fountain, a whipping at the eyes, an undertow at the ankles; it was a rain to drown all rains and the memory of rains. It came by the pound and the ton, it hacked at the jungle and cut the trees like scissors and shaved the grass and tunneled the soil and molted the bushes. It shrank men's hands into the hands of wrinkled apes; it rained a solid glassy rain, and it never stopped.

"How much farther, Lieutenant?"

"I don't know. A mile, ten miles, a thousand."

"Aren't you sure?"

"How can I be sure?"

"I don't like this rain. If we only knew how far it is to the Sun Dome, I'd feel better."

"Another hour or two from here."

"You really think so, Lieutenant?"

"Of course."

"Or are you lying to keep us happy?"

"I'm lying to keep you happy. Shut up!"

The two men sat together in the rain. Behind them sat two other men who were wet and tired and slumped like clay that was melting.

The lieutenant looked up. He had a face that once had been brown and now the rain had washed it pale, and the rain had washed the color from his eyes and they were white, as were his teeth, and as was his hair. He was all white. Even his uniform was beginning to turn white, and perhaps a little green with fungus.

The lieutenant felt the rain on his cheeks. "How many million years since the rain stopped raining here on Venus?"

"Don't be crazy," said one of the two other men. "It never stops raining on Venus. It just goes on and on. I've lived here for ten years and I never saw a minute, or even a second, when it wasn't pouring."

"It's like living under water," said the lieutenant, and rose up, shrugging his guns into place. "Well, we'd better get going. We'll find that Sun Dome yet."

"Or we won't find it," said the cynic.

"It's an hour or so."

"Now you're lying to me, Lieutenant."

"No, now I'm lying to myself. This is one of those times when you've got to lie. I can't take much more of this."

They walked down the jungle trail, now and then looking at their compasses. There was no direction anywhere, only what the compass said. There was a gray sky and rain falling and jungle and a path, and, far back behind them somewhere, a rocket in which they had ridden and fallen. A rocket in which lay two of their friends, dead and dripping rain.

They walked in single file, not speaking. They came to

a river which lay wide and flat and brown, flowing down to the great Single Sea. The surface of it was stippled in a billion places by the rain.

"All right, Simmons."

The lieutenant nodded and Simmons took a small packet from his back which, with a pressure of hidden chemical, inflated into a large boat. The lieutenant directed the cutting of wood and the quick making of paddles and they set out into the river, paddling swiftly across the smooth surface in the rain.

The lieutenant felt the cold rain on his cheeks and on his neck and on his moving arms. The cold was beginning to seep into his lungs. He felt the rain on his ears, on his eyes, on his legs.

"I didn't sleep last night," he said.

"Who could? Who has? When? How many nights *have* we slept? Thirty nights, thirty days! Who can sleep with rain slamming their head, banging away. . . . I'd give anything for a hat. Anything at all, just so it wouldn't hit my head anymore. I get headaches. My head is sore; it hurts all the time."

"I'm sorry I came to China," said one of the others.

"First time I ever heard Venus called China."

"Sure, China. Chinese water cure. Remember the old torture? Rope you against a wall. Drop one drop of water on your head every half hour. You go crazy waiting for the next one. Well, that's Venus, but on a big scale. We're not made for water. You can't sleep, you can't breathe right, and you're crazy from just being soggy. If we'd been ready for a crash, we'd have brought waterproofed uniforms and hats. It's this beating rain on your head gets you, most of all. It's so heavy. It's like BB shot. I don't know how long I can take it."

"Boy, me for the Sun Dome! The man who thought *them* up, thought of something."

They crossed the river, and in crossing they thought of the Sun Dome, somewhere ahead of them, shining in the jungle rain. A yellow house, round and bright as the sun. A house fifteen feet high by one hundred feet in diameter, in which was warmth and quiet and hot food and freedom from rain. And in the center of the Sun Dome, of course, was a sun. A small floating free globe of yellow fire, drifting in a space at the top of the building where you could look at it from where you sat, smoking or reading a book or drinking your hot chocolate crowned with marshmallow dollops. There it would be, the yellow sun, just the size of the Earth sun, and it was warm and continuous, and the rain world of Venus would be forgotten as long as they stayed in that house and idled their time.

The lieutenant turned and looked back at the three men using their oars and gritting their teeth. They were as white as mushrooms, as white as he was. Venus bleached everything away in a few months. Even the jungle was an immense cartoon nightmare, for how could the jungle be green with no sun, with always rain falling and always dusk? The white, white jungle with the pale cheese-colored leaves, and the earth carved of wet Camembert, and the tree boles like immense toadstools—everything black and white. And how often could you see the soil itself? Wasn't it mostly a creek, a stream, a puddle, a pool, a lake, a river, and then, at last, the sea?

"Here we are!"

They leaped out on the farthest shore, splashing and sending up showers. The boat was deflated and stored in a cigarette packet. Then, standing on the rainy shore, they tried to light up a few smokes for themselves, and it was five minutes or so before, shuddering, they worked the inverted lighter and cupping their hands, managed a few drags upon cigarettes that all too quickly were limp and beaten away from their lips by a sudden slap of rain.

They walked on.

"Wait just a moment," said the lieutenant. "I thought I saw something ahead."

"The Sun Dome?"

"I'm not sure. The rain closed in again."

Simmons began to run. "The Sun Dome!"

"Come back, Simmons!"

"The Sun Dome!"

Simmons vanished in the rain. The others ran after him.

They found him in a little clearing, and they stopped and looked at him and what he had discovered.

The rocket ship.

It was lying where they had left it. Somehow they had circled back and were where they had started. In the ruin of the ship green fungus was growing up out of the mouths of the two dead men. As they watched, the fungus took flower, the petals broke away in the rain, and the fungus died.

"How did we do it?"

"An electrical storm must be nearby. Threw our compasses off. That explains it."

"You're right."

"What'll we do now?"

"Start out again."

"Good lord, we're not any closer to anywhere!"

"Let's try to keep calm about it, Simmons."

"Calm, calm! This rain's driving me wild!"

"We've enough food for another two days if we're careful."

The rain danced on their skin, on their wet uniforms; the rain streamed from their noses and ears, from their fingers and knees. They looked like stone fountains frozen in the jungle, issuing forth water from every pore.

And, as they stood, from a distance they heard a roar.

And the monster came out of the rain.

The monster was supported upon a thousand electric blue legs. It walked swiftly and terribly. It struck down a leg with a driving blow. Everywhere a leg struck a tree fell and burned. Great whiffs of ozone filled the rainy air, and smoke blew away and was broken up by the rain. The monster was a half mile wide and a mile high and it felt of the ground like a great blind thing. Sometimes, for a moment, it had no legs at all. And then, in an instant, a thousand whips would fall out of its belly, white-blue whips, to sting the jungle.

"There's the electrical storm," said one of the men. "There's the thing ruined our compasses. And it's coming this way."

"Lie down, everyone," said the lieutenant.

"Run!" cried Simmons.

"Don't be a fool. Lie down. It hits the highest points. We may get through unhurt. Lie down about fifty feet from the rocket. It may very well spend its force there and leave us be. Get down!"

The men flopped.

"Is it coming?" they asked each other, after a moment.

"Coming."

"Is it nearer?"

"Two hundred yards off."

"Nearer?"

"Here she is!"

The monster came and stood over them. It dropped down ten blue bolts of lightning which struck the rocket. The rocket flashed like a beaten gong and gave off a metal ringing. The monster let down fifteen more bolts which danced about in a ridiculous pantomime, feeling of the jungle and the watery soil.

"No, no!" One of the men jumped up.

"Get down, you fool!" said the lieutenant.

"No!"

The lightning struck the rocket another dozen times. The lieutenant turned his head on his arm and saw the blue blazing flashes. He saw trees split and crumple into ruin. He saw the monstrous dark cloud turn like a black disk overhead and hurl down a hundred other poles of electricity.

The man who had leaped up was now running, like someone in a great hall of pillars. He ran and dodged between the pillars and then at last a dozen of the pillars slammed down and there was the sound a fly makes when landing upon the grill wires of an exterminator. The lieutenant remembered this from his childhood on a farm. And there was a smell of a man burned to a cinder.

The lieutenant lowered his head. "Don't look up," he told the others. He was afraid that he too might run at any moment.

The storm above them flashed down another series of bolts and then moved on away. Once again there was only the rain, which rapidly cleared the air of the charred smell, and in a moment the three remaining men were sitting and waiting for the beat of their hearts to subside into quiet once more.

They walked over to the body, thinking that perhaps

they could still save the man's life. They couldn't believe that there wasn't some way to help the man. It was the natural act of men who have not accepted death until they have touched it and turned it over and made plans to bury it or leave it there for the jungle to bury in an hour of quick growth.

The body was twisted steel, wrapped in burned leather. It looked like a wax dummy that had been thrown into an incinerator and pulled out after the wax had sunk to the charcoal skeleton. Only the teeth were white, and they shone like a strange white bracelet dropped half through a clenched black fist.

"He shouldn't have jumped up." They said it almost at the same time.

Even as they stood over the body it began to vanish, for the vegetation was edging in upon it, little vines and ivy and creepers, and even flowers for the dead.

At a distance the storm walked off on blue bolts of lightning and was gone.

They crossed a river and a creek and a stream and a dozen other rivers and creeks and streams. Before their eyes rivers appeared, rushing, new rivers, while old rivers changed their courses—rivers the color of mercury, rivers the color of silver and milk.

They came to the sea.

The Single Sea. There was only one continent on Venus. This land was three thousand miles long by a thousand miles wide, and about this island was the Single Sea, which covered the entire raining planet. The Single Sea, which lay upon the pallid shore with little motion . . .

*   *   *

"This way." The lieutenant nodded south. "I'm sure there are two Sun Domes down that way."

"While they were at it, why didn't they build a hundred more?"

"There's a hundred and twenty of them now, aren't there?"

"One hundred and twenty-six, as of last month. They tried to push a bill through Congress back on Earth a year ago to provide for a couple dozen more, but oh no, you know how *that* is. They'd rather a few men went crazy with the rain."

They started south.

The lieutenant and Simmons and the third man, Pickard, walked in the rain, in the rain that fell heavily and lightly, heavily and lightly; in the rain that poured and hammered and did not stop falling upon the land and the sea and the walking people.

Simmons saw it first. "There it is!"

"There's what?"

"The Sun Dome!"

The lieutenant blinked the water from his eyes and raised his hands to ward off the stinging blows of the rain.

At a distance there was a yellow glow on the edge of the jungle, by the sea. It was, indeed, the Sun Dome.

The men smiled at each other.

"Looks like you were right, Lieutenant."

"Luck."

"Brother, that puts muscle in me, just seeing it. Come on! Last one there's a son-of-a-bitch!" Simmons began to trot. The others automatically fell in with this, gasping, tired, but keeping pace.

"A big pot of coffee for me," panted Simmons, smiling.

"And a pan of cinnamon buns, by God! And just lie there and let the old sun hit you. The guy that invented the Sun Domes, he should have got a medal!"

They ran faster. The yellow glow grew brighter.

"Guess a lot of men went crazy before they figured out the cure. Think it'd be obvious! Right off." Simmons panted the words in cadence to his running. "Rain, rain! Years ago. Found a friend. Of mine. Out in the jungle. Wandering around. In the rain. Saying over and over, 'Don't know enough, to come in, outta the rain. Don't know enough, to come in, outta the rain. Don't know enough—' On and on. Like that. Poor crazy bastard."

"Save your breath!"

They ran.

They all laughed. They reached the door of the Sun Dome, laughing.

Simmons yanked the door wide. "Hey!" he yelled. "Bring on the coffee and buns!"

There was no reply.

They stepped through the door.

The Sun Dome was empty and dark. There was no synthetic yellow sun floating in a high gaseous whisper at the center of the blue ceiling. There was no food waiting. It was cold as a vault. And through a thousand holes which had been newly punctured in the ceiling water streamed, the rain fell down, soaking into the thick rugs and the heavy modern furniture and splashing on the glass tables. The jungle was growing up like a moss in the room, on top of the bookcases and the divans. The rain slashed through the holes and fell upon the three men's faces.

Pickard began to laugh quietly.

"Shut up, Pickard!"

"Ye gods, look what's here for us—no food, no sun, nothing. The Venusians—they did it! Of course!"

Simmons nodded, with the rain funneling down on his face. The water ran in his silvered hair and on his white eyebrows. "Every once in a while the Venusians come up out of the sea and attack a Sun Dome. They know if they ruin the Sun Domes they can ruin us."

"But aren't the Sun Domes protected with guns?"

"Sure." Simmons stepped aside to a place that was relatively dry. "But it's been five years since the Venusians tried anything. Defense relaxes. They caught this Dome unaware."

"Where are the bodies?"

"The Venusians took them all down into the sea. I hear they have a delightful way of drowning you. It takes about eight hours to drown the way they work it. Really delightful."

"I bet there isn't any food here at all." Pickard laughed.

The lieutenant frowned at him, nodded at him so Simmons could see. Simmons shook his head and went back to a room at one side of the oval chamber. The kitchen was strewn with soggy loaves of bread, and meat that had grown a faint green fur. Rain came through a hundred holes in the kitchen roof.

"Brilliant." The lieutenant glanced up at the holes. "I don't suppose we can plug up all those holes and get snug here."

"Without food, sir?" Simmons retorted. "I notice the sun machine's torn apart. Our best bet is to make our way to the next Sun Dome. How far is that from here?"

"Not far. As I recall, they built two rather close together here. Perhaps if we waited here, a rescue mission from the other might—"

"It's probably been here and gone already, some days

ago. They'll send a crew to repair this place in about six months, when they get the money from Congress. I don't think we'd better wait."

"All right then, we'll eat what's left of our rations and get on to the next Dome."

Pickard said, "If only the rain wouldn't hit my head, just for a few minutes. If I could only remember what it's like not to be bothered." He put his hands on his skull and held it tight. "I remember when I was in school a bully used to sit in back of me and pinch me and pinch me and pinch me every five minutes, all day long. He did that for weeks and months. My arms were sore and black and blue all the time. And I thought I'd go crazy from being pinched. One day I must have gone a little mad from being hurt and hurt, and I turned around and took a metal trisquare I used in mechanical drawing and I almost killed that bastard. I almost cut his lousy head off. I almost took his eye out before they dragged me out of the room, and I kept yelling, 'Why don't he leave me alone? why don't he leave me alone?' Brother!" His hands clenched the bone of his head, shaking, tightening, his eyes shut. "But what do I do *now*? Who do I hit, who do I tell to lay off, stop bothering me, this damn rain, like the pinching, always *on* you, that's all you hear, that's all you feel!"

"We'll be at the other Sun Dome by four this afternoon."

"Sun Dome? Look at this one! What if all the Sun Domes on Venus are gone? What then? What if there are holes in all the ceilings, and the rain coming in!"

"We'll have to chance it."

"I'm tired of chancing it. All I want is a roof and some quiet. I want to be alone."

"That's only eight hours off, if you hold on."

"Don't worry, I'll hold on all right." And Pickard laughed, not looking at them.

"Let's eat," said Simmons, watching him.

They set off down the coast, southward again. After four hours they had to cut inland to go around a river that was a mile wide and so swift it was not navigable by boat. They had to walk inland six miles to a place where the river boiled out of the earth, suddenly, like a mortal wound. In the rain, they walked on solid ground and returned to the sea.

"I've got to sleep," said Pickard at last. He slumped. "Haven't slept in four weeks. Tried, but couldn't. Sleep here."

The sky was getting darker. The night of Venus was setting in and it was so completely black that it was dangerous to move. Simmons and the lieutenant fell to their knees also, and the lieutenant said, "All right, we'll see what we can do. We've tried it before, but I don't know. Sleep doesn't seem one of the things you can get in this weather."

They lay out full, propping their heads up so the water wouldn't come to their mouths, and they closed their eyes. The lieutenant twitched.

He did not sleep.

There were things that crawled on his skin. Things grew upon him in layers. Drops fell and touched other drops and they became streams that trickled over his body, and while these moved down his flesh, the small growths of the forest took root in his clothing. He felt the ivy cling and make a second garment over him; he felt the small flowers bud and open and petal away, and still the rain pattered on his body and on his head. In the luminous night—for the vegetation glowed in the darkness—he could see the other two men outlined, like logs that had fallen and taken upon themselves velvet coverings of grass and flowers. The rain hit his face. He covered his face with his hands. The rain hit his neck. He turned over on his stomach in the mud, on the rubbery plants, and the rain hit his back and hit his legs.

Suddenly he leaped up and began to brush the water from himself. A thousand hands were touching him and he no longer wanted to be touched. He no longer could stand being touched. He floundered and struck something else and knew that it was Simmons, standing up in the rain, sneezing moisture, coughing and choking. And then Pickard was up, shouting, running about.

"Wait a minute, Pickard!"

"Stop it, stop it!" Pickard screamed. He fired off his gun six times at the night sky. In the flashes of powdery illumination they could see armies of raindrops, suspended as in a vast motionless amber, for an instant, hesitating as if shocked by the explosion, fifteen billion droplets, fifteen billion tears, fifteen billion ornaments, jewels standing out against a white velvet viewing board. And then, with the light gone, the drops which had waited to have their pictures taken, which had suspended their downward rush, fell upon them, stinging, in an insect cloud of coldness and pain.

"Stop it! Stop it!"

"Pickard!"

But Pickard was only standing now, alone. When the lieutenant switched on a small hand lamp and played it over Pickard's wet face, the eyes of the man were dilated. and his mouth was open, his face turned up, so the water hit and splashed on his tongue, and hit and drowned the wide eyes, and bubbled in a whispering froth on the nostrils.

"Pickard!"

The man would not reply. He simply stood there for a

long while with the bubbles of rain breaking out in his whit-
ened hair and manacles of rain jewels dripping from his wrists
and his neck.

"Pickard! We're leaving. We're going on. Follow us."

The rain dripped from Pickard's ears.

"Do you hear me, Pickard!"

It was like shouting down a well.

"Pickard!"

"Leave him alone," said Simmons.

"We can't go on without him."

"What'll we do, carry him?" Simmons spat. "He's no
good to us or himself. You know what he'll do? He'll just
stand here and drown."

"What?"

"You ought to know that by now. Don't you know the
story? He'll just stand here with his head up and let the rain
come in his nostrils and his mouth. He'll breathe the water."

"No."

"That's how they found General Mendt that time. Sitting
on a rock with his head back, breathing the rain. His lungs
were full of water."

The lieutenant turned the light back to the unblinking
face. Pickard's nostrils gave off a tiny whispering wet sound.

"Pickard!" The lieutenant slapped the face.

"He can't even feel you," said Simmons. "A few days in
this rain and you don't have any face or any legs or hands."

The lieutenant looked at his own hand in horror. He
could no longer feel it.

"But we can't leave Pickard here."

"I'll show you what we can do." Simmons fired his gun.

Pickard fell into the raining earth.

Simmons said, "Don't move, Lieutenant. I've got my gun

ready for you too. Think it over; he would only have stood or sat there and drowned. It's quicker this way."

The lieutenant blinked at the body. "But you killed him."

"Yes, because he'd have killed us by being a burden. You saw his face. Insane."

After a moment the lieutenant nodded. "All right."

They walked off into the rain.

It was dark and their hand lamps threw a beam that pierced the rain for only a few feet. After a half hour they had to stop and sit through the rest of the night, aching with hunger, waiting for the dawn to come; when it did come it was gray and continually raining as before, and they began to walk again.

"We've miscalculated," said Simmons.

"No. Another hour."

"Speak louder. I can't hear you." Simmons stopped and smiled. "By Christ," he said, and touched his ears. "My ears. They've gone out on me. All the rain pouring finally numbed me right down to the bone."

"Can't you hear anything?" said the lieutenant.

"What?" Simmon's eyes were puzzled.

"Nothing. Come on."

"I think I'll wait here. You go on ahead."

"You can't do that."

"I can't hear you. You go on. I'm tired. I don't think the Sun Dome is down this way. And, if it is, it's probably got holes in the roof, like the last one. I think I'll just sit here."

"Get up from there!"

"So long, Lieutenant."

"You can't give up now."

"I've got a gun here that says I'm staying. I just don't give a damn anymore. I'm not crazy yet, but I'm the next thing to it. I don't want to go out that way. As soon as you get out of sight I'm going to use this gun on myself."

"Simmons!"

"You said my name. I can read that much off your lips."

"Simmons."

"Look, it's a matter of time. Either I die now or in a few hours. Wait'll you get to that next Dome, if you ever get there, and find rain coming in through the roof. Won't that be nice?"

The lieutenant waited and then splashed off in the rain. He turned and called back once, but Simmons was only sitting there with the gun in his hands, waiting for him to get out of sight. He shook his head and waved the lieutenant on.

The lieutenant didn't even hear the sound of the gun.

He began to eat the flowers as he walked. They stayed down for a time, and weren't poisonous; neither were they particularly sustaining, and he vomited them up, sickly, a minute or so later.

Once he took some leaves and tried to make himself a hat, but he had tried that before; the rain melted the leaves from his head. Once picked, the vegetation rotted quickly and fell away into gray masses in his fingers.

"Another five minutes," he told himself. "Another five minutes and then I'll walk into the sea and keep walking. We weren't made for this; no Earthman was or ever will be able to take it. Your nerves, your nerves."

He floundered his way through a sea of slush and foliage and came to a small hill.

At a distance there was a faint yellow smudge in the cold veils of water.

The next Sun Dome.

Through the trees, a long round yellow building, far away. For a moment he only stood, swaying, looking at it.

He began to run and then he slowed down, for he was afraid. He didn't call out. What if it's the same one? What if it's the dead Sun Dome, with no sun in it? he thought.

He slipped and fell. Lie here, he thought; it's the wrong one. Lie here. It's no use. Drink all you want.

But he managed to climb to his feet again and crossed several creeks, and the yellow light grew very bright, and he began to run again, his feet crashing into mirrors and glass, his arms flailing at diamonds and precious stones.

He stood before the yellow door. The printed letters over it said THE SUN DOME. He put his numb hand up to feel it. Then he twisted the doorknob and stumbled in.

He stood for a moment looking about. Behind him the rain whirled at the door. Ahead of him, upon a low table, stood a silver pot of hot chocolate, steaming, and a cup, full, with a marshmallow in it. And beside that, on another tray, stood thick sandwiches of rich chicken meat and fresh-cut tomatoes and green onions. And on a rod just before his eyes was a great thick green Turkish towel, and a bin in which to throw wet clothes, and, to his right, a small cubicle in which heat rays might dry you instantly. And upon a chair, a fresh change of uniform, waiting for anyone—himself, or any lost one—to make use of it. And farther over, coffee in steaming copper urns, and a phonograph from which music was playing quietly, and books bound in red and brown leather. And near the books a cot, a soft deep cot upon which one might lie, exposed and bare, to drink in the rays of the one great bright thing which dominated the long room.

He put his hands to his eyes. He saw other men moving toward him, but said nothing to them. He waited, and opened his eyes, and looked. The water from his uniform pooled at his feet, and he felt it drying from his hair and his face and his chest and his arms and his legs.

He was looking at the sun.

It hung in the center of the room, large and yellow and warm. It made not a sound, and there was no sound in the room. The door was shut and the rain only a memory to his tingling body. The sun hung high in the blue sky of the room, warm, hot, yellow, and very fine.

He walked forward, tearing off his clothes as he went.

The Rocket Man

The electrical fireflies were hovering above Mother's dark hair to light her path. She stood in her bedroom door looking out at me as I passed in the silent hall. "You *will* help me keep him here this time, won't you?" she asked.

"I guess so," I said.

"Please." The fireflies cast moving bits of light on her white face. "This time he mustn't go away again."

"All right," I said, after standing there a moment. "But it won't do any good; it's no use."

She went away, and the fireflies, on their electric circuits, fluttered after her like an errant constellation, showing her how to walk in darkness. I heard her say, faintly, "We've got to try, anyway."

Other fireflies followed me to my room. When the weight of my body cut a circuit in the bed, the fireflies winked out. It was midnight, and my mother and I waited, our rooms separated by darkness, in bed. The bed began to rock me and sing to me. I touched a switch; the singing and rocking stopped. I didn't want to sleep. I didn't want to sleep at all.

This night was no different from a thousand others in our time. We would wake nights and feel the cool air turn hot, feel the fire in the wind, or see the walls burned a bright color for an instant, and then we knew *his* rocket was over our house—his rocket, and the oak trees swaying from the concussion. And I would lie there, eyes wide, panting, and mother in her room. Her voice would come to me over the interroom radio:

"Did you feel it?"

And I would answer, "That was him, all right."

That was my father's ship passing over our town, a small town where *space* rockets never came, and we would lie awake for the next two hours, thinking, "Now Dad's landed in Springfield, now he's on the tarmac, now he's signing the papers, now he's in the helicopter, now he's over the river, now the hills, now he's settling the helicopter in at the little airport at Green Village here. . . ." And the night would be half over when, in our separate cool beds, Mother and I would be listening, listening. "Now he's walking down Bell Street. He always walks . . . never takes a cab . . . now across the park, now turning the corner of Oakhurst and *now* . . ."

I lifted my head from my pillow. Far down the street, coming closer and closer, smartly, quickly, briskly—footsteps. Now turning in at our house, up the porch steps. And we were both smiling in the cool darkness, Mom and I, when we heard the front door open in recognition, speak a quiet word of welcome, and shut, downstairs. . . .

Three hours later I turned the brass knob to their room quietly, holding my breath, balancing in a darkness as big as the space between the planets, my hand out to reach the small black case at the foot of my parents' sleeping bed.

Taking it, I ran silently to my room, thinking. He won't tell me, he doesn't want me to *know*.

And from the opened case spilled his black uniform, like a black nebula, stars glittering here or there, distantly, in the material. I kneaded the dark stuff in my warm hands; I smelled the planet Mars, an iron smell, and the planet Venus, a green ivy smell, and the planet Mercury, a scent of sulphur and fire; and I could smell the milky mood and the hardness of stars. I pushed the uniform into a centrifuge machine I'd built in my ninth-grade shop that year, set it whirling. Soon a fine powder precipitated into a retort. This I slid under a microscope. And while my parents slept unaware, and while our house was asleep, all the automatic bakers and servers and robot cleaners in an electric slumber, I stared down upon brilliant motes of meteor dust, comet tail, and loam from far Jupiter glistening like worlds themselves which drew me down the tube a billion miles into space, at terrific accelerations.

At dawn, exhausted with my journey and fearful of discovery, I returned the boxed uniform to their sleeping room.

Then I slept, only to waken at the sound of the horn of the dry-cleaning car which stopped in the yard below. They took the black uniform box with them. It's good I didn't wait, I thought. For the uniform would be back in an hour, clean of all its destiny and travel.

I slept again, with the little vial of magical dust in my pajama pocket, over my beating heart.

When I came downstairs, there was Dad at the breakfast table, biting into his toast. "Sleep good, Doug?" he said, as if he had been there all the time, and hadn't been gone for three months.

"All right," I said.

"Toast?"

He pressed a button and the breakfast table made me four pieces, golden brown.

I remember my father that afternoon, digging and digging in the garden, like an animal after something, it seemed. There he was with his long dark arms moving swiftly, planting, tamping, fixing, cutting, pruning, his dark face always down to the soil, his eyes always down to what he was doing, never up to the sky, never looking at me, or Mother, even, unless we knelt with him to feel the earth soak up through the overalls at our knees, to put our hands into the black dirt and not look at the bright, crazy sky. Then he would glance to either side, to Mother or me, and give us a gentle wink, and go on, bent down, face down, the sky staring at his back.

That night we sat on the mechanical porch swing which swung us and blew a wind upon us and sang to us. It was summer and moonlight and we had lemonade to drink, and we held the cold glasses in our hands, and Dad read the stereo-newspapers inserted into the special hat you put on your head and which turned the microscopic page in front of the magnifying lens if you blinked three times in succession. Dad smoked cigarettes and told me about how it was when he was a boy in the year 1997. After a while he said, as he had always said, "Why aren't you out playing kick-the-can, Doug?"

I didn't say anything, but Mom said, "He does, on nights when you're not here."

Dad looked at me and then, for the first time that day, at the sky. Mother always watched him when he glanced at the stars. The first day and night when he got home he wouldn't look at the sky much. I thought about him garden-ing and gardening so furiously, his face almost driven into the earth. But the second night he looked at the stars a little more. Mother wasn't afraid of the sky in the day so much, but it was the night stars that she wanted to turn off, and sometimes I could almost see her reaching for a switch in her mind, but never finding it. And by the third night maybe Dad'd be out here on the porch until way after we were all ready for bed, and then I'd hear Mom call him in, almost like she called me from the street at times. And then I would hear Dad fitting the electric-eye door lock in place, with a sigh. And the next morning at breakfast I'd glance down and see his little black case near his feet as he buttered his toast and Mother slept late.

"Well, be seeing you, Doug," he'd say, and we'd shake hands.

"In about three months?"

"Right."

And he'd walk away down the street, not taking a heli-copter or beetle or bus, just walking with his uniform hidden in his small underarm case; he didn't want anyone to think he was vain about being a Rocket Man.

Mother would come out to eat breakfast, one piece of dry toast, about an hour later.

But now it was tonight, the first night, the good night, and he wasn't looking at the stars much at all.

"Let's go to the television carnival," I said.

"Fine," said Dad.

Mother smiled at me.

And we rushed off to town in a helicopter and took Dad through a thousand exhibits, to keep his face and head down with us and not looking anywhere else. And as we laughed at the funny things and looked serious at the serious ones, I thought, My father goes to Saturn and Neptune and Pluto, but he never brings me presents. Other boys whose fathers go into space bring back bits of ore from Callisto and hunks of black meteor or blue sand. But I have to get my own collection, trading from other boys, the Martian rocks and Mercurian sands which filled my room, but about which Dad would never comment.

On occasion, I remembered, he brought something for Mother. He planted some Martian sunflowers once in our yard, but after he was gone a month and the sunflowers grew large, Mom ran out one day and cut them all down.

Without thinking, as we paused at one of the three-dimensional exhibits, I asked Dad the question I always asked:

"What's it like, out in space?"

Mother shot me a frightened glance. It was too late.

Dad stood there for a full half minute trying to find an answer, then he shrugged.

"It's the best thing in a lifetime of best things." Then he caught himself. "Oh, it's really nothing at all. Routine. You wouldn't like it." He looked at me, apprehensively.

"But *you* always go back."

"Habit."

"Where're you going next?"

"I haven't decided yet. I'll think it over."

He always thought it over. In those days rocket pilots were rare and he could pick and choose, work when he liked. On the third night of his homecoming you could see him picking and choosing among the stars.

"Come on," said Mother, "let's go home."

It was still early when we got home. I wanted Dad to put on his uniform. I shouldn't have asked—it always made Mother unhappy—but I could not help myself. I kept at him, though he had always refused. I had never seen him in it, and at last he said, "Oh, all right."

We waited in the parlor while he went upstairs in the air flue. Mother looked at me dully, as if she couldn't believe that her own son could do this to her. I glanced away. "I'm sorry," I said.

"You're not helping at all," she said. "At all."

There was a whisper in the air flue a moment later.

"Here I am," said Dad quietly.

We looked at him in his uniform.

It was glossy black with silver buttons and silver rims to the heels of the black boots, and it looked as if someone had cut the arms and legs and body from a dark nebula, with little faint stars glowing through it. It fit as close as a glove fits to a slender long hand, and it smelled like cool air and metal and space. It smelled of fire and time.

Father stood, smiling awkwardly, in the center of the room.

"Turn around," said Mother.

Her eyes were remote, looking at him.

When he was gone, she never talked of him. She never said anything about anything but the weather or the condition of my neck and the need of a washcloth for it, or the fact that she didn't sleep nights. Once she said the light was too strong at night.

"But there's no moon this week," I said.

"There's starlight," she said.

I went to the store and bought her some darker, greener shades. As I lay in bed at night, I could hear her pull them down tight to the bottom of the windows. It made a long rustling noise.

Once I tried to mow the lawn.

"No." Mom stood in the door. "Put the mower away."

So the grass went three months at a time without cutting. Dad cut it when he came home.

She wouldn't let me do anything else either, like repairing the electrical breakfast maker or the mechanical book reader. She saved everything up, as if for Christmas. And then I would see Dad hammering or tinkering, and always smiling at his work, and Mother smiling over him, happy.

No, she never talked of him when he was gone. And as for Dad, he never did anything to make a contact across the millions of miles. He said once, "If I called you, I'd want to be with you. I wouldn't be happy."

Once Dad said to me, "Your mother treats me, sometimes, as if I weren't here—as if I were invisible."

I had seen her do it. She would look just beyond him, over his shoulder, at his chin or hands, but never into his eyes. If she did look at his eyes, her eyes were covered with a film, like an animal going to sleep. She said yes at the right times, and smiled, but always a half second later than expected.

"I'm not there for her," said Dad.

But other days she would be there and he would be there for her, and they would hold hands and walk around the block, or take rides, with Mom's hair flying like a girl's behind her, and she would cut off all the mechanical devices in the kitchen and bake him incredible cakes and pies and cookies, looking deep into his face, her smile a real smile. But at the end of such days when he was there to her, she would always cry. And Dad would stand helpless, gazing about the room as if to find the answer, but never finding it.

Dad turned slowly, in his uniform, for us to see.

"Turn around again," said Mom.

The next morning Dad came rushing into the house with handfuls of tickets. Pink rocket tickets for California, blue tickets for Mexico.

"Come on!" he said. "We'll buy disposable clothes and burn them when they're soiled. Look, we take the noon rocket to L.A., the two-o'clock helicopter to Santa Barbara, the nine-o'clock plane to Ensenada, sleep overnight!"

And we went to California and up and down the Pacific Coast for a day and a half, settling at last on the sands of Malibu to cook wieners at night. Dad was always listening or singing or watching things on all sides of him, holding onto things as if the world were a centrifuge going so swiftly that he might be flung off away from us at any instant.

The last afternoon at Malibu Mom was up in the hotel room. Dad lay on the sand beside me for a long time in the hot sun. "Ah," he sighed, "this is it." His eyes were gently closed; he lay on his back, drinking the sun. "You *miss* this," he said.

He meant "on the rocket," of course. But he never said "the rocket" or mentioned the rocket and all the things you couldn't have on the rocket. You couldn't have a salt wind on the rocket or a blue sky or a yellow sun or Mom's cooking. You couldn't talk to your fourteen-year-old boy on a rocket.

"Let's hear it," he said at last.

And I knew that now we would talk, as we had always talked, for three hours straight. All afternoon we would murmur back and forth in the lazy sun about my school grades, how high I could jump, how fast I could swim.

Dad nodded each time I spoke and smiled and slapped my chest lightly in approval. We talked. We did not talk of rockets or space, but we talked of Mexico, where we had driven once in an ancient car, and of the butterflies we had caught in the rain forests of green warm Mexico at noon, seeing the hundred butterflies sucked to our radiator, dying there, beating their blue and crimson wings, twitching, beautiful, and sad. We talked of such things instead of the things I wanted to talk about. And he listened to me. That was the thing he did, as if he was trying to fill himself up with all the sound he could hear. He listened to the wind and the falling ocean and my voice, always with a rapt attention, a concentration that almost excluded physical bodies themselves and kept only the sounds. He shut his eyes to listen. I would see him listening to the lawn mower as he cut the grass by hand instead of using the remote-control device, and I would see him smelling the cut grass as it sprayed up at him behind the mower in a green fount.

"Doug," he said, about five in the afternoon, as we were picking up our towels and heading back along the beach near the surf, "I want you to promise me something."

"What?"

"Don't ever be a Rocket Man."

I stopped.

"I mean it," he said. "Because when you're out there you want to be here, and when you're here you want to be out there. Don't start that. Don't let it get hold of you."

"But—"

"You don't know what it is. Every time I'm out there I

think, If I ever get back to Earth I'll stay there; I'll never go out again. But I go out, and I guess I'll always go out."

"I've thought about being a Rocket Man for a long time," I said.

He didn't hear me. "I try to stay here. Last Saturday when I got home I started trying so damned hard to stay here."

I remembered him in the garden, sweating, and all the traveling and doing and listening, and I knew that he did this to convince himself that the sea and the towns and the land and his family were the only real things and the good things. But I knew where he would be tonight: looking at the jewelry in Orion from our front porch.

"Promise me you won't be like me," he said.

I hesitated awhile. "Okay," I said.

He shook my hand. "Good boy," he said.

The dinner was fine that night. Mom had run about the kitchen with handfuls of cinnamon and dough and pots and pans tinkling, and now a great turkey fumed on the table, with dressing, cranberry sauce, peas, and pumpkin pie.

"In the middle of August?" said Dad, amazed.

"You won't be here for Thanksgiving."

"So I won't."

He sniffed it. He lifted each lid from each tureen and let the flavor steam over his sunburned face. He said "Ah" to each. He looked at the room and his hands. He gazed at the pictures on the wall, the chairs, the table, me, and Mom. He cleared his throat. I saw him make up his mind. "Lilly?"

"Yes?" Mom looked across her table which she had set like a wonderful silver trap, a miraculous gravy pit into which, like a struggling beast of the past caught in a tar pool, her husband might at last be caught and held, gazing out through a jail of wishbones, safe forever. Her eyes sparkled.

"Lilly," said Dad.

Go on, I thought crazily. Say it quick: say you'll stay home this time, for good, and never go away; say it!

Just then a passing helicopter jarred the room and the windowpane shook with a crystal sound. Dad glanced at the window.

The blue stars of evening were there, and the red planet Mars was rising in the East.

Dad looked at Mars a full minute. Then he put his hand out blindly toward me. "May I have some peas," he said.

"Excuse me," said Mother. "I'm going to get some bread." She rushed out into the kitchen.

"But there's bread on the table," I said.

Dad didn't look at me as he began his meal.

I couldn't sleep that night. I came downstairs at one in the morning and the moonlight was like ice on all the house-tops, and dew glittered in a snow field on our grass. I stood in the doorway in my pajamas, feeling the warm night wind, and then I knew that Dad was sitting in the mechanical porch swing, gliding gently. I could see his profile tilted back, and he was watching the stars wheel over the sky. His eyes were like gray crystal there, the moon in each one.

I went out and sat beside him.

We glided awhile in the swing.

At last I said, "How many ways are there to die in space?"

"A million."

"Name some."

"The meteors hit you. The air goes out of your rocket.

Or comets take you along with them. Concussion. Strangulation. Explosion. Centrifugal force. Too much acceleration. Too little. The heat, the cold, the sun, the moon, the stars, the planets, the asteroids, the planetoids, radiation . . ."

"And do they bury you?"

"They never find you."

"Where do you go?"

"A billion miles away. Traveling graves, they call them. You become a meteor or a planetoid traveling forever through space."

I said nothing.

"One thing," he said later, "it's quick in space. Death. It's over like that. You don't linger. Most of the time you don't even know it. You're dead and that's it."

We went up to bed.

It was morning.

Standing in the doorway, Dad listened to the yellow canary singing in its golden cage.

"Well, I've decided," he said. "Next time I come home, I'm home to stay."

"Dad!" I said.

"Tell your mother that when she gets up," he said.

"You *mean* it!"

He nodded gravely. "See you in about three months."

And there he went off down the street, carrying his uniform in its secret box, whistling and looking at the tall green trees and picking chinaberries off the chinaberry bush as he brushed by, tossing them ahead of him as he walked away into the bright shade of early morning. . . .

*   *   *

I asked Mother about a few things that morning after Father had been gone a number of hours. "Dad said that sometimes you don't act as if you hear or see him," I said.

And then she explained everything to me quietly.

"When he went off into space ten years ago, I said to myself, 'He's dead.' Or as good as dead. So think of him dead. And when he comes back, three or four times a year, it's not him at all, it's only a pleasant little memory or a dream. And if a memory stops or a dream stops, it can't hurt half as much. So most of the time I think of him dead—"

"But other times—"

"Other times I can't help myself. I bake pies and treat him as if he were alive, and then it hurts. No, it's better to think he hasn't been here for ten years and I'll never see him again. It doesn't hurt as much."

"Didn't he say next time he'd settle down?"

She shook her head slowly. "No, he's dead. I'm very sure of that."

"He'll come alive again, then," I said.

"Ten years ago," said Mother, "I thought, What if he dies on Venus? Then we'll never be able to see Venus again. What if he dies on Mars? We'll never be able to look at Mars again, all red in the sky, without wanting to go in and lock the door. Or what if he died on Jupiter or Saturn or Neptune? On those nights when those planets were high in the sky, we wouldn't want to have anything to do with the stars."

"I guess not," I said.

The message came the next day.

The messenger gave it to me and I read it standing on the porch. The sun was setting. Mom stood in the screen

door behind me, watching
in my pocket.

"Mom," I said.

"Don't tell me anyt

She didn't cry.

Well, it wasn't M

Jupiter or Saturn that

of him every time Jupit

ning sky.

This was different.

His ship had fallen into the sun.

And the sun was big and fiery and merciless, a..
always in the sky and you couldn't get away from it.

So for a long time after my father died my mother slept
through the days and wouldn't go out. We had breakfast at
midnight and lunch at three in the morning, and dinner at
the cold dim hour of 6 A.M. We went to all-night shows and
went to bed at sunrise.

And, for a long while, the only days we ever went out
to walk were the days when it was raining and there was
no sun.

The Last Night of the World

"What would you do if you knew that this was the last night of the world?"

"What would I do? You mean seriously?"

"Yes, seriously."

"I don't know. I hadn't thought."

He poured some coffee. In the background the two girls were playing blocks on the parlor rug in the light of the green hurricane lamps. There was an easy, clean aroma of the brewed coffee in the evening air.

"Well, better start thinking about it," he said.

"You don't mean it!"

He nodded.

"A war?"

He shook his head.

"Not the hydrogen or atom bomb?"

"No."

"Or germ warfare?"

"None of those at all," he said, stirring his coffee slowly. "But just, let's say, the closing of a book."

"I don't think I understand."

"No, nor do I, really; it's just a feeling. Sometimes it frightens me, sometimes I'm not frightened at all but at peace." He glanced in at the girls and their yellow hair shining in the lamplight. "I didn't say anything to you. It first happened about four nights ago."

"What?"

"A dream I had. I dreamed that it was all going to be over, and a voice said it was; not any kind of voice I can remember, but a voice anyway, and it said things would stop here on Earth. I didn't think too much about it the next day, but then I went to the office and caught Stan Willis looking out the window in the middle of the afternoon, and I said a penny for your thoughts, Stan, and he said, I had a dream last night, and before he even told me the dream I knew what it was. I could have told him, but he told me and I listened to him."

"It was the same dream?"

"The same. I told Stan I had dreamed it too. He didn't seem surprised. He relaxed, in fact. Then we started walking through the office, for the hell of it. It wasn't planned. We didn't say, 'Let's walk around.' We just walked around on our own, and everywhere we saw people looking at their desks or their hands or out windows. I talked to a few. So did Stan."

"And they all had dreamed?"

"All of them. The same dream, with no difference."

"Do you believe in it?"

"Yes. I've never been more certain."

"And when will it stop? The world, I mean."

"Sometime during the night for us, and then as the night goes on around the world, that'll go too. It'll take twenty-four hours for it all to go."

They sat awhile not touching their coffee. Then they lifted it slowly and drank, looking at each other.

"Do we deserve this?" she said.

"It's not a matter of deserving, it's just that things didn't work out. I notice you didn't even argue about this. Why not?"

"I guess I've a reason," she said.

"The same one everyone at the office had?"

She nodded slowly. "I didn't want to say anything. It happened last night. And the women on the block talked about it, among themselves, today. They dreamed. I thought it was only a coincidence." She picked up the evening paper. "There's nothing in the paper about it."

"Everyone knows, so there's no need."

He sat back in his chair, watching her. "Are you afraid?"

"No. I always thought I would be, but I'm not."

"Where's that spirit called self-preservation they talk so much about?"

"I don't know. You don't get too excited when you feel things are logical. This is logical. Nothing else but this could have happened from the way we've lived."

"We haven't been too bad, have we?"

"No, nor enormously good. I suppose that's the trouble—we haven't been very much of anything except us, while a big part of the world was busy being lots of quite awful things."

The girls were laughing in the parlor.

"I always thought people would be screaming in the streets at a time like this."

"I guess not. You don't scream about the real thing."

"Do you know, I won't miss anything but you and the girls. I never liked cities or my work or anything except you three. I won't miss a thing except perhaps the change in the weather, and a glass of ice water when it's hot, and I might miss sleeping. How can we sit here and talk this way?"

"Because there's nothing else to do."

"That's it, of course; for if there were, we'd be doing it. I suppose this is the first time in the history of the world that everyone has known just what they were going to do during the night."

"I wonder what everyone else will do now, this evening, for the next few hours."

"Go to a show, listen to the radio, watch television, play cards, put the children to bed, go to bed themselves, like always."

"In a way that's something to be proud of—like always."

They sat a moment and then he poured himself another coffee. "Why do you suppose it's tonight?"

"Because."

"Why not some other night in the last century, or five centuries ago, or ten?"

"Maybe it's because it was never October 19, 1969, ever before in history, and now it is and that's it; because it's the year when things are as they are all over the world and that's why it's the end."

"There are bombers on their schedules both ways across the ocean tonight that'll never see land."

"That's part of the reason why."

"Well," he said, getting up, "what shall it be? Wash the dishes?"

They washed the dishes and stacked them away with special neatness. At eight-thirty the girls were put to bed and kissed good night and the little lights by their beds turned on and the door left open just a trifle.

"I wonder," said the husband, coming from the bedroom and glancing back, standing there with his pipe for a moment.

"What?"

"If the door will be shut all the way, or if it'll be left just a little ajar so some light comes in."

"I wonder if the children know."

"No, of course not."

They sat and read the papers and talked and listened to some radio music and then sat together by the fireplace watching the charcoal embers as the clock struck ten-thirty and eleven and eleven-thirty. They thought of all the other people in the world who had spent their evening each in his own special way.

"Well," he said at last.

He kissed his wife for a long time.

"We've been good for each other, anyway."

"Do you want to cry?" he asked.

"I don't think so."

They moved through the house and turned out the lights and went into the bedroom and stood in the night cool darkness undressing and pushing back the covers. "The sheets are so clean and nice."

"I'm tired."

"We're *all* tired."

They got into bed and lay back.

"Just a moment," she said.

He heard her get out of bed and go into the kitchen. A moment later, she returned. "I left the water running in the sink," she said.

Something about this was so very funny that he had to laugh.

She laughed with him, knowing what it was that she had done that was funny. They stopped laughing at last and lay in their cool night bed, their hands clasped, their heads together.

"Good night," he said, after a moment.

"Good night," she said.

The Exiles

Their eyes were fire and the breath flamed out the witches' mouths as they bent to probe the caldron with greasy stick and bony finger.

> *"When shall we three meet again*
> *In thunder, lightning, or in rain?"*

They danced drunkenly on the shore of an empty sea, fouling the air with their three tongues, and burning it with their cats' eyes malevolently aglitter:

> *"Round about the cauldron go;*
> *In the poison'd entrails throw. . . .*
> *Double, double, toil and trouble;*
> *Fire burn, and cauldron bubble!"*

They paused and cast a glance about. *"Where's the crystal? Where's the needles?"*

"Here!"

"Good!"

"Is the yellow wax thickened?"

"Yes!"

"Pour it in the iron mold!"

"Is the wax figure done?" They shaped it like molasses adrip on their green hands.

"Shove the needle through the heart!"

"The crystal, the crystal; fetch it from the tarot bag. Dust it off; have a look!"

They bent to the crystal, their faces white.

"See, see, see. . ."

A rocket ship moved through space from the planet Earth to the planet Mars. On the rocket ship men were dying.

The captain raised his head, tiredly. "We'll have to use the morphine."

"But, Captain—"

"You see yourself this man's condition." The captain lifted the wool blanket and the man restrained beneath the wet sheet moved and groaned. The air was full of sulphurous thunder.

"I saw it—I saw it." The man opened his eyes and stared at the port where there were only black spaces, reeling stars, Earth far removed, and the planet Mars rising large and red. "I saw it—a bat, a huge thing, a bat with a man's face, spread over the front port. Fluttering and fluttering, fluttering and fluttering."

"Pulse?" asked the captain.

The orderly measured it. "One hundred and thirty."

"He can't go on with that. Use the morphine. Come along, Smith."

They moved away. Suddenly the floor plates were laced with bone and white skulls that screamed. The captain did not dare look down, and over the screaming he said, "Is this where Perse is?" turning in at a hatch.

A white-smocked surgeon stepped away from a body. "I just don't understand it."

"How did Perse die?"

"We don't know, Captain. It wasn't his heart, his brain, or shock. He just—died."

The captain felt the doctor's wrist, which changed to a hissing snake and bit him. The captain did not flinch. "Take care of yourself. You've a pulse too."

The doctor nodded. "Perse complained of pains—needles, he said—in his wrists and legs. Said he felt like wax, melting. He fell. I helped him up. He cried like a child. Said he had a silver needle in his heart. He died. Here he is. We can repeat the autopsy for you. Everything's physically normal."

"That's impossible! He died of *something!*"

The captain walked to a port. He smelled of menthol and iodine and green soap on his polished and manicured hands. His white teeth were dentrificed, and his ears scoured to a pinkness, as were his cheeks. His uniform was the color of new salt, and his boots were black mirrors shining below him. His crisp crew-cut hair smelled of sharp alcohol. Even his breath was sharp and new and clean. There was no spot to him. He was a fresh instrument, honed and ready, still hot from the surgeon's oven.

The men with him were from the same mold. One expected huge brass keys spiraling slowly from their backs.

They were expensive, talented, well-oiled toys, obedient and quick.

The captain watched the planet Mars grow very large in space.

"We'll be landing in an hour on that damned place, Smith, did you see any bats, or have other nightmares?"

"Yes, sir. The month before our rocket took off from New York, sir. White rats biting my neck, drinking my blood. I didn't tell. I was afraid you wouldn't let me come on this trip."

"Never mind," sighed the captain. "I had dreams too. In all of my fifty years I never had a dream until that week before we took off from Earth. And then every night I dreamed I was a white wolf. Caught on a snowy hill. Shot with a silver bullet. Buried with a stake in my heart." He moved his head toward Mars. "Do you think, Smith, *they* know we're coming?"

"We don't know if there *are* Martian people, sir."

"Don't we? They began frightening us off eight weeks ago, before we started. They've killed Perse and Reynolds now. Yesterday they made Grenville go blind. How? I don't know. Bats, needles, dreams, men dying for no reason. I'd call it witchcraft in another day. But this is the year 2120, Smith. We're rational men. This all can't be happening. But it is! Whoever they are, with their needles and their bats, they'll try to finish us all." He swung about. "Smith, fetch those books from my file. I want them when we land."

Two hundred books were piled on the rocket desk.

"Thank you, Smith. Have you glanced at them? Think I'm insane? Perhaps. It's a crazy hunch. At that last moment I ordered these books from the Historical Museum. Because of my dreams. Twenty nights I was stabbed, butchered, a

screaming bat pinned to a surgical mat, a thing rotting under-
ground in a black box, bad, wicked dreams. Our whole crew
dreamed of witch-things and were-things, vampires and phan-
toms, things they *couldn't* know anything about. Why? Because books on such ghastly subjects were destroyed a
century ago. By law. Forbidden for anyone to own the grisly
volumes. These books you see here are the *last* copies, kept
for historical purposes in the locked museum vaults."

Smith bent to read the dusty titles:

"*Tales of Mystery and Imagination*, by Edgar Allan Poe. *Dra-
cula*, by Bram Stoker. *Frankenstein*, by Mary Shelley. *The Turn
of the Screw*, by Henry James. *The Legend of Sleepy Hollow*, by
Washington Irving. *Rappaccini's Daughter*, by Nathaniel Hawthorne. *An Occurrence at Owl Creek Bridge*, by Ambrose Bierce.
Alice in Wonderland, by Lewis Carroll. *The Willows*, by Algernon
Blackwood. *The Wizard of Oz*, by L. Frank Baum. *The Weird
Shadow Over Innsmouth*, by H. P. Lovecraft. And more! Books
by Walter de la Mare, Wakefield, Harvey, Wells, Asquith,
Huxley—all forbidden authors. All burned in the same year
that Halloween was outlawed and Christmas was banned! But,
sir, what good are these to us on the rocket?"

"I don't know," sighed the captain, "yet."

The three hags lifted the crystal where the captain's
image flickered, his tiny voice tinkling out of the glass:

"I don't know," sighed the captain, "yet."

The three witches glared redly into one another's faces.

"We haven't much time," said one.

"Better warn *Them* in the City."

"They'll want to know about the books. It doesn't look
good. That fool of a captain!"

"In an hour they'll land their rocket."

The three hags shuddered and blinked up at the Emerald City by the edge of the dry Martian sea. In its highest window a small man held a blood-red drape aside. He watched the wastelands where the three witches fed their caldron and shaped the waxes. Farther along, ten thousand other blue fires and laurel incenses, black tobacco smokes and fir weeds, cinnamons and bone dusts rose soft as moths through the Martian night. The man counted the angry, magical fires. Then, as the three witches stared, he turned. The crimson drape, released, fell, causing the distant portal to wink, like a yellow eye.

Mr. Edgar Allan Poe stood in the tower window, a faint vapor of spirits upon his breath. "Hecate's friends are busy tonight," he said, seeing the witches, far below.

A voice behind him said, "I saw Will Shakespeare at the shore, earlier, whipping them on. All along the sea Shakespeare's army alone, tonight, numbers thousands: the three witches, Oberson, Hamlet's father, Puck—all, all of them— thousands! Good lord, a regular sea of people."

"Good William." Poe turned. He let the crimson drape fall shut. He stood for a moment to observe the raw stone room, the black-timbered table, the candle flame, the other man, Mr. Ambrose Bierce, sitting very idly there, lighting matches and watching them burn down, whistling under his breath, now and then laughing to himself.

"We'll have to tell Mr. Dickens now," said Mr. Poe. "We've put it off too long. It's a matter of hours. Will you go down to his home with me, Bierce?"

Bierce glanced up merrily. "I've just been thinking— what'll happen to us?"

"If we can't kill the rocket men off, frighten them away,

then we'll have to leave, of course. We'll go on to Jupiter, and when they come to Jupiter, we'll go on to Saturn, and when they come to Saturn, we'll go to Uranus, or Neptune, and then on out to Pluto—"

"Where then?"

Mr. Poe's face was weary; there were fire coals remaining, fading, in his eyes, and a sad wildness in the way he talked, and a uselessness of his hands and the way his hair fell lanky over his amazing white brow. He was like a satan of some lost dark cause, a general arrived from a derelict invasion. His silky, soft, black mustache was worn away by his musing lips. He was so small his brow seemed to float, vast and phosphorescent, by itself, in the dark room.

"We have the advantages of superior forms of travel," he said. "We can always hope for one of their atomic wars, dissolution, the dark ages come again. The return of superstition. We could go back then to Earth, all of us, in one night." Mr. Poe's black eyes brooded under his round and luminant brow. He gazed at the ceiling. "So they're coming to ruin *this* world too? They won't leave *anything* undefiled, will they?"

"Does a wolf pack stop until it's killed its prey and eaten the guts? It should be quite a war. I shall sit on the side lines and be the scorekeeper. So many Earthmen boiled in oil, so many Mss. Found in Bottles burnt, so many Earthmen stabbed with needles, so many Red Deaths put to flight by a batter of hypodermic syringes—ha!"

Poe swayed angrily, faintly drunk with wine. "What did we do? Be *with* us, Bierce, in the name of God! Did we have a fair trial before a company of literary critics? No! Our books were plucked up by neat, sterile, surgeon's pliers, and flung into vats, to boil, to be killed of all their mortuary germs. Damn them all!"

"I find our situation amusing," said Bierce.

They were interrupted by a hysterical shout from the tower stair.

"Mr. Poe! Mr. Bierce!"

"Yes, yes, we're coming!" Poe and Bierce descended to find a man gasping against the stone passage wall.

"Have you heard the news?" he cried immediately, clawing at them like a man about to fall over a cliff. "In an hour they'll land! They're bringing books with them—*old* books, the witches said! What're you doing in the tower at a time like this? Why aren't you acting?"

Poe said: "We're doing everything we can, Blackwood. You're new to all this. Come along, we're going to Mr. Charles Dickens' place—"

"—to contemplate our doom, our black doom," said Bierce, with a wink.

They moved down the echoing throats of the castle, level after dim green level, down into mustiness and decay and spiders and dreamlike webbing. "Don't worry," said Poe, his brow like a huge white lamp before them, descending, sinking. "All along the dead sea tonight I've called the others. Your friends and mine, Blackwood—Bierce. They're all there. The animals and the old women and the tall men with the sharp white teeth. The traps are waiting; the pits, yes, and the pendulums. The Red Death." Here he laughed quietly. "Yes, even the Red Death. I never thought—no, I never thought the time would come when a thing like the Red Death would actually *be*. But *they* asked for it, and they shall have it!"

"But are we strong enough?" wondered Blackwood.

"How strong is strong? They won't be prepared for us,

at least. They haven't the imagination. Those clean young rocket men with their antiseptic bloomers and fish-bowl helmets, with their new religion. About their necks, on gold chains, scalpels. Upon their heads, a diadem of microscopes. In their holy fingers, steaming incense urns which in reality are only germicidal ovens for steaming out superstition. The names of Poe, Bierce, Hawthorne, Blackwood—blasphemy to their clean lips."

Outside the castle they advanced through a watery space, a tarn that was not a tarn, which misted before them like the stuff of nightmares. The air filled with wing sounds and a whirring, a motion of winds and blacknesses. Voices changed, figures swayed at campfires. Mr. Poe watched the needles knitting, knitting, knitting, in the firelight; knitting pain and misery, knitting wickedness into wax marionettes, clay puppets. The caldron smells of wild garlic and cayenne and saffron hissed up to fill the night with evil pungency.

"Get on with it!" said Poe. "I'll be back!"

All down the empty seashore black figures spindled and waned, grew up and blew into black smoke on the sky. Bells rang in mountain towers and licorice ravens spilled out with the bronze sounds and spun away to ashes.

Over a lonely moor and into a small valley Poe and Bierce hurried, and found themselves quite suddenly on a cobbled street, in cold, bleak, biting weather, with people stomping up and down stony courtyards to warm their feet; foggy withal, and candles flaring in the windows of offices and shops where hung the Yuletide turkeys. At a distance some boys, all bundled up, snorting their pale breaths on the wintry air, were trilling, "God Rest Ye Merry, Gentlemen," while the immense tones of a great clock continuously sounded midnight. Children dashed by from the baker's with dinners all asteam in their grubby fists, on trays and under silver bowls.

At a sign which read SCROOGE, MARLEY AND DICKENS. Poe gave the Marley-faced knocker a rap, and from within, as the door popped open a few inches, a sudden gust of music almost swept them into a dance. And there, beyond the shoulder of the man who was sticking a trim goatee and mustaches at them, was Mr. Fezziwig clapping his hands, and Mrs. Fezziwig, one vast substantial smile, dancing and colliding with other merrymakers, while the fiddle chirped and laughter ran about a table like chandelier crystals given a sudden push of wind. The large table was heaped with brawn and turkey and holly and geese; with mince pies, suckling pigs, wreaths of sausages, oranges and apples; and there was Bob Cratchit and Little Dorrit and Tiny Tim and Mr. Fagin himself, and a man who looked as if he might be an undigested bit of beef, a blot of mustard, a crumb of cheese, a fragment of an underdone potato—who else but Mr. Marley, chains and all, while the wine poured and the brown turkeys did their excellent best to steam!

"What do you want?" demanded Mr. Charles Dickens.

"We've come to plead with you again, Charles; we need your help," said Poe.

"Help? Do you think I would help you fight against those good men coming in the rocket? I don't belong here, anyway. My books were burned by mistake. I'm no supernaturalist, no writer of horrors and terrors like you, Poe; you, Bierce, or the others. I'll have nothing to do with you terrible people!"

"You are a persuasive talker," reasoned Poe. "You could

go to meet the rocket men, lull them, lull their suspicions and then—then we would take care of them."

Mr. Dickens eyed the folds of the black cape which hid Poe's hands. From it, smiling, Poe drew forth a black cat. "For *one* of our visitors."

"And for the others?"

Poe smiled again, well pleased. "The Premature Burial?"

"You are a grim man, Mr. Poe."

"I am a frightened and an angry man. I am a god, Mr. Dickens, even as you are a god, even as we all are gods, and our inventions—our people, if you wish—have not only been threatened, but banished and burned, torn up and censored, ruined and done away with. The worlds we created are falling into ruin. Even gods must fight!"

"So?" Mr. Dickens tilted his head, impatient to return to the party, the music, the food. "Perhaps you can explain why we are here? How did we come here?"

"War begets war. Destruction begets destruction. On Earth, a century ago, in the year 2020 they outlawed our books. Oh, what a horrible thing—to destroy our literary creations that way! It summoned us out of—what? Death? The Beyond? I don't like abstract things. I don't know. I only know that our worlds and our creations called us and we tried to save them, and the only saving thing we could do was wait out the century here on Mars, hoping Earth might overweight itself with these scientists and their doubtings; but now they're coming to clean us out of here, us and our dark things, and all the alchemists, witches, vampires, and were-things that, one by one, retreated across space as science made inroads through every country on Earth and finally left no alternative at all but exodus. You must help us. You have a good speaking manner. We need you."

"I repeat, I am not of you, I don't approve of you and the others," cried Dickens angrily. "I was no player with witches and vampires and midnight things."

"What of *A Christmas Carol?*"

"Ridiculous! *One* story. Oh, I wrote a few others about ghosts, perhaps, but what of that? My basic works had none of that nonsense!"

"Mistaken or not, they grouped you with us. They destroyed your books—your worlds too. You must hate them, Mr. Dickens!"

"I admit they are stupid and rude, but that is all. Good day!"

"Let Mr. Marley come, at least!"

"*No!*"

The door slammed. As Poe turned away, down the street, skimming over the frosty ground, the coachman playing a lively air on a bugle, came a great coach, out of which, cherry-red, laughing and singing, piled the Pickwickians, banging on the door, shouting Merry Christmas good and loud, when the door was opened by the fat boy.

Mr. Poe hurried along the midnight shore of the dry sea. By fires and smoke he hesitated, to shout orders, to check the bubbling caldrons, the poisons and the chalked pentagrams. "Good!" he said, and ran on. "Fine!" he shouted, and ran again. People joined him and ran with him. Here were Mr. Coppard and Mr. Machen running with him now. And there were hating serpents and angry demons and fiery bronze dragons and spitting vipers and trembling witches like the barbs and nettles and thorns and all the vile flotsam and jetsam of the retreating sea of imagination, left on the melancholy shore, whining and frothing and spitting.

Mr. Machen stopped. He sat like a child on the cold sand. He began to sob. They tried to soothe him, but he would not listen. "I just thought," he said. "What happens to us on the day when the *last* copies of our books are destroyed?"

The air whirled.

"Don't speak of it!"

"We must," wailed Mr. Machen. "Now, now, as the rocket comes down, you, Mr. Poe; you, Coppard; you, Bierce—all of you grow faint. Like wood smoke. Blowing away. Your faces melt—"

"Death! *Real* death for all of us."

"We exist only through Earth's sufferance. If a final edict tonight destroyed our last few works we'd be like lights put out."

Coppard brooded gently. "I wonder who I am. In what Earth mind tonight do I exist? In some African hut? Some hermit, reading my tales? Is he the lonely candle in the wind of time and science? The flickering orb sustaining me here in rebellious exile? Is it him? Or some boy in a discarded attic, finding me, only just in time! Oh, last night I felt ill, ill, ill to the marrows of me, for there is a body of the soul as well as a body of the body, and this soul body ached in all of its glowing parts, and last night I felt myself a candle, guttering. When suddenly I sprang up, given new light! As some child, sneezing with dust, in some yellow garret on Earth once more found a worn, time-specked copy of me! And so I'm given a short respite!"

A door banged wide in a little hut by the shore. A thin short man, with flesh hanging from him in folds, stepped out and, paying no attention to the others, sat down and stared into his clenched fists.

"There's the one I'm sorry for," whispered Blackwood. "Look at him, dying away. He was once more real than we, who were men. They took him, a skeleton thought, and clothed him in centuries of pink flesh and snow beard and red velvet suit and black boot; made him reindeers, tinsel, holly. And after centuries of manufacturing him they drowned him in a vat of Lysol, you might say."

The men were silent.

"What must it be on Earth?" wondered Poe. "Without Christmas? No hot chestnuts, no tree, no ornaments or drums or candles—nothing; nothing but the snow and wind and the lonely, factual people. . . ."

They all looked at the thin little old man with the scraggly beard and faded red velvet suit.

"Have you heard his story?"

"I can imagine it. The glitter-eyed psychiatrist, the clever sociologist, the resentful, froth-mouthed educationalist, the antiseptic parents—"

"A regrettable situation," said Bierce, smiling, "for the Yuletide merchants who, toward the last there, as I recall, were beginning to put up holly and sing Noel the day before Halloween. With any luck at all this year they might have started on Labor Day!"

Bierce did not continue. He fell forward with a sigh. As he lay upon the ground he had time to say only, "How interesting." And then, as they all watched, horrified, his body burned into blue dust and charred bone, the ashes of which fled through the air in black tatters.

"Bierce, Bierce!"

"Gone!"

"His last book gone. Someone on Earth just now burned it."

"God rest him. Nothing of him left now. For what are we but books, and when those are gone, nothing's to be seen."

A rushing sound filled the sky.

They cried out, terrified, and looked up. In the sky, dazzling it with sizzling fire clouds, was the rocket! Around the men on the seashore lanterns bobbed; there was a squealing and a bubbling and an odor of cooked spells. Candle-eyed pumpkins lifted into the cold clear air. Thin fingers clenched into fists and a witch screamed from her withered mouth:

> "Ship, ship, break, fall!
> Ship, ship, burn all!
> Crack. flake, shake, melt!
> Mummy dust, cat pelt!"

"Time to go," murmured Blackwood. "On to Jupiter, on to Saturn or Pluto."

"Run away?" shouted Poe in the wind. "Never!"

"I'm a tired old man!"

Poe gazed into the old man's face and believed him. He climbed atop a huge boulder and faced the ten thousand gray shadows and green lights and yellow eyes on the hissing wind.

"The powders!" he shouted.

A thick hot smell of bitter almond, civet, cumin, worm-seed and orris!

The rocket came down—steadily down, with the shriek of a damned spirit! Poe raged at it! He flung his fists up and the orchestra of heat and smell and hatred answered in symphony! Like stripped tree fragments, bats flew upward!

Burning hearts, flung like missiles, burst in bloody fireworks on the singed air. Down, down, relentlessly down, like a pendulum the rocket came. And Poe howled, furiously, and shrank back with every sweep and sweep of the rocket cutting and ravening the air! All the dead sea seemed a pit in which, trapped, they waited the sinking of the dread machinery, the glistening ax; they were people under the avalanche!

"The snakes!" screamed Poe.

And luminous serpentines of undulant green hurtled toward the rocket. But it came down, a sweep, a fire, a motion, and it lay panting out exhaustions of red plumage on the sand, a mile away.

"At it!" shrieked Poe. "The plan's changed! Only one chance! Run! At it! At it! Drown them with our bodies! Kill them!"

And as if he had commanded a violent sea to change its course, to suck itself free from primeval beds, the whirls and savage gouts of fire spread and ran like wind and rain and stark lightning over the sea sands, down empty river deltas, shadowing and screaming, whistling and whining, sputtering and coalescing toward the rocket which, extinguished, lay like a clean metal torch in the farthest hollow. As if a great charred caldron of sparkling lava had been overturned, the boiling people and snapping animals churned down the dry fathoms.

"Kill them!" screamed Poe, running.

The rocket men leaped out of their ship, guns ready. They stalked about, sniffing the air like hounds. They saw nothing. They relaxed.

The captain stepped forth last. He gave sharp commands. Wood was gathered, kindled, and a fire leapt up in an instant. The captain beckoned his men into a half circle about him.

"A new world," he said, forcing himself to speak deliberately, though he glanced nervously, now and again, over his shoulder at the empty sea. "The old world left behind. A new start. What more symbolic than that we here dedicate ourselves all the more firmly to science and progress." He nodded crisply to his lieutenant. "The books."

Firelight limned the faded gilt titles: *The Willows, The Outsider, Behold, The Dreamer, Dr. Jekyll and Mr. Hyde, The Land of Oz, Pellucidar, The Land That Time Forgot, A Midsummer Night's Dream,* and the monstrous names of Machen and Edgar Allen Poe, and Cabell and Dunsany and Blackwood and Lewis Carroll; the names, the old names, the evil names.

"A new world. With a gesture, we burn the last of the old."

The captain ripped pages from the books. Leaf by seared leaf, he fed them into the fire.

A scream!

Leaping back, the men stared beyond the firelight at the edges of the encroaching and uninhabited sea.

Another scream! A high and wailing thing, like the death of a dragon and the thrashing of a bronzed whale left gasping when the waters of a leviathan's sea drain down the shingles and evaporate.

It was the sound of air rushing in to fill a vacuum, where, a moment before, there had been *something!*

The captain neatly disposed of the last book by putting it into the fire.

The air stopped quivering.

Silence!

The rocket men leaned and listened.

"Captain, did you hear it?"

"No."

"Like a wave, sir. On the sea bottom! I thought I saw something. Over there. A black wave. Big. Running at us."

"You were mistaken."

"There, sir!"

"What?"

"See it? There! The city! Way over! That green city near the lake! It's splitting in half. It's falling!"

The men squinted and shuffled forward.

Smith stood trembling among them. He put his hand to his head as if to find a thought there. "I remember. Yes, now I do. A long time back. When I was a child. A book I read. A story. Oz, I think it was. Yes, Oz. *The Emerald City of Oz* . . ."

"Oz? Never heard of it."

"Yes, Oz, that's what it was. I saw it just now, like in the story. I saw it fall."

"Smith!"

"Yes, sir?"

"Report for psychoanalysis tomorrow."

"Yes, sir!" A brisk salute.

"Be careful."

Then men tiptoed, guns alert, beyond the ship's aseptic light to gaze at the long sea and the low hills.

"Why," whispered Smith, disappointed, "there's no one here at all, is there? No one here at all."

The wind blew sand over his shoes, whining.

No Particular Night or Morning

He had smoked a packet of cigarettes in two hours.

"How far out in space are we?"

"A billion miles."

"A billion miles from where?" said Hitchcock.

"It all depends," said Clemens, not smoking at all. "A billion miles from home, you might say."

"Then *say* it."

"Home. Earth. New York. Chicago. Wherever you were from."

"I don't even remember," said Hitchcock. "I don't even believe there is an Earth now, do you?"

"Yes," said Clemens. "I dreamt about it this morning."

"There is no morning in space."

"During the night then."

"It's always night." said Hitchcock quietly. "Which night do you mean?"

"Shut up," said Clemens irritably. "Let me finish."

Hitchcock lit another cigarette. His hand did not shake, but it looked as if, inside the sunburned flesh, it might be tremoring all to itself, a small tremor in each hand and a large invisible tremor in his body. The two men sat on the observation corridor floor, looking out at the stars. Clemens's eyes flashed, but Hitchcock's eyes focused on nothing; they were blank and puzzled.

"I woke up at 0500 hours myself," said Hitchcock, as if he were talking to his right hand. "And I heard myself screaming, 'Where am I? where am I?' And the answer was 'Nowhere!' And I said, 'Where've I been?' And I said, 'Earth!' 'What's Earth?' I wondered. 'Where I was born,' I said. But it was nothing and worse than nothing. I don't believe in anything I can't see or hear or touch. I can't see Earth, so why should I believe in it? It's safer this way, not to believe."

"There's Earth." Clemens pointed, smiling. "That point of light there."

"That's not Earth; that's our sun. You can't see Earth from here."

"I can see it. I have a good memory."

"It's not the *same*, you fool," said Hitchcock suddenly. There was a touch of anger in his voice. "I mean *see* it. I've always been that way. When I'm in Boston, New York is dead. When I'm in New York, Boston is dead. When I don't see a man for a day, he's dead. When he comes walking down the street, my God, it's a resurrection. I do a dance, almost, I'm so glad to see him. I used to, anyway. I don't dance anymore. I just look. And when the man walks off, he's dead again."

Clemens laughed. "It's simply that your mind works on a primitive level. You can't hold to things. You've got no imagination, Hitchcock old man. You've got to learn to hold on."

"Why should I hold onto things I can't use?" said Hitchcock, his eyes wide, still staring into space. "I'm practical. If Earth isn't here for me to walk on, you want me to walk on a memory? That *hurts*. Memories, as my father once said, are porcupines. To hell with them! Stay away from them. They make you unhappy. They ruin your work. They make you cry."

"I'm walking on Earth right now," said Clemens, squinting to himself, blowing smoke.

"You're kicking porcupines. Later in the day you won't be able to eat lunch, and you'll wonder why," said Hitchcock in a dead voice. "And it'll be because you've got a footful of quills aching in you. To hell with it! If I can't drink it, pinch it, punch it, or lie on it, then I say drop it in the sun. I'm dead to Earth. It's dead to me. There's no one in New York weeping for me tonight. Shove New York. There isn't any season here; winter and summer are gone. So is spring, and autumn. It isn't any particular night or morning; it's space and space. The only thing right now is you and me and this rocket ship. And the only thing I'm positive of is *me*. That's all of it."

Clemens ignored this. "I'm putting a dime in the phone slot right now," he said, pantomiming it with a slow smile. "And calling my girl in Evanston. Hello, Barbara!"

The rocket sailed on through space.

The lunch bell rang at 1305 hours. The men ran by on soft rubber sneakers and sat at the cushioned tables.

Clemens wasn't hungry.

"See, what did I tell you!" said Hitchcock. "You and your damned porcupines! Leave them alone, like I told you. Look at me, shoveling away food." He said this with a mechanical, slow, and unhumorous voice. "Watch me." He put a big piece of pie in his mouth and felt it with his tongue. He looked at the pie on his plate as if to see the texture. He moved it with his fork. He felt the fork handle. He mashed the lemon filling and watched it jet up between the tines. Then he touched a bottle of milk all over and poured out half a quart into a glass, listening to it. He looked at the milk as if to make it whiter. He drank the milk so swiftly that he couldn't have tasted it. He had eaten his entire lunch in a few minutes, cramming it in feverishly, and now he looked around for more, but it was gone. He gazed out the window of the rocket, blankly. "Those aren't real, either," he said.

"What?" asked Clemens.

"The stars. Who's ever touched one? I can see them, sure, but what's the use of seeing a thing that's a million or a billion miles away? Anything that far off isn't worth bothering with."

"Why did you come on this trip?" asked Clemens suddenly.

Hitchcock peered into his amazingly empty milk glass and clenched it tight, then relaxed his hand and clenched it again. "I don't know." He ran his tongue on the glass rim. "I just had to, is all. How do you know why you do anything in this life?"

"You liked the idea of space travel? Going places?"

"I don't know. Yes. No. It wasn't going places. It was being *between*." Hitchcock for the first time tried to focus his eyes upon something, but it was so nebulous and far off that his eyes couldn't make the adjustment, though he worked his face and hands. "Mostly it was space. So much space. I liked the idea of nothing on top, nothing on the bottom, and a lot of nothing in between, and me in the middle of the nothing."

"I never heard it put that way before."

"*I* just put it that way; I hope you listened."

Hitchcock took out his cigarettes and lit up and began to suck and blow the smoke, again and again.

Clemens said, "What sort of childhood did you have, Hitchcock?"

"I was never young. Whoever I was then is dead. That's more of your quills. I don't want a hide full, thanks. I've always figured it that you die each day and each day is a box, you see, all numbered and neat; but never go back and lift the lids, because you've died a couple of thousand times in your life, and that's a lot of corpses, each dead a different way, each with a worse expression. Each of those days is a different you, somebody you don't know or understand or want to understand."

"You're cutting yourself off, that way."

"Why should I have anything to do with that younger Hitchcock? He was a fool, and he was yanked around and taken advantage of and used. His father was no good, and he was glad when his mother died, because she was the same. Should I go back and see his face on that day and gloat over it? He was a fool."

"We're all fools," said Clemens, "all the time. It's just we're a different kind each day. We think, I'm not a fool today. I've learned my lesson. I was a fool yesterday but not this morning. Then tomorrow we find out that, yes, we were a fool today too. I think the only way we can grow and get on in this world is to accept the fact we're not perfect and live accordingly."

"I don't want to remember imperfect things," said Hitchcock. "I can't shake hands with that younger Hitchcock, can I? Where is he? Can you find him for me? He's dead, so to hell with him! I won't shape what I do tomorrow by some lousy thing I did yesterday."

"You've got it wrong."

"Let me have it then." Hitchcock sat, finished with his meal, looking out the port. The other men glanced at him.

"Do meteors exist?" asked Hitchcock.

"You know damn well they do."

"In our radar machines—yes, as streaks of light in space. No, I don't believe in anything that doesn't exist and act in my presence. Sometimes"—he nodded at the men finishing their food—"sometimes I don't believe in anyone or anything but me." He sat up. "Is there an upstairs to this ship?"

"Yes."

"I've got to see it immediately."

"Don't get excited."

"You wait here; I'll be right back." Hitchcock walked out swiftly. The other men sat nibbling their food slowly. A moment passed. One of the men raised his head. "How long's this been going on? I mean Hitchcock."

"Just today."

"He acted funny the other day too."

"Yes, but it's worse today."

"Has anyone told the psychiatrist?"

"We thought he'd come out of it. Everyone has a little touch of space the first time out. I've had it. You get wildly philosophical, then frightened. You break into a sweat, then you doubt your parentage, you don't believe in Earth, you get drunk, wake up with a hang-over, and that's it."

"But Hitchcock don't get drunk," said someone. "I wish he would."

"How'd he ever get past the examining board?"

"How'd we all get past? They need men. Space scares

the hell out of most people. So the board lets a lot of border-lines through."

"That man isn't a borderline," said someone. "He's a fall-off-a-cliff-and-no-bottom-to-hit."

They waited for five minutes. Hitchcock didn't come back.

Clemens finally got up and went out and climbed the circular stairs to the flight deck above. Hitchcock was there, touching the wall tenderly.

"It's here," he said.

"Of course it is."

"I was afraid it might not be." Hitchcock peered at Clemens. "And you're alive."

"I have been for a long time."

"No," said Hitchcock. "Now, just *now*, this *instant*, while you're here with me, you're alive. A moment ago you weren't anything."

"I was to me," said the other.

"That's not important. You weren't here with me," said Hitchcock. "Only that's important. Is the crew down below?"

"Yes."

"Can you prove it?"

"Look, Hitchcock, you'd better see Dr. Edwards. I think you need a little servicing."

"No, I'm all right. Who's the doctor, anyway? Can you prove he's on this ship?"

"I can. All I have to do is call him."

"No. I mean, standing here, in this instant, you can't prove he's here, can you?"

"Not without moving. I can't."

"You see. You have no mental evidence. That's what I want, a mental evidence I can *feel*. I don't want physical evidence, proof you have to go out and drag in. I want evidence that you can carry in your mind and always touch and smell and feel. But there's no way to do that. In order to believe in a thing you've got to carry it with you. You can't carry the Earth, or a man, in your pocket. I want a way to do that, carry things with me always, so I can believe in them. How clumsy to have to go to all the trouble of going out and bringing in something terribly physical to *prove* something. I hate physical things because they can be left behind and become impossible to believe in them."

"Those are the rules of the game."

"I want to change them. Wouldn't it be fine if we could *prove* things with our mind, and know for certain that things are always in their place. I'd like to know what a place is *like* when I'm *not there*. I'd like to be *sure*."

"That's not possible."

"You know," said Hitchcock, "I first got the idea of coming out into space about five years ago. About the time I lost my job. Did you know I wanted to be a writer? Oh yes, one of those men who always talk about writing but rarely write. And too much temper. So I lost my good job and left the editorial business and couldn't get another job and went on down hill. Then my wife died. You see, nothing stays where you put it—you can't trust material things. I had to put my boy in an aunt's trust, and things got worse; then one day I had a story published with my name on it, but it wasn't me."

"I don't get you."

Hitchcock's face was pale and sweating.

"I can only say that I looked at the page with my name under the title. By Joseph Hitchcock. But it was some other man. There was no way to *prove*—actually *prove*, *really* prove—that that man was me. The story was familiar—I knew I had written it—but that name on the paper still was not me. It was a symbol, a name. It was alien. And then I realized that even if I did become successful at writing, it would never mean a thing to me, because I couldn't identify myself with that name. It would be soot and ashes. So I didn't write any more. I was never sure, anyway, that the stories I had in my desk a few days later were mine, though I remembered typing them. There was always that gap of proof. That gap between doing and having done. What is done is dead and is not proof, for it is not an action. Only actions are important. And pieces of paper were remains of actions done and over and now unseen. The proof of doing was over and done. Nothing but memory remained, and I didn't trust my memory. Could I actually *prove* I'd written these stories? No. Can *any* author? I mean *proof.* I mean action as proof. No. Not really. Not unless someone sits in the room while you type, and then maybe you're doing it from memory. And once a thing is accomplished there is no proof, only memory. So then I began to find gaps between everything. I doubted I was married or had a child or ever had a job in my life. I doubted that I had been born in Illinois and had a drunken father and swinish mother. I couldn't prove anything. Oh yes, people could say, 'You are thus and so and such and such,' but that was nothing."

"You should get your mind off stuff like that," said Clemens.

"I can't. All the gaps and spaces. And that's how I got to thinking about the stars. I thought how I'd like to be in a rocket ship in space, in nothing, in *nothing*, going on into nothing, with just a thin something, a thin eggshell of metal holding me, going on away from all the somethings with gaps in them that couldn't prove themselves. I knew then that the only happiness for me was space. When I get to Aldebaran II I'll sign up to return on the five-year journey to Earth and so go back and forth like a shuttlecock all the rest of my life."

"Have you talked about this to the psychiatrist?"

"So he could try to mortar up the gaps for me, fill in the gulfs with noise and warm water and words and hands touching me, and all that? No, thanks." Hitchcock stopped. "I'm getting worse, aren't I? I thought so. This morning when I woke up I thought, I'm getting worse. Or is it better?" He paused again and cocked an eye at Clemens. "Are you there? Are you *really* there? Go on, prove it."

Clemens slapped him on the arm, hard.

"Yes," said Hitchcock, rubbing his arm, looking at it very thoroughly, wonderingly, massaging it. "You were there. For a brief fraction of an instant. But I wonder if you are— *now*."

"See you later," said Clemens. He was on his way to find the doctor. He walked away.

A bell rang. Two bells, three bells rang. The ship rocked as if a hand had slapped it. There was a sucking sound, the sound of a vacuum cleaner turned on. Clemens heard the screams and felt the air thin. The air hissed away about his ears. Suddenly there was nothing in his nose or lungs. He stumbled and then the hissing stopped.

He heard someone cry. "A meteor." Another said, "It's patched!" And this was true. The ship's emergency spider, running over the outside of the hull, had slapped a hot patch on the hole in the metal and welded it tight.

Someone was talking and talking and then beginning to shout at a distance. Clemens ran along the corridor through the freshening, thickening air. As he turned in at a bulkhead he saw the hole in the steel wall, freshly sealed; he saw the meteor fragments lying about the room like bits of a toy. He saw the captain and the members of the crew and a man lying on the floor. It was Hitchcock. His eyes were closed and he was crying. "It tried to kill me," he said, over and over. "It tried to kill me." They got him on his feet. "It can't do that," said Hitchcock. "That's not how it should be. Things like that can't happen, can they? It came in after *me*. Why did it do that?"

"All right, all right, Hitchcock," said the captain.

The doctor was bandaging a small cut on Hitchcock's arm. Hitchcock looked up, his face pale, and saw Clemens there looking at him. "It tried to *kill* me," he said.

"I know," said Clemens.

Seventeen hours passed. The ship moved on in space.

Clemens stepped through a bulkhead and waited. The psychiatrist and the captain were there. Hitchcock sat on the floor with his legs drawn up to his chest, arms wrapped tight about them.

"Hitchcock," said the captain.

No answer.

"Hitchcock, listen to me," said the psychiatrist.

They turned to Clemens. "You're his friend?"

"Yes."

"Do you want to help us?"

"If I can."

"It was that damned meteor," said the captain. "This might not have happened if it hadn't been for that."

"It would've come anyway, sooner or later," said the doctor. To Clemens: "You might talk to him."

Clemens walked quietly over and crouched by Hitchcock and began to shake his arm gently, calling in a low voice, "Hey there, Hitchcock."

No reply.

"Hey, it's me. Me, Clemens," said Clemens. "Look, I'm here." He gave the arm a little slap. He massaged the rigid neck, gently, and the back of the bent-down head. He glanced at the psychiatrist, who sighed very softly. The captain shrugged.

"Shock treatment, Doctor?"

The psychiatrist nodded. "We'll start within the hour."

Yes, thought Clemens, shock treatment. Play a dozen jazz records for him, wave a bottle of fresh green chlorophyll and dandelions under his nose, put grass under his feet, squirt Chanel on the air, cut his hair, clip his fingernails, bring him a woman, shout, bang and crash at him, fry him with electricity, fill the gap and the gulf, but where's your proof? You can't keep proving to him forever. You can't entertain a baby with rattles and sirens all night every night for the next thirty years. Sometime you've got to stop. When you do that, he's lost again. That is, if he pays any attention to you at all.

"Hitchcock!" he cried, as loud as he could, almost frantically, as if he himself were falling over a cliff. "It's me. It's your pal! Hey!"

Clemens turned and walked away out of the silent room.

Twelve hours later another alarm bell rang.

After all of the running had died down, the captain explained: "Hitchcock snapped out of it for a minute or so. He was alone. He climbed into a space suit. He opened an airlock. Then he walked out into space—alone."

Clemens blinked through the immense glass port, where

there was a blur of stars and distant blackness. "He's out there now?"

"Yes. A million miles behind us. We'd never find him. First time I knew he was outside the ship was when his helmet radio came in on our control-room beam. I heard him talking to himself."

"What did he say?"

"Something like 'No more space ship now. Never was any. No people. No people in all the universe. Never were any. No plants. No stars.' That's what he said. And then he said something about his hands and feet and legs. 'No hands,' he said. 'I haven't any hands anymore. Never had any. No feet. Never had any. Can't prove it. No body. Never had any. No lips. No face. No head. Nothing. Only space. Only space. Only the gap.' "

The men turned quietly to look from the glass port out into the remote and cold stars.

Space, thought Clemens. The space that Hitchcock loved so well. Space, with nothing on top, nothing on the bottom, a lot of empty nothings between, and Hitchcock falling in the middle of the nothing, on his way to no particular night and no particular morning. . . .

The Fox and the Forest

There were fireworks the very first night, things that you
should be afraid of perhaps, for they might remind you
of other more horrible things, but these were beautiful, rockets
that ascended into the ancient soft air of Mexico and shook
the stars apart in blue and white fragments. Everything was
good and sweet, the air was that blend of the dead and the
living, of the rains and the dusts, of the incense from the church,
and the brass smell of the tubas on the bandstand which pulsed
out vast rhythms of "La Paloma." The church doors were thrown
wide and it seemed as if a giant yellow constellation had fallen
from the October sky and lay breathing fire upon the church
walls; a million candles sent their color and fumes about. Newer
and better fireworks scurried like tight-rope walking comets
across the cool-tiled square, banged against adobe café walls,
then rushed on hot wires to bash the high church tower, in
which boys' naked feet alone could be seen kicking and re-
kicking, clanging and tilting and retilting the monster bells into
monstrous music. A flaming bull blundered about the plaza chas-
ing laughing men and screaming children.

"The year is 1938," said William Travis, standing by his wife on the edge of the yelling crowd, smiling. "A good year."

The bull rushed upon them. Ducking, the couple ran, with fire balls pelting them, past the music and riot, the church, the band, under the stars, clutching each other, laughing. The bull passed, carried lightly on the shoulders of a charging Mexican, a framework of bamboo and sulphurous gunpowder.

"I've never enjoyed myself so much in my life." Susan Travis had stopped for her breath.

"It's amazing," said William.

"It will go on, won't it?"

"All night."

"No, I mean our trip."

He frowned and patted his breast pocket. "I've enough traveler's checks for a lifetime. Enjoy yourself. Forget it. They'll never find us."

"Never?"

"Never."

Now someone was setting off giant crackers, hurling them from the great bell-tolling tower of the church in a sputter of smoke, while the crowd below fell back under the threat and the crackers exploded in wonderful concussions among their dancing feet and flailing bodies. A wondrous smell of frying tortillas hung all about, and in the cafés men sat at tables looking out, mugs of beer in their brown hands.

The bull was dead. The fire was out of the bamboo tubes and he was expended. The laborer lifted the framework from his shoulders. Little boys clustered to touch the magnificent papier-mâché head, the real horns.

"Let's examine the bull," said William.

As they walked past the café entrance Susan saw the

man looking out at them, a white man in a salt-white suit, with a blue tie and blue shirt, and a thin, sunburned face! His hair was blond and straight and his eyes were blue, and he watched them as they walked.

She would never have noticed him if it had not been for the bottles at his immaculate elbow; a fat bottle of crème de menthe, a clear bottle of vermouth, a flagon of cognac, and seven other bottles of assorted liqueurs, and, at his finger tips, ten small half-filled glasses from which, without taking his eyes off the street, he sipped, occasionally squinting, pressing his thin mouth shut upon the savor. In his free hand a thin Havana cigar smoked, and on a chair stood twenty cartons of Turkish cigarettes, six boxes of cigars, and some packaged colognes.

"Bill—" whispered Susan.

"Take it easy," he said. "He's nobody."

"I saw him in the plaza this morning."

"Don't look back, keep walking. Examine the papier-mâché bull here. That's it, ask questions."

"Do you think he's from the Searchers?"

"They couldn't follow us!"

"They might!"

"What a nice bull," said William to the man who owned it.

"He couldn't have followed us back through two hundred years, could he?"

"Watch yourself, for God's sake," said William.

She swayed. He crushed her elbow tightly, steering her away.

"Don't faint." He smiled, to make it look good. "You'll be all right. Let's go right in that café, drink in front of him, so if he *is* what we think he is, he won't suspect."

"No, I couldn't."

"We've *got* to. Come on now. And so I said to David, that's ridiculous!" This last in a loud voice as they went up the cafe steps.

We are here, thought Susan. Who are we? Where are we going? What do we fear? Start at the beginning, she told herself, holding to her sanity, as she felt the adobe floor underfoot.

My name is Ann Kristen; my husband's name is Roger. We were born in the year 2155 A.D. And we lived in a world that was evil. A world that was like a great black ship pulling away from the shore of sanity and civilization, roaring its black horn in the night, taking two billion people with it, whether they wanted to go or not, to death, to fall over the edge of the earth and the sea into radioactive flame and madness.

They walked into the café. The man was staring at them.

A phone rang.

The phone startled Susan. She remembered a phone ringing two hundred years in the future, on that blue April morning in 2155, and herself answering it.

"Ann, this is Rene! Have you heard? I mean about Travel in Time, Incorporated? Trips to Rome in 21 B.C., trips to Napoleon's Waterloo—any time, any place!"

"Rene, you're joking."

"No. Clinton Smith left this morning for Philadelphia in 1776. Travel in Time, Inc., arranges everything. Costs money. But, *think*—to actually *see* the burning of Rome, Kubla Khan, Moses and the Red Sea! You've probably got an ad in your tube mail now."

She had opened the suction mail tube and there was the metal foil advertisement:

ROME AND THE BORGIAS!
THE WRIGHT BROTHERS AT KITTY HAWK!

Travel in Time, Inc., can costume you, put you in a crowd
during the assassination of Lincoln or Caesar! We guarantee to teach you any language you need to move freely in
any civilization, in any year, without friction. Latin, Greek,
ancient American colloquial. Take your vacation in *Time* as
well as Place!

Rene's voice was buzzing on the phone. "Tom and I
leave for 1492 tomorrow. They're arranging for Tom to sail
with Columbus. Isn't it amazing!"

"Yes," murmured Ann, stunned. "What does the Govern-
ment say about this Time Machine company?"

"Oh, the police have an eye on it. Afraid people might
evade the draft, run off and hide in the Past. Everyone has
to leave a security bond behind, his house and belongings,
to guarantee return. After all, the war's on."

"Yes, the war," murmured Ann. "The war."

Standing there, holding the phone, she had thought,
Here is the chance my husband and I have talked and prayed
over for so many years. We don't like this world of 2155.
We want to run away from his work at the bomb factory, I
from my position with disease-culture units. Perhaps there is
a chance for us to escape, to run for centuries into a wild
country of years where they will never find and bring us back
to burn our books, censor our thoughts, scald our minds with
fear, march us, scream at us with radios . . .

They were in Mexico in the year 1938.

She looked at the stained café wall.

Good workers for the Future State were allowed vacations

into the Past to escape fatigue. And so she and her husband had moved back into 1938, a room in New York City, and enjoyed the theaters and the Statue of Liberty which still stood green in the harbor. And on the third day they had changed their clothes, their names, and had flown off to hide in Mexico!

"It *must* be him," whispered Susan, looking at the stranger seated at the table. "Those cigarettes, the cigars, the liquor. They give him away. Remember *our* first night in the Past?"

A month ago, their first night in New York, before their flight, drinking all the strange drinks, savoring and buying odd foods, perfumes, cigarettes of ten dozen rare brands, for they were rare in the Future, where war was everything. So they had made fools of themselves, rushing in and out of stores, salons, tobacconists, going up to their room to get wonderfully ill.

And now here was this stranger doing likewise, doing a thing that only a man from the Future would do who had been starved for liquors and cigarettes for many years.

Susan and William sat and ordered a drink.

The stranger was examining their clothes, their hair, their jewelry—the way they walked and sat.

"Sit easily," said William under his breath. "Look as if you've worn this clothing style all your life."

"We should never have tried to escape."

"My God!" said William, "he's coming over. Let me do the talking."

The stranger bowed before them. There was the faintest tap of heels knocking together. Susan stiffened. That military sound!—unmistakable as that certain ugly rap on your door at midnight.

"Mr. Roger Kristen," said the stranger, "you did not pull up your pant legs when you sat down."

William froze. He looked at his hands lying on either leg, innocently. Susan's heart was beating swiftly.

"You've got the wrong person," said William quickly. "My name's not Krisler."

"Kristen," corrected the stranger.

"I'm William Travis," said William. "And I don't see what my pant legs have to do with you."

"Sorry." The stranger pulled up a chair. "Let us say I thought I knew you because you did *not* pull your trousers up. *Everyone* does. If they don't, the trousers bag quickly. I am a long way from home, Mr.—Travis, and in need of company. My name is Simms."

"Mr. Simms, we appreciate your loneliness, but we're tired. We're leaving for Acapulco tomorrow."

"A charming spot. I was just there, looking for some friends of mine. They are somewhere. I shall find them yet. Oh, is the lady a bit sick?"

"Good night, Mr. Simms."

They started out the door, William holding Susan's arm firmly. They did not look back when Mr. Simms called, "Oh, just one other thing." He paused and then slowly spoke the words:

"2155 A.D."

Susan shut her eyes and felt the earth falter under her. She kept going, into the fiery plaza, seeing nothing.

They locked the door of their hotel room. And then she was crying and they were standing in the dark, and the room tilted under them. Far away firecrackers exploded, and there was laughter in the plaza.

"What a damned, loud nerve," said William. "Him sitting there, looking us up and down like animals, smoking his damn cigarettes, drinking his drinks. I should have killed him then!" His voice was nearly hysterical. "He even had the nerve to use his real name to us. The Chief of the Searchers. And the thing about my pant legs. My God, I should have pulled them up when I sat. It's an automatic gesture of this day and age. When I didn't do it, it set me off from the others; it made *him* think. Here's a man who never wore pants, a man used to breech uniforms and future styles. I could kill myself for giving us away!"

"No, no, it was my walk—these high heels—that did it. Our haircuts—so new, so fresh. Everything about us odd and uneasy."

He turned on the light. "He's still testing us. He's not positive of us—not completely. We can't run out on him, then. We can't make him certain. We'll go to Acapulco leisurely."

"Maybe he *is* sure of us, but is just playing."

"I wouldn't put it past him. He's got all the time in the world. He can dally here if he wants and bring us back to the Future sixty seconds after we left it. He might keep us wondering for days, laughing at us."

Susan sat on the bed, wiping the tears from her face. smelling the old smell of charcoal and incense.

"They won't make a scene, will they?"

"They won't dare. They'll have to get us alone to put us in that Time Machine and send us back."

"There's a solution then," she said. "We'll never be alone; we'll always be in crowds. We'll make a million friends, visit markets, sleep in the Official Palaces in each town, pay the Chief of Police to guard us until we find a way to kill Simms and escape, disguise ourselves in new clothes, perhaps as Mexicans."

Footsteps sounded outside their locked door.

They turned out the light and undressed in silence. The footsteps went away. A door closed.

Susan stood by the window looking down at the plaza in the darkness. "So that building there is a church?"

"Yes."

"I've often wondered what a church looked like. It's been so long since anyone saw one. Can we visit it tomorrow?"

"Of course. Come to bed."

They lay in the dark room.

Half an hour later their phone rang. She lifted the receiver.

"Hello?"

"The rabbits may hide in the forest," said a voice, "but a fox can always find them."

She replaced the receiver and lay back straight and cold in the bed.

Outside, in the year 1938, a man played three tunes upon a guitar, one following another.

During the night she put her hand out and almost touched the year 2155. She felt her fingers slide over cool spaces of time, as over a corrugated surface, and she heard the insistent thump of marching feet, a million bands playing a million military tunes, and she saw the fifty thousand rows of disease cultures in their aseptic glass tubes, her hand reaching out to them at her work in that huge factory in the Future; the tubes of leprosy, bubonic, typhoid, tuberculosis, and then the great explosion. She saw her hand burned to a wrinkled plum, felt it recoil from a concussion so immense that the world was lifted and let fall and all the buildings broke and people hemorrhaged and lay silent. Great volcanoes, machines, winds, avalanches slid down to silence and she awoke, sobbing, in the bed, in Mexico, many years away. . . .

In the early morning, drugged with the single hour's sleep they had finally been able to obtain, they awoke to the sound of loud automobiles in the street. Susan peered down from the iron balcony at a small crowd of eight people only now emerging, chattering, yelling, from trucks and cars with red lettering on them. A crowd of Mexicans had followed the trucks.

"*Qué pasa?*" Susan called to a little boy.

The boy replied.

Susan turned back to her husband. "An American motion-picture company, here on location."

"Sounds interesting." William was in the shower. "Let's watch them. I don't think we'd better leave today. We'll try to lull Simms. Watch the films being made. They say the primitive film make was something. Get our minds off ourselves."

Ourselves, thought Susan. For a moment, in the bright sun, she had forgotten that somewhere in the hotel, waiting, was a man smoking a thousand cigarettes, it seemed. She saw the eight loud happy Americans below and wanted to call to them: "Save me, hide me, help me! Color my hair, my eyes; clothe me in strange clothes. I need your help. I'm from the year 2155!"

But the words stayed in her throat. The functionaries of Travel in Time, Inc., were not foolish. In your brain, before you left on your trip, they placed a psychological block. You could tell no one your true time or birthplace, nor could you reveal any of the Future to those in the Past. The Past and the Future must be protected from each other. Only with this psychological block were people allowed to travel unguarded through the ages. The Future must be protected from any change brought about by her people traveling in the Past. Even if she wanted to with all her heart, she could not tell any of those happy people below in the plaza who she was, or what her predicament had become.

"What about breakfast?" said William.

Breakfast was being served in the immense dining room. Ham and eggs for everyone. The place was full of tourists. The film people entered, all eight of them—six men and two women, giggling, shoving chairs about. And Susan sat near them, feeling the warmth and protection they offered, even when Mr. Simms came down the lobby stairs, smoking his Turkish cigarette with great intensity. He nodded at them from a distance, and Susan nodded back, smiling, because he couldn't do anything to them here, in front of eight film people and twenty other tourists.

"Those actors," said William. "Perhaps I could hire two of them, say it was a joke, dress them in our clothes, have them drive off in our car when Simms is in such a spot where he can't see their faces. If two people pretending to be us could lure him off for a few hours, we might make it to Mexico City. It'd take him years to find us there!"

"Hey!"

A fat man, with liquor on his breath, leaned on their table.

"American tourists!" he cried. "I'm so sick of seeing Mexicans, I could kiss you!" He shook their hands. "Come on, eat with us. Misery loves company. I'm Misery, this is Miss Gloom and Mr. and Mrs. Do-We-Hate-Mexico! We all hate it. But we're here for some preliminary shots for a damn film. The rest of the crew arrives tomorrow. My name's Joe Melton. I'm a director. And if this ain't a hell of a country! Funerals in the streets, people dying. Come on, move over. Join the party; cheer us up!"

Susan and William were both laughing.

"Am I funny?" Mr. Melton asked the immediate world.

"Wonderful!" Susan moved over.

Mr. Simms was glaring across the dining room at them. She made a face at him.

Mr. Simms advanced among the tables.

"Mr. and Mrs. Travis," he called. "I thought we were breakfasting together, alone."

"Sorry," said William.

"Sit down, pal," said Mr. Melton. "Any friend of theirs is a pal of mine."

Mr. Simms sat. The film people talked loudly, and while they talked, Mr. Simms said quietly, "I hope you slept well."

"Did you?"

"I'm not used to spring mattresses," replied Mr. Simms wryly. "But there are compensations. I stayed up half the night trying new cigarettes and foods. Odd, fascinating. A whole new spectrum of sensation, these ancient vices."

"We don't know what you're talking about," said Susan.

"Always the play acting," Simms laughed. "It's no use. Nor is this stratagem of crowds. I'll get you alone soon enough. I'm immensely patient."

"Say," Mr. Melton broke in, his face flushed, "is this guy giving you any trouble?"

"It's all right."

"Say the word and I'll give him the bum's rush."

Melton turned back to yell at his associates. In the

laughter, Mr. Simms went on: "Let us come to the point. It took me a month of tracing you through towns and cities to find you, and all of yesterday to be sure of you. If you come with me quietly, I might be able to get you off with no punishment, if you agree to go back to work on the hydrogen-plus bomb."

"Science this guy talks at breakfast!" observed Mr. Melton, half listening.

Simms went on, imperturbably. "Think it over. You can't escape. If you kill me, others will follow you."

"We don't know what you're talking about."

"Stop it!" cried Simms irritably. "Use your intelligence! You know we can't let you get away with this escape. Other people in the year 2155 might get the same idea and do what you've done. We need people."

"To fight your wars," said William at last.

"Bill!"

"It's all right, Susan. We'll talk on his terms now. We can't escape."

"Excellent," said Simms. "Really, you've both been incredibly romantic, running away from your responsibilities."

"Running away from horror."

"Nonsense. Only a war."

"What are you guys talking about?" asked Mr. Melton.

Susan wanted to tell him. But you could only speak in generalities. The psychological block in your mind allowed that. Generalities, such as Simms and William were now discussing.

"Only *the* war," said William. "Half the world dead of leprosy bombs!"

"Nevertheless," Simms pointed out, "the inhabitants of the Future resent you two hiding on a tropical isle, as it were,

while they drop off the cliff into hell. Death loves death,
not life. Dying people love to know that others die with
them. It is a comfort to learn you are not alone in the kiln,
in the grave. I am the guardian of their collective resentment
against you two."

"Look at the guardian of resentments!" said Mr. Melton
to his companions.

"The longer you keep me waiting, the harder it will go
for you. We need you on the bomb project, Mr. Travis.
Return now—no torture. Later, we'll force you to work, and
after you've finished the bomb, we'll try a number of compli-
cated new devices on you, sir."

"I've a proposition," said William. "I'll come back with
you if my wife stays here alive, safe, away from that war."

Mr. Simms considered it. "All right. Meet me in the
plaza in ten minutes. Pick me up in your car. Drive me to a
deserted country spot. I'll have the Travel Machine pick us
up there."

"Bill!" Susan held his arm tightly.

"Don't argue." He looked over at her. "It's settled." To
Simms: "One thing. Last night you could have gotten in our
room and kidnaped us. Why didn't you?"

"Shall we say that I was enjoying myself?" replied Mr.
Simms languidly, sucking his new cigar. "I hate giving up this
wonderful atmosphere, this sun, this vacation. I regret leaving
behind the wine and the cigarettes. Oh, how I regret It. The
plaza then, in ten minutes. Your wife will be protected and
may stay here as long as she wishes. Say your good-bys."

Mr. Simms arose and walked out.

"There goes Mr. Big Talk!" yelled Mr. Melton at the
departing gentleman. He turned and looked at Susan. "Hey.

Someone's crying. Breakfast's no time for people to cry. Now *is* it?"

At nine-fifteen Susan stood on the balcony of their room, gazing down at the plaza. Mr. Simms was seated there, his neat legs crossed, on a delicate bronze bench. Biting the tip from a cigar, he lit it tenderly.

Susan heard the throb of a motor, and far up the street, out of a garage and down the cobbled hill, slowly, came William in his car.

The car picked up speed. Thirty, now forty, now fifty miles an hour. Chickens scattered before it.

Mr. Simms took off his white panama hat and mopped his pink forehead, put his hat back on, and then saw the car.

It was rushing sixty miles an hour, straight on for the plaza.

"William!" screamed Susan.

The car hit the low plaza curb, thundering; it jumped up, sped across the tiles toward the green bench where Mr. Simms now dropped his cigar, shrieked, flailed his hands, and was hit by the car. His body flew up and up in the air, and down and down, crazily, into the street.

On the far side of the plaza, one front wheel broken, the car stopped. People were running.

Susan went in and closed the balcony doors.

They came down the Official Palace steps together, arm in arm, their faces pale, at twelve noon.

"*Adiós, señor,*" said the mayor behind them. "*Señora.*"

They stood in the plaza where the crowd was pointing at the blood.

"Will they want to see you again?" asked Susan.

"No, we went over and over it. It was an accident. I lost control of the car. I wept for them. God knows I had to get my relief out somewhere. I *felt* like weeping. I hated to kill him. I've never wanted to do anything like that in my life."

"They won't prosecute you?"

"They talked about it, but no. I talked faster. They believe me. It was an accident. It's over."

"Where will we go? Mexico City? Uruapan?"

"The car's in the repair shop. It'll be ready at four this afternoon. Then we'll get the hell out."

"Will we be followed? Was Simms working alone?"

"I don't know. We'll have a little head start on them, I think."

The film people were coming out of the hotel as they approached. Mr. Melton hurried up, scowling. "Hey I heard what happened. Too bad. Everything okay now? Want to get your minds off it? We're doing some preliminary shots up the street. You want to watch, you're welcome. Come on, do you good."

They went.

They stood on the cobbled street while the film camera was being set up. Susan looked at the road leading down and away, and the highway going to Acapulco and the sea, past pyramids and ruins and little adobe towns with yellow walls, blue walls, purple walls and flaming bougainvillea, and she thought, We shall take the roads, travel in clusters and crowds, in markets, in lobbies, bribe police to sleep near, keep double locks, but always the crowds, never alone again, always afraid the next person who passes may be another Simms. Never knowing if we've tricked and lost the Searchers. And always up ahead, in the Future, they'll wait for us to be brought back, waiting with their bombs to burn us and disease to rot us, and their police to tell us to roll over, turn around, jump through the hoop! And so we'll keep running through the forest, and we'll never ever stop or sleep well again in our lives.

A crowd gathered to watch the film being made. And Susan watched the crowd and the streets.

"Seen anyone suspicious?"

"No. What time is it?"

"Three o'clock. The car should be almost ready."

The test film was finished at three forty-five. They all walked down to the hotel, talking. William paused at the garage. "The car'll be ready at six," he said, coming out, worried.

"But no later than that?"

"It'll be ready, don't worry."

In the hotel lobby they looked around for other men traveling alone, men who resembled Mr. Simms, men with new haircuts and too much cigarette smoke and cologne smell about them, but the lobby was empty. Going up the stairs, Mr. Melton said, "Well, it's been a long hard day. Who'd like to put a header on it? You folks? Martini? Beer?"

"Maybe one."

The whole crowd pushed into Mr. Melton's room and the drinking began.

"Watch the time," said William.

Time, thought Susan. If only they had time. All she wanted was to sit in the plaza all of a long bright day in October, with not a worry or a thought, with the sun on her face and arms, her eyes closed, smiling at the warmth, and never move. Just sleep in the Mexican sun, and sleep warmly and easily and slowly and happily for many, many days. . . .

Mr. Melton opened the champagne.

"To a very beautiful lady, lovely enough for films," he said, toasting Susan. "I might even give you a test."

She laughed.

"I mean it," said Melton. "You're very nice. I could make you a movie star."

"And take me to Hollywood?" cried Susan.

"Get the hell out of Mexico, sure!"

Susan glanced at William and he lifted an eyebrow and nodded. It would be a change of scene, clothing, locale, name, perhaps; and they would be traveling with eight other people, a good shield against any interference from the Future.

"It sounds wonderful," said Susan.

She was feeling the champagne now. The afternoon was slipping by; the party was whirling about her. She felt safe and good and alive and truly happy for the first time in many years.

"What kind of film would my wife be good for?" asked William, refilling his glass.

Melton appraised Susan. The party stopped laughing and listened.

"Well, I'd like to do a story of suspense," said Melton. "A story of a man and wife, like yourselves."

"Go on."

"Sort of a war story, maybe," said the director, examining the color of his drink against the sunlight.

Susan and William waited.

"A story about a man and wife, who live in a little house on a little street in the year 2155, maybe," said Melton. "This is ad lib, understand. But this man and wife are faced with a terrible war, super-plus hydrogen bombs, censorship, death in that year, and—here's the gimmick—they escape into the Past, followed by a man who they think is evil, but who is only trying to show them what their duty is."

William dropped his glass to the floor.

Mr. Melton continued: "And this couple take refuge with a group of film people whom they learn to trust. Safety in numbers, they say to themselves."

Susan felt herself slip down into a chair. Everyone was watching the director. He took a little sip of wine. "Ah, that's a fine wine. Well, this man and woman, it seems, don't realize how important they are to the Future. The man, especially, is the keystone to a new bomb metal. So the Searchers, let's call them, spare no trouble or expense to find, capture, and take home the man and wife, once they get them totally alone, in a hotel room, where no one can see. Strategy. The Searchers work alone, or in groups of eight. One trick or another will do it. Don't you think it would make a wonderful film, Susan? Don't you, Bill?" He finished his drink.

Susan sat with her eyes straight ahead of her.

"Have a drink?" said Mr. Melton.

William's gun was out and fired three times, and one of the men fell, and the others ran forward. Susan screamed. A hand was clamped to her mouth. Now the gun was on the floor and William was struggling, held.

Mr. Melton said, "Please," standing there where he had stood, blood showing on his fingers. "Let's not make matters worse."

Someone pounded on the hall door.

"Let me in!"

"The manager," said Mr. Melton dryly. He jerked his head. "Everyone, let's move!"

"Let me in! I'll call the police!"

Susan and William looked at each other quickly, and then at the door.

"The manager wishes to come in," said Mr. Melton. "Quick!"

A camera was carried forward. From it shot a blue light which encompassed the room instantly. It widened out and the people of the party vanished, one by one.

"Quickly!"

Outside the window, in the instant before she vanished, Susan saw the green land and the purple and yellow and blue and crimson walls and the cobbles flowing down like a river, a man upon a burro riding into the warm hills, a boy drinking Orange Crush, she could feel the sweet liquid in her throat, a man standing under a cool plaza tree with a guitar, she could feel her hand upon the strings, and, far away, the sea, the blue and tender sea, she could feel it roll her over and take her in.

And then she was gone. Her husband was gone.

The door burst wide open. The manager and his staff rushed in.

The room was empty.

"But they were just here! I saw them come in, and now—gone!" cried the manager. "The windows are covered with iron grating. They couldn't get out that way!"

In the late afternoon the priest was summoned and they opened the room again and aired it out, and had him sprinkle holy water through each corner and give it his blessing.

"What shall we do with these?" asked the charwoman.

She pointed to the closet, where there were 67 bottles of chartreuse, cognac, *crème de cacao*, absinthe, vermouth, tequila, 106 cartons of Turkish cigarettes, and 198 yellow boxes of fifty-cent pure Havana-filler cigars. . . .

The Visitor

Saul Williams awoke to the still morning. He looked wearily out of his tent and thought about how far away Earth was. Millions of miles, he thought. But then what could you do about it? Your lungs were full of the "blood rust." You coughed all the time.

Saul arose this particular morning at seven o'clock. He was a tall man, lean, thinned by his illness. It was a quiet morning on Mars, with the dead sea bottom-flat and silent— no wind on it. The sun was clear and cool in the empty sky. He washed his face and ate breakfast.

After that he wanted very much to be back on Earth. During the day he tried every way that it was possible to be in New York City. Sometimes, if he sat right and held his hands a certain way, he did it. He could almost smell New York. Most of the time, though, it was impossible.

Later in the morning Saul tried to die. He lay on the sand and told his heart to stop. It continued beating. He imagined himself leaping from a cliff or cutting his wrists, but laughed to himself—he knew he lacked the nerve for either act.

Maybe if I squeeze tight and think about it enough, I'll just sleep and never wake, he thought. He tried it. An hour later he awoke with a mouth full of blood. He got up and spat it out and felt very sorry for himself. This blood rust— it filled your mouth and your nose; it ran from your ears, your fingernails; and it took a year to kill you. The only cure was shoving you in a rocket and shooting you out to exile on Mars. There was no known cure on Earth, and remaining there would contaminate and kill others. So here he was, bleeding all the time, and lonely.

Saul's eyes narrowed. In the distance, by an ancient city ruin, he saw another man lying on a filthy blanket.

When Saul walked up, the man on the blanket stirred weakly.

"Hello, Saul," he said.

"Another morning," said Saul. "Christ, I'm lonely!"

"It is an affliction of the rusted ones," said the man on the blanket, not moving, very pale and as if he might vanish if you touched him.

"I wish to God," said Saul, looking down at the man, "that you could at least talk. Why is it that intellectuals never get the blood rust and come up here?"

"It is a conspiracy against you, Saul," said the man, shutting his eyes, too weary to keep them open. "Once I had the strength to be an intellectual. Now, it's a job to think."

"If only we could talk," said Saul Williams.

The other man merely shrugged indifferently.

"Come tomorrow. Perhaps I'll have enough strength to talk about Aristotle then. I'll try. Really I will." The man sank down under the worn tree. He opened one eye. "Remember, once we did talk on Aristotle, six months ago, on that good day I had."

"I remember," said Saul, not listening. He looked at the dead sea. "I wish I were as sick as you, then maybe I wouldn't worry about being an intellectual. Then maybe I'd get some peace."

"You'll get just as bad as I am now in about six months," said the dying man. "Then you won't care about anything but sleep and more sleep. Sleep will be like a woman to you. You'll always go back to her, because she's fresh and good and faithful and she always treats you kindly and the same. You only wake up so you can think about going back to sleep. It's a nice thought." The man's voice was a bare whisper. Now it stopped and a light breathing took over.

Saul walked off.

Along the shores of the dead sea, like so many emptied bottles flung up by some long-gone wave, were the huddled bodies of sleeping men. Saul could see them all down the curve of the empty sea. One, two, three—all of them sleeping alone, most of them worse off than he, each with his little cache of food, each grown into himself, because social converse was weakening and sleep was good.

At first there had been a few nights around mutual campfires. And they had all talked about Earth. That was the only thing they talked about. Earth and the way the waters ran in town creeks and what homemade strawberry pie tasted like and how New York looked in the early morning coming over on the Jersey ferry in the salt wind.

I want Earth, thought Saul. I want it so bad it hurts. I want something I can never have again. And they all want it and it hurts them not to have it. More than food or a woman or anything, I just want Earth. This sickness puts women away forever; they're not things to be wanted. But Earth, yes. That's a thing for the mind and not the weak body.

The bright metal flashed on the sky.

Saul looked up.

The bright metal flashed again.

A minute later the rocket landed on the sea bottom. A valve opened, a man stepped out, carrying his luggage with him. Two other men, in protective germicide suits, accompanied him, bringing out vast cases of food, setting up a tent for him.

Another minute and the rocket returned to the sky. The exile stood alone.

Saul began to run. He hadn't run in weeks, and it was very tiring, but he ran and yelled.

"Hello, hello!"

The young man looked Saul up and down when he arrived.

"Hello. So this is Mars. My name's Leonard Mark."

"I'm Saul Williams."

They shook hands. Leonard Mark was very young— only eighteen, very blond, pink-faced, blue-eyed and fresh in spite of his illness.

"How are things in New York?" said Saul.

"Like this," said Leonard Mark. And he looked at Saul.

New York grew up out of the desert, made of stone and filled with March winds. Neons exploded in electric color. Yellow taxis glided in a still night. Bridges rose and tugs chanted in the midnight harbors. Curtains rose on spangled musicals.

Saul put his hands to his head, violently.

"Hold on, hold on!" he cried. "What's happening to me? What's wrong with me? I'm going crazy!"

Leaves sprouted from trees in Central Park, green and new. On the pathway Saul strolled along, smelling the air.

"Stop it, stop it, you fool!" Saul shouted at himself. He pressed his forehead with his hands. "This can't be!"

"It is," said Leonard Mark.

The New York towers faded. Mars returned. Saul stood on the empty sea bottom, staring limply at the young newcomer.

"You," he said, putting his hand out to Leonard Mark. "You did it. You did it with your mind."

"Yes," said Leonard Mark.

Silently they stood facing each other. Finally, trembling, Saul seized the other exile's hand and wrung it again and again, saying, "Oh, but I'm glad you're here. You can't know how glad I am!"

They drank their rich brown coffee from the tin cups.

It was high noon. They had been talking all through the warm morning time.

"And this ability of yours?" said Saul over his cup, looking steadily at the young Leonard Mark.

"It's just something I was born with," said Mark, looking into his drink. "My mother was in the blowup of London back in '57. I was born ten months later. I don't know what you'd call my ability. Telepathy and thought transference, I suppose. I used to have an act, I traveled all around the world. Leonard Mark, the mental marvel, they said on the billboards. I was pretty well off. Most people thought I was a charlatan. You know what people think of theatrical folks. Only I knew I was really genuine, but I didn't let anybody know. It was safer not to let it get around too much. Oh, a few of my close friends knew about my *real* ability. I had a lot of talents that will come in handy now that I'm here on Mars."

"You sure scared the hell out of me," said Saul, his cup rigid in his hand. "When New York came right up out of the ground that way, I thought I was insane."

"It's a form of hypnotism which affects all of the sensual

organs at once—eyes, ears, nose, mouth, skin—all of them. What would you like to be doing now most of all?"

Saul put down his cup. He tried to hold his hands very steady. He wet his lips. "I'd like to be in a little creek I used to swim in in Mellin Town, Illinois, when I was a kid. I'd like to be stark-naked and swimming."

"Well," said Leonard Mark and moved his head ever so little.

Saul fell back on the sand, his eyes shut.

Leonard Mark sat watching him.

Saul lay on the sand. From time to time his hands moved, twitched excitedly. His mouth spasmed open; sounds issued from his tightening and relaxing throat.

Saul began to make slow movements of his arms, out and back, out and back, gasping with his head to one side, his arms going and coming slowly on the warm air, stirring the yellow sand under him, his body turning slowly over.

Leonard Mark quietly finished his coffee. While he drank he kept his eyes on the moving, whispering Saul lying there on the dead sea bottom.

"All right," said Leonard Mark.

Saul sat up, rubbing his face.

After a moment he told Leonard Mark, "I saw the creek. I ran along the bank and I took off my clothes," he said breathlessly, his smile incredulous. "And I *dived in* and swam around!"

"I'm pleased," said Leonard Mark.

"Here!" Saul reached into his pocket and drew forth his last bar of chocolate. "This is for you."

"What's this?" Leonard Mark looked at the gift. "Chocolate? Nonsense, I'm not doing this for pay. I'm doing it because it makes you happy. Put that thing back in your pocket before I turn it into a rattlesnake and it bites you."

"Thank you, thank you!" Saul put it away. "You don't know how good that water was." He fetched the coffeepot. "More?"

Pouring the coffee, Saul shut his eyes a moment.

I've got Socrates here, he thought; Socrates and Plato, and Nietzsche and Schopenhauer. This man, by his talk, is a genius. By his talent, he's incredible! Think of the long, easy days and the cool nights of talk we'll have. It won't be a bad year at all. Not half.

He spilled the coffee.

"What's wrong?"

"Nothing." Saul himself was confused, startled.

We'll be in Greece, he thought. In Athens. We'll be in Rome, if we want, when we study the Roman writers. We'll stand in the Parthenon and the Acropolis. It won't be just talk, but it'll be a place to be, besides. This man can do it. He has the power to do it. When we talk the plays of Racine, he can make a stage and players and all of it for me. By Christ, this is better than life ever was! How much better to be sick and here than well on Earth without these abilities! How many people have ever seen a Greek drama played in a Greek amphitheater in the year 31 B.C.?

And if I ask, quietly and earnestly, will this man take on the aspect of Schopenhauer and Darwin and Bergson and all the other thoughtful men of the ages . . . ? Yes, why not? To sit and talk with Nietzsche in person, with Plato himself . . . !

There was only one thing wrong. Saul felt himself swaying.

The other men. The other sick ones along the bottom of this dead sea.

In the distance men were moving, walking toward them. They had seen the rocket flash, land, dislodge a passenger. Now they were coming, slowly, painfully, to greet the new arrival.

Saul was cold. "Look," he said. "Mark, I think we'd better head for the mountains."

"Why?"

"See those men coming? Some of them are insane."

"Really?"

"Yes."

"Isolation and all make them that way?"

"Yes, that's it. We'd better get going."

"They don't look very dangerous. They move slowly."

"You'd be surprised."

Mark looked at Saul. "You're trembling. Why's that?"

"There's no time to talk," said Saul, getting up swiftly. "Come on. Don't you realize what'll happen once they discover your talent? They'll fight over you. They'll kill each other—kill you—for the right to own you."

"Oh, but I don't belong to anybody," said Leonard Mark. He looked at Saul. "No. Not even you."

Saul jerked his head. "I didn't even think of that."

"Didn't you now?" Mark laughed.

"We haven't time to argue," answered Saul, eyes blinking, cheeks blazing. "Come on!"

"I don't want to. I'm going to sit right here until those men show up. You're a little too possessive. My life's my own."

Saul felt an ugliness in himself. His face began to twist. "You *heard* what I said."

"How very quickly you changed from a friend to an enemy," observed Mark.

Saul hit at him. It was a neat quick blow, coming down. Mark ducked aside, laughing. "No, you don't!"

They were in the center of Times Square. Cars roared, hooting, upon them. Buildings plunged up, hot, into the blue air.

"It's a lie!" cried Saul, staggering under the visual impact. "For God's sake, don't, Mark! The men are coming. You'll be killed!"

Mark sat there on the pavement, laughing at his joke. "Let them come. I can fool them all!"

New York distracted Saul. It was meant to distract— meant to keep his attention with its unholy beauty, after so many months away from it. Instead of attacking Mark he could only stand, drinking in the alien but familiar scene.

He shut his eyes. "No." And fell forward, dragging Mark with him. Horns screamed in his ears. Brakes hissed and caught violently. He smashed at Mark's chin.

Silence.

Mark lay on the sea bottom.

Taking the unconscious man in his arms, Saul began to run, heavily.

New York was gone. There was only the wide sound-lessness of the dead sea. The men were closing in around him. He headed for the hills with his precious cargo, with New York and green country and fresh springs and old friends held in his arms. He fell once and struggled up. He did not stop running.

Night filled the cave. The wind wandered in and out, tugging at the small fire, scattering ashes.

Mark opened his eyes. He was tied with ropes and lean-ing against the dry wall of the cave, facing the fire.

Saul put another stick on the fire, glancing now and again with a catlike nervousness at the cave entrance.

"You're a fool."

Saul started.

"Yes," said Mark, "you're a fool. They'll find us. If they have to hunt for six months they'll find us. They saw New York, at a distance, like a mirage. And us in the center of it. It's too much to think they won't be curious and follow our trail."

"I'll move on with you then," said Saul, staring into the fire.

"And they'll come after."

"Shut up!"

Mark smiled. "Is that the way to speak to your wife?"

"You heard me!"

"Oh, a fine marriage this is—your greed and my mental ability. What do you want to see now? Shall I show you a few more of your childhood scenes?"

Saul felt the sweat coming out on his brow. He didn't know if the man was joking or not. "Yes," he said.

"All right," said Mark, "watch!"

Flame gushed out of the rocks. Sulphur choked him. Pits of brimstone exploded, concussions rocked the cave. Heaving up, Saul coughed and blundered, burned, withered by hell!

Hell went away. The cave returned.

Mark was laughing.

Saul stood over him. "You," he said coldly, bending down.

"What else do you expect?" cried Mark. "To be tied up,

toted off, made the intellectual bride of a man insane with loneliness—do you think I enjoy this?"

"I'll untie you if you promise not to run away."

"I couldn't promise that. I'm a free agent. I don't belong to anybody."

Saul got down on his knees. "But you've *got* to belong, do you hear? You've *got* to belong. I can't let you go away!"

"My dear fellow, the more you say things like that, the more remote I am. If you'd had any sense and done things intelligently, we'd have been friends. I'd have been glad to do you these little hypnotic favors. After all, they're no trouble for me to conjure up. Fun, really. But you've botched it. You wanted me all to yourself. You were afraid the others would take me away from you. Oh, how mistaken you were. I have enough power to keep them all happy. You could have shared me, like a community kitchen. I'd have felt quite like a god among children, being kind, doing favors, in return for which you might bring me little gifts, special tidbits of food."

"I'm sorry, I'm sorry!" Saul cried. "But I know those men too well."

"Are you any different? Hardly! Go out and see if they're coming. I thought I heard a noise."

Saul ran. In the cave entrance he cupped his hands, peering down into the night-filled gully. Dim shapes stirred. Was it only the wind blowing the roving clumps of weeds? He began to tremble a fine, aching tremble.

"I don't see anything." He came back into an empty cave.

He stared at the fireplace. "Mark!"

Mark was gone.

There was nothing but the cave, filled with boulders,

stones, pebbles, the lonely fire flickering, the wind sighing. And Saul standing there, incredulous and numb.

"Mark! Mark! Come back!"

The man had worked free of his bonds, slowly, carefully, and using the ruse of imagining he heard other men approaching, had gone—where?

The cave was deep, but ended in a blank wall. And Mark could not have slipped past him into the night. How then?

Saul stepped around the fire. He drew his knife and approached a large boulder that stood against the cave wall. Smiling, he pressed the knife against the boulder. Smiling, he tapped the knife there. Then he drew his knife back to plunge it into the boulder.

"Stop!" shouted Mark.

The boulder vanished. Mark was there.

Saul suspended his knife. The fire played on his cheeks. His eyes were quite insane.

"It didn't work," he whispered. He reached down and put his hands on Mark's throat and closed his fingers. Mark said nothing, but moved uneasily in the grip, his eyes ironic, telling things to Saul that Saul knew.

If you kill me, the eyes said, where will all your dreams be? If you kill me, where will all the streams and brook trout be? Kill me, kill Plato, kill Aristotle, kill Einstein; yes, kill all of us! Go ahead, strangle me. I dare you.

Saul's fingers released the throat.

Shadows moved into the cave mouth.

Both men turned their heads.

The other men were there. Five of them, haggard with travel, panting, waiting in the outer rim of light.

"Good evening," called Mark, laughing. "Come in, come in, gentlemen!"

*   *   *

By dawn the arguments and ferocities still continued. Mark sat among the glaring men, rubbing his wrists, newly released from his bonds. He created a mahogany-paneled conference hall and a marble table at which they all sat, ridiculously bearded, evil-smelling, sweating and greedy men, eyes bent upon their treasure.

"The way to settle it," said Mark at last, "is for each of you to have certain hours of certain days for appointments with me. I'll treat you all equally. I'll be city property, free to come and go. That's fair enough. As for Saul here, he's on probation. When he's proved he can be a civil person once more, I'll give him a treatment or two. Until that time, I'll have nothing more to do with him."

The other exiles grinned at Saul.

"I'm sorry," Saul said. "I didn't know what I was doing. I'm all right now."

"We'll see," said Mark. "Let's give ourselves a month, shall we?"

The other men grinned at Saul.

Saul said nothing. He sat staring at the floor of the cave.

"Let's see now," said Mark. "On Mondays it's your day, Smith."

Smith nodded.

"On Tuesdays I'll take Peter there, for an hour or so."

Peter nodded.

"On Wednesdays I'll finish up with Johnson, Holtzman, and Jim, here."

The last three men looked at each other.

"The rest of the week I'm to be left strictly alone, do you hear?" Mark told them. "A little should be better than nothing. If you don't obey, I won't perform at all."

"Maybe we'll *make* you perform," said Johnson. He caught the other men's eye. "Look, we're five against his one. We can make him do anything we want. If we co-operate, we've got a great thing here."

"Don't be idiots," Mark warned the other men.

"Let me talk," said Johnson. "He's telling us what he'll do. Why don't we tell *him!* Are we bigger than him, or not? And him threatening not to perform! Well, just let me get a sliver of wood under his toenails and maybe burn his fingers a bit with a steel file, and we'll see if he performs! Why shouldn't we have performances, I want to know, every night in the week?"

"Don't listen to him!" said Mark. "He's crazy. He can't be depended on. You know what he'll do, don't you? He'll get you all off guard, one by one, and kill you, yes, kill all of you, so that when he's done, he'll be alone—just him and me! That's his sort."

The listening men blinked. First at Mark, then at Johnson.

"For that matter," observed Mark, "none of you can trust the others. This is a fool's conference. The minute your back is turned one of the other men will murder you. I dare say, at the week's end, you'll all be dead or dying."

A cold wind blew into the mahogany room. It began to dissolve and became a cave once more. Mark was tired of his joke. The marble table splashed and rained and evaporated.

The men gazed suspiciously at each other with little bright animal eyes. What was spoken was true. They saw each other in the days to come, surprising one another, killing—until that last lucky one remained to enjoy the intellectual treasure that walked among them.

Saul watched them and felt alone and disquieted. Once

you have made a mistake, how hard to admit your wrongness, to go back, start fresh. They were *all* wrong. They had been lost a long time. Now they were worse than lost.

"And to make matters very bad," said Mark at last, "one of you has a gun. All the rest of you have only knives. But one of you, I know, has a gun."

Everybody jumped up. "Search!" said Mark. "Find the one with the gun or you're all dead!"

That did it. The men plunged wildly about, not knowing whom to search first. Their hands grappled, they cried out, and Mark watched them in contempt.

Johnson fell back, feeling in his jacket. "All right," he said. "We might as well have it over now! Here, you, Smith."

And he shot Smith through the chest. Smith fell. The other men yelled. They broke apart. Johnson aimed and fired twice more.

"Stop!" cried Mark.

New York soared up around them, out of rock and cave and sky. Sun glinted on high towers. The elevated thundered; tugs blew in the harbor. The green lady stared across the bay, a torch in her hand.

"Look, you fools!" said Mark. Central Park broke out constellations of spring blossoms. The wind blew fresh-cut lawn smells over them in a wave.

And in the center of New York, bewildered, the men stumbled. Johnson fired his gun three times more. Saul ran forward. He crashed against Johnson, bore him down, wrenched the gun away. It fired again.

The men stopped milling.

They stood. Saul lay across Johnson. They ceased struggling.

There was a terrible silence. The men stood watching.

New York sank down into the sea. With a hissing, bubbling, sighing; with a cry of ruined metal and old time, the great structures leaned, warped, flowed, collapsed.

Mark stood among the buildings. Then, like a building; a neat red hole drilled into his chest, wordless, he fell.

Saul lay staring at the men, at the body.

He got up, the gun in his hand.

Johnson did not move—was afraid to move.

They all shut their eyes and opened them again, thinking that by so doing they might reanimate the man who lay before them.

The cave was cold.

Saul stood up and looked, remotely, at the gun in his hand. He took it and threw it far out over the valley and did not watch it fall.

They looked down at the body as if they could not believe it. Saul bent down and took hold of the limp hand. "Leonard!" he said softly. "Leonard?" He shook the hand. "Leonard!"

Leonard Mark did not move. His eyes were shut; his chest had ceased going up and down. He was getting cold.

Saul got up. "We've killed him," he said, not looking at the men. His mouth was filling with a raw liquor now. "The only one we didn't want to kill, we killed." He put his shaking hand to his eyes. The other men stood waiting.

"Get a spade," said Saul. "Bury him." He turned away. "I'll have nothing to do with you."

Somebody walked off to find a spade.

Saul was so weak he couldn't move. His legs were grown into the earth, with roots feeding deep of loneliness and fear and the cold of the night. The fire had almost died out and now there was only the double moonlight riding over the blue mountains.

There was the sound of someone digging in the earth with a spade.

"We don't need him anyhow," said somebody, much too loudly.

The sound of digging went on. Saul walked off slowly and let himself slide down the side of a dark tree until he reached and was sitting blankly on the sand, his hands blindly in his lap.

Sleep, he thought. We'll all go to sleep now. We have that much, anyway. Go to sleep and try to dream of New York and all the rest.

He closed his eyes wearily, the blood gathering in his nose and his mouth and in his quivering eyes.

"How did he do it?" he asked in a tired voice. His head fell forward on his chest. "How did he bring New York up here and make us walk around in it? Let's try. It shouldn't be too hard. Think! Think of New York," he whispered, falling down into sleep. "New York and Central Park and then Illinois in the spring, apple blossoms and green grass."

It didn't work. It wasn't the same. New York was gone and nothing he could do would bring it back. He would rise every morning and walk on the dead sea looking for it, and walk forever around Mars, looking for it, and never find it. And finally lie, too tired to walk, trying to find New York in his head, but not finding it.

The last thing he heard before he slept was the spade rising and falling and digging a hole into which, with a tremendous crash of metal and golden mist and odor and color and sound, New York collapsed, fell, and was buried.

He cried all night in his sleep.

The Concrete Mixer

He listened to the dry-grass rustle of the old witches' voices beneath his open window:

"Ettil, the coward! Ettil, the refuser! Ettil, who will not wage the glorious war of Mars against Earth!"

"Speak on, witches!" he cried.

The voices dropped to a murmur like that of water in the long canals under the Martian sky.

"Ettil, the father of a son who must grow up in the shadow of this horrid knowledge!" said the old wrinkled women. They knocked their sly-eyed heads gently together. "Shame, shame!"

His wife was crying on the other side of the room. Her tears were as rain, numerous and cool on the tiles. "Oh, Ettil, how can you think this way?"

Ettil laid aside his metal book which, at his beckoning, had been singing him a story all morning from its thin golden-wired frame.

"I've tried to explain," he said. "This is a foolish thing, Mars invading Earth. We'll be destroyed, utterly."

Outside, a banging, crashing boom, a surge of brass, a drum, a cry, marching feet, pennants and songs. Through the stone streets the army, fire weapons to shoulder, stamped. Children skipped after. Old women waved dirty flags.

"I shall remain on Mars and read a book." said Ettil.

A blunt knock on the door. Tylla answered. Father-in-law stormed in. "What's this I hear about my son-in-law? A traitor?"

"Yes, Father."

"You're not fighting in the Martian Army?"

"No, Father."

"Gods!" The old father turned very red. "A plague on your name! You'll be shot."

"Shoot me, then, and have it over."

"Who ever heard of a Martian *not* invading? Who!"

"Nobody. It is, I admit, quite incredible."

"Incredible," husked the witch voices under the window.

"Father, can't you reason with him?" demanded Tylla.

"Reason with a dung heap," cried Father, eyes blazing. He came and stood over Ettil. "Bands playing, a fine day, women weeping, children jumping, everything right, men marching bravely, and you sit here! Oh, shame!"

"Shame," sobbed the faraway voices in the hedge.

"Get the devil out of my house with your inane chatter," said Ettil, exploding. "Take your medals and your drums and run!"

He shoved Father-in-law past a screaming wife, only to have the door thrown wide at this moment, as a military detail entered.

A voice shouted, "Ettil Vrye?"

"Yes!"

"You are under arrest!"

"Good-by, my dear wife. I am off to the wars with these fools!" shouted Ettil, dragged through the door by the men in bronze mesh.

"Good-by, good-by," said the town witches, fading away. . . .

The cell was neat and clean. Without a book, Ettil was nervous. He gripped the bars and watched the rockets shoot up into the night air. The stars were cold and numerous; they seemed to scatter when every rocket blasted up among them.

"Fools," whispered Ettil. "Fools!"

The cell door opened. One man with a kind of vehicle entered, full of books; books here, there, everywhere in the chambers of the vehicle. Behind him the Military Assignor loomed.

"Ettil Vrye, we want to know why you had these illegal Earth books in your house. These copies of *Wonder Stories*, *Scientific Tales*, *Fantastic Stories*. Explain." The man gripped Ettil's wrist.

Ettil shook him free. "If you're going to shoot me, shoot me. That literature, from Earth, is the very reason why I won't try to invade them. It's the reason why your invasion will fail."

"How so?" The assignor scowled and turned to the yellowed magazines.

"Pick any copy," said Ettil. "Any one at all. Nine out of ten stories in the years 1929, '30 to '50, Earth calendar, have every Martian invasion successfully invading Earth."

"Ah!" The assignor smiled, nodded.

"And then," said Ettil, "failing."

"That's treason! Owning such literature!"

"So be it, if you wish. But let me draw a few conclusions. Invariably, each invasion is thwarted by a young man, usually lean, usually Irish, usually alone, named Mick or Rick, or Jick or Bannon, who destroys the Martians."

"You don't believe that!"

"No, I don't believe Earthmen can actually do that— no. But they have a background, understand, Assignor, of generations of children reading just such fiction, absorbing it. They have nothing but a literature of invasions successfully thwarted. Can you say the same for Martian literature?"

"Well—"

"No."

"I guess not."

"You know not. We never wrote stories of such a fantastic nature. Now we rebel, we attack, and we shall die."

"I don't see your reasoning on that. Where does this tie in with the magazine stories?"

"Morale. A big thing. The Earthmen know they can't fail. It is in them like blood beating in their veins. They cannot fail. They will repel each invasion, no matter how well organized. Their youth of reading just such fiction as this has given them a faith we cannot equal. We Martians? We are uncertain; we know that we might fail. Our morale is low, in spite of the banged drums and tooted horns."

"I won't listen to this treason," cried the assignor. "This fiction will be burned, as you will be, within the next ten minutes. You have a choice, Ettil Vrye. Join the Legion of War, or burn."

"It is a choice of deaths. I choose to burn."

"Men!"

He was hustled out into the courtyard. There he saw his carefully hoarded reading matter set to the torch. A special pit was prepared, with oil five feet deep in it. This, with a great thunder, was set afire. Into this, in a minute, he would be pushed.

On the far side of the courtyard, in shadow, he noticed the solemn figure of his son standing alone, his great yellow eyes luminous with sorrow and fear. He did not put out his hand or speak, but only looked at his father like some dying animal, a wordless animal seeking rescue.

Ettil looked at the flaming pit. He felt the rough hands seize him, strip him, push him forward to the hot perimeter of death. Only then did Ettil swallow and cry out, "Wait!"

The assignor's face, bright with the orange fire, pushed forward in the trembling air. "What is it?"

"I will join the Legion of War," replied Ettil.

"Good! Release him!"

The hands fell away.

As he turned he saw his son standing far across the court, waiting. His son was not smiling, only waiting. In the sky a bronze rocket leaped across the stars, ablaze . . .

"And now we bid good-by to these stalwart warriors," said the assignor. The band thumped and the wind blew a fine sweet rain of tears gently upon the sweating army. The children cavorted. In the chaos Ettil saw his wife weeping with pride, his son solemn and silent at her side.

They marched into the ship, everybody laughing and brave. They buckled themselves into their spiderwebs. All through the tense ship the spiderwebs were filled with lounging, lazy men. They chewed on bits of food and waited. A great lid slammed shut. A valve hissed.

"Off to Earth and destruction," whispered Ettil.

"What?" asked someone.

"Off to glorious victory," said Ettil, grimacing.

The rocket jumped.

Space, thought Ettil. Here we are banging across black inks and pink lights of space in a brass kettle. Here we are, a celebratory rocket heaved out to fill the Earthmen's eyes with fear flames as they look up to the sky. What is it like, being far, far away from your home, your wife, your child, here and now?

He tried to analyze his trembling. It was like tying your most inward working organs to Mars and then jumping out a million miles. Your heart was still on Mars, pumping, glowing. Your brain was still on Mars, thinking, crenulated, like an abandoned torch. Your stomach was still on Mars, somnolent, trying to digest the final dinner. Your lungs were still in the cool blue wine air of Mars, a soft folded bellows screaming for release, one part of you longing for the rest.

For here you were, a meshless, cogless automaton, a body upon which officials had performed clinical autopsy and left all of you that counted back upon the empty seas and strewn over the darkened hills. Here you were, bottle-empty, fireless, chill, with only your hands to give death to Earthmen. A pair of hands is all you are now, he thought in cold remoteness.

Here you lie in the tremendous web. Others are about you, but they are whole—whole hearts and bodies. But all of you that lives is back there walking the desolate seas in evening winds. This thing here, this cold clay thing, is already dead.

"Attack stations, attack stations, attack!"

"Ready, ready, ready!"

"Up!"

"Out of the webs, quick!"

Ettil moved. Somewhere before him his two cold hands moved.

How swift it has all been, he thought. A year ago one

Earth rocket reached Mars. Our scientists, with their incredible telepathic ability, copied it; our workers, with their incredible plants, reproduced it a hundredfold. No other Earth ship has reached Mars since then, and yet we know their language perfectly, all of us. We know their culture, their logic. And we shall pay the price of our brilliance. . . .

"Guns on the ready!"

"Right!"

"Sights!"

"Reading by miles?"

"Ten thousand!"

"Attack!"

A humming silence. A silence of insects throbbing in the walls of the rocket. The insect singing of tiny bobbins and levers and whirls of wheels. Silence of waiting men. Silence of glands emitting the slow steady pulse of sweat under arm, on brow, under staring pale eyes!

"Wait! Ready!"

Ettil hung onto his sanity with his fingernails, hung hard and long.

Silence, silence, silence. Waiting.

Teeee-e-ee!

"What's that?"

"Earth radio!"

"Cut them in!"

"They're trying to reach us, call us. Cut them in!"

Eee-e-e!

"Here they are! Listen!"

"Calling Martian invasion fleet!"

The listening silence, the insect hum pulling back to let the sharp Earth voice crack in upon the rooms of waiting men.

"This is Earth calling. This is William Sommers, president of the Association of United American Producers!"

Ettil held tight to his station, bent forward, eyes shut.

"Welcome to Earth."

"What?" the men in the rocket roared. "What did he say?"

"Yes, welcome to Earth."

"It's a trick!"

Ettil shivered, opened his eyes to stare in bewilderment at the unseen voice from the ceiling source.

"Welcome! Welcome to green, industrial Earth!" declared the friendly voice. "With open arms we welcome you, to turn a bloody invasion into a time of friendships that will last through all of Time."

"A trick!"

"Hush, listen!"

"Many years ago we of Earth renounced war, destroyed our atom bombs. Now, unprepared as we are, there is nothing for us but to welcome you. The planet is yours. We ask only mercy from you good and merciful invaders."

"It can't be true!" a voice whispered.

"It must be a trick!"

"Land and be welcomed, all of you," said Mr. William Sommers of Earth. "Land anywhere. Earth is yours; we are all brothers!"

Ettil began to laugh. Everyone in the room turned to see him. The other Martians blinked. "He's gone mad!"

He did not stop laughing until they hit him.

The tiny fat man in the center of the hot rocket tarmac at Green Town, California, jerked out a clean white handkerchief and touched it to his wet brow. He squinted blindly from the fresh plank platform at the fifty thousand people

restrained behind a fence of policemen, arm to arm. Everybody looked at the sky.

"There they are!"

A gasp.

"No, just sea gulls!"

A disappointed grumble.

"I'm beginning to think it would have been better to
have declared war on them," whispered the mayor. "Then we
could all go home."

"*Sh-h!*" said his wife.

"There!" The crowd roared.

Out of the sun came the Martian rockets.

"Everybody ready?" The mayor glanced nervously about.

"Yes, sir," said Miss California 1965.

"Yes," said Miss America 1940, who had come rushing
up at the last minute as a substitute for Miss America 1966,
who was ill at home.

"Yes siree," said Mr. Biggest Grapefruit in San Fernando
Valley 1956, eagerly.

"Ready, band?"

The band poised its brass like so many guns.

"Ready!"

The rockets landed. "Go!"

The band played, "California, Here I Come" ten times.

From noon until one o'clock the mayor made a speech,
shaking his hands in the direction of the silent, apprehen-
sive rockets.

At one-fifteen the seals of the rockets opened.

The band played "Oh, You Golden State" three times.

Ettil and fifty other Martians leaped out, guns at the ready.

The mayor ran forward with the key to Earth in his hands.

The band played "Santa Claus Is Coming to Town," and

a full chorus of singers imported from Long Beach sang different words to it, something about "Martians Are Coming to Town."

Seeing no weapons about, the Martians relaxed, but kept their guns out.

From one-thirty until two-fifteen the mayor made the same speech over for the benefit of the Martians.

At two-thirty Miss America of 1940 volunteered to kiss all the Martians if they lined up.

At two-thirty and ten seconds the band played "How Do You Do, Everybody," to cover the confusion caused by Miss America's suggestion.

At two thirty-five Mr. Biggest Grapefruit presented the Martians with a two-ton truck full of grapefruit.

At two thirty-seven the mayor gave them all free passes to the Elite and Majestic theaters, combining this gesture with another speech which lasted until after three.

The band played, and the fifty thousand people sang, "For They Are Jolly Good Fellows."

It was over at four o'clock.

Ettil sat down in the shadow of the rocket, two of his fellows with him. "So this is Earth!"

"I say kill the filthy rats," said one Martian. "I don't trust them. They're sneaky. What's their motive for treating us this way?" He held up a box of something that rustled. "What's this stuff they gave me? A sample, they said." He read the label. BLIX, *the new sudsy soap.*

The crowd had drifted about, was mingling with the Martians like a carnival throng. Everywhere was the buzzing murmur of people fingering the rockets, asking questions.

Ettil was cold. He was beginning to tremble even more now. "Don't you feel it?" he whispered. "The tenseness, the evilness of all this. Something's going to happen to us. They have some plan. Something subtle and horrible. They're going to do something to us—I know."

"I say kill every one of them!"

"How can you kill people who call you 'pal' and 'buddy'?" asked another Martian.

Ettil shook his head. "They're sincere. And yet I feel as if we were in a big acid vat melting away, away. I'm frightened." He put his mind out to touch among the crowd. "Yes, they're really friendly, hail-fellows-well-met (one of their terms). One huge mass of common men, loving dogs and cats and Martians equally. And yet—and yet—"

The band played "Roll Out the Barrel." Free beer was being distributed through the courtesy of Hagenback Beer, Fresno, California.

The sickness came.

The men poured out fountains of slush from their mouths. The sound of sickness filled the land.

Gagging, Ettil sat beneath a sycamore tree. "A plot, a plot—a horrible plot," he groaned, holding his stomach.

"What did you eat?" The assignor stood over him.

"Something that they called popcorn," groaned Ettil.

"And?"

"And some sort of long meat on a bun, and some yellow liquid in an iced vat, and some sort of fish and something called pastrami," sighed Ettil, eyelids flickering.

The moans of the Martian invaders sounded all about.

"Kill the plotting snakes!" somebody cried weakly.

"Hold on," said the assignor. "It's merely hospitality. They overdid it. Up on your feet now, men. Into the town. We've got to place small garrisons of men about to make sure all is well. Other ships are landing in other cities. We've our job to do here."

The men gained their feet and stood blinking stupidly about.

"Forward, march!"

One, two, three, *four!* One, two, three, *four!* . . .

The white stores of the little town lay dreaming in shimmering heat. Heat emanated from everything—poles, concrete, metal, awnings, roofs, tar paper—everything.

The sound of Martian feet sounded on the asphalt.

"Careful, men!" whispered the assignor.

They walked past a beauty shop.

From inside, a furtive giggle.

"Look!"

A coppery head bobbed and vanished like a doll in the window. A blue eye glinted and winked at a keyhole.

"It's a plot," whispered Ettil. "A plot, I tell you!"

The odors of perfume were fanned out on the summer air by the whirling vents of the grottoes where the women hid like undersea creatures, under electric cones, their hair curled into wild whorls and peaks, their eyes shrewd and glassy, animal and sly, their mouths painted a neon red. Fans were whirring, the perfumed wind issuing upon the stillness, moving among green trees, creeping among the amazed Martians.

"For God's sake!" screamed Ettil, his nerves suddenly breaking loose. "Let's get in our rockets—go home! They'll get us! Those horrid things in there. See them? Those evil undersea things, those women in their cool little caverns of artificial rock!"

"Shut up!"

Look at them in there, he thought, drifting their dresses like cool green gills over their pillar legs. He shouted.

"Someone shut his mouth!"

"They'll rush out on us, hurling boxes and copies of *Kleig Love* and *Holly Pick-ture,* shrieking with their red greasy mouths! Inundate us with banality, destroy our sensibilities! Look at them, being electrocuted by devices, their voices like hums and chants and murmurs! Do you dare go in there?"

"Why not?" asked the other Martians.

"They'll fry you, bleach you, change you! Crack you, flake you away until you're nothing but a husband, a working man, the one with the money who pays so they can come sit in there devouring their evil chocolates! Do you think you could control them?"

"Yes, by the gods!"

From a distance a voice drifted, a high and shrill voice, a woman's voice saying, "Ain't that middle one there cute?"

"Martians ain't so bad after all. Gee, they're just men." said another, fading.

"Hey, there. *Yoo-hoo!* Martians! Hey!"

Yelling, Ettil ran. . . .

He sat in a park and trembled steadily. He remembered what he had seen. Looking up at the dark night sky, he felt so far from home, so deserted. Even now, as he sat among the still trees, in the distance he could see Martian warriors walking the streets with the Earth women, vanishing into the phantom darknesses of the little emotion palaces to hear the ghastly sounds of white things moving on gray screens, with little frizz-haired women beside them, wads of gelatinous gum working in their jaws, other wads under the seats, hardening with the fossil imprints of the women's tiny cat teeth forever imbedded therein. The cave of winds—the cinema.

"Hello."

He jerked his head in terror.

A woman sat on the bench beside him, chewing gum lazily. "Don't run off; I don't bite," she said.

"Oh," he said.

"Like to go to the pictures?" she said.

"No."

"Aw, come on," she said. "Everybody else is."

"No," he said. "Is that all you do in this world?"

"All? Ain't that enough?" Her blue eyes widened suspiciously. "What you want me to do—sit home, read a book? Ha, ha! That's rich."

Ettil stared at her a moment before asking a question.

"Do you do anything else?" he asked.

"Ride in cars. You got a car? You oughta get you a big new convertible Podler Six. Gee, they're fancy! Any man with a Podler Six can go out with any gal, you bet!" she said, blinking at him. "I bet you got all kinds of money—you come from Mars and all. I bet if you really wanted you could get a Podler Six and travel everywhere."

"To the show maybe?"

"What's wrong with 'at?"

"Nothing—nothing."

"You know what you talk like, mister?" she said. "A Communist! Yes, sir, that's the kinda talk nobody stands for, by gosh. Nothing wrong with our little old system. We was good enough to let you Martians invade, and we never raised even our bitty finger, did we?"

"That's what I've been trying to understand," said Ettil. "Why did you let us?"

"Cause we're bighearted, mister; that's why! Just remember that, bighearted." She walked off to look for someone else.

Gathering courage to himself, Ettil began to write a letter to his wife, moving the pen carefully over the paper on his knee.

"Dear Tylla—"

But again he was interrupted. A small-little-girl-of-an-old-woman, with a pale round wrinkled little face, shook her tambourine in front of his nose, forcing him to glance up.

"Brother," she cried, eyes blazing. "Have you been saved?"

"Am I in danger?" Ettil dropped his pen, jumping.

"Terrible danger!" she wailed, clanking her tambourine, gazing at the sky. "You need to be saved, brother, in the worst way!"

"I'm inclined to agree," he said, trembling.

"We saved lots already today. I saved three myself, of you Mars people. Ain't that nice?" She grinned at him.

"I guess so."

She was acutely suspicious. She leaned forward with her secret whisper. "Brother," she wanted to know, "you been baptized?"

"I don't know," he whispered back.

"You don't know?" she cried, flinging up hand and tambourine.

"Is it like being shot?" he asked.

"Brother," she said, "you are in a bad and sinful condition. I blame it on your ignorant bringing up. I bet those schools on Mars are terrible—don't teach you no truth at all. Just a pack of made-up lies. Brother, you got to be baptized if you want to be happy."

"Will it make me happy even in this world here?" he said.

"Don't ask for everything on your platter," she said. "Be

satisfied with a wrinkled pea, for there's another world we're all going to that's better than this one."

"I know that world," he said.

"It's peaceful," she said.

"Yes."

"There's quiet," she said.

"Yes."

"There's milk and honey flowing."

"Why, yes," he said.

"And everybody's laughing."

"I can see it now," he said.

"A better world," she said.

"Far better," he said. "Yes, Mars is a great planet."

"Mister," she said, tightening up and almost flinging the tambourine in his face, "you been joking with me?"

"Why, no." He was embarrassed and bewildered. "I thought you were talking about—"

"Not about mean old nasty Mars, I tell you, mister! It's your type that is going to boil for years, and suffer and break out in black pimples and be tortured—"

"I must admit Earth isn't very nice. You've described it beautifully."

"Mister, you're funning me again!" she cried angrily.

"No, no—please. I plead ignorance."

"Well," she said, "you're a heathen, and heathens are improper. Here's a paper. Come to this address tomorrow night and be baptized and be happy. We shouts and we stomps and we talk in voices, so if you want to hear our all-cornet, all-brass band, you come, won't you now?"

"I'll try," he said hesitantly.

Down the street she went, patting her tambourine, singing at the top of her voice, "Happy Am I, I'm Always Happy."

Dazed, Ettil returned to his letter.

"Dear Tylla: To think that in my naïveté I imagined that the Earthmen would have to counterattack with guns and bombs. No, no. I was sadly wrong. There is no Rick or Mick or Jick or Bannon—those lever fellows who save worlds. No.

"There are blond robots with pink rubber bodies, real, but somehow unreal, alive but somehow automatic in all responses, living in caves all of their lives. Their *derrières* are incredible in girth. Their eyes are fixed and motionless from an endless time of staring at picture screens. The only muscles they have occur in their jaws from their ceaseless chewing of gum.

"And it is not only these, my dear Tylla, but the entire civilization into which we have been dropped like a shovelful of seeds into a large concrete mixer. Nothing of us will survive. We will be killed not by the gun but by the glad-hand. We will be destroyed not by the rocket but by the automobile . . ."

Somebody screamed. A crash, another crash. Silence.

Ettil leaped up from his letter. Outside, on the street, two cars had crashed. One full of Martians, another with Earthmen. Ettil returned to his letter:

"Dear, dear Tylla, a few statistics if you will allow. Forty-five thousand people killed every year on this continent of America; made into jelly right in the can, as it were, in the automobiles. Red blood jelly, with white marrow bones like sudden thoughts, ridiculous horror thoughts, transfixed in the immutable jelly. The cars roll up in tight neat sardine rolls—all sauce, all silence.

"Blood manure for green buzzing summer flies, all over the highways. Faces made into Halloween masks by sudden stops. Halloween is one of their holidays. I think they worship the automobile on that night—something to do with death, anyway.

"You look out your window and see two people lying atop each other in friendly fashion who, a moment ago, had never before, dead. I foresee our army mashed, diseased, trapped in cinemas by witches and gum. Sometime in the next day I shall try to escape back to Mars before it is too late.

"Somewhere on Earth tonight, my Tylla, there is a Man with a Lever, which, when he pulls it, Will Save the World. The man is now unemployed. His switch gathers dust. He himself plays pinochle.

"The women of this evil planet are drowning us in a tide of banal sentimentality, misplaced romance, and one last fling before the makers of glycerin boil them down for usage. Good night, Tylla. Wish me well, for I shall probably die trying to escape. My love to our child."

Weeping silently, he folded the letter and reminded himself to mail it later at the rocket post.

He left the park. What was there to do? Escape? But how? Return to the post late tonight, steal one of the rockets alone and go back to Mars? Would it be possible? He shook his head. He was much too confused.

All that he really knew was that if he stayed here he would soon be the property of a lot of things that buzzed and snorted and hissed, that gave off fumes or stenches. In six months he would be the owner of a large pink, trained ulcer, a blood pressure of algebraic dimensions, a myopia this side of blindness, and nightmares as deep as oceans and infested with improbable lengths of dream intestines through which he must violently force his way each night. No, no.

He looked at the haunted faces of the Earthmen drifting

violently along in their mechanical death boxes. Soon—yes, very soon—they would invent an auto with six silver handles on it!

"Hey, there!"

An auto horn. A large long hearse of a car, black and ominous, pulled to the curb. A man leaned out.

"You a Martian?"

"Yes."

"Just the man I gotta see. Hop in quick—the chance of a lifetime. Hop in. Take you to a real nice joint where we can talk. Come on—don't stand there."

As if hypnotized, Ettil opened the door of the car, got in.

They drove off.

"What'll it be, E.V.? How about a manhattan? Two manhattans, waiter. Okay, E.V. This is my treat. This is on me and Big Studios! Don't even touch your wallet. Pleased to meet you, E.V. My name's R. R. Van Plank. Maybe you hearda me? No? Well, shake anyhow."

Ettil felt his hand massaged and dropped. They were in a dark hole with music and waiters drifting about. Two drinks were set down. It had all happened so swiftly. Now Van Plank, hands crossed on his chest, was surveying his Martian discovery.

"What I want you for, E.V., is this. It's the most magnanimous idea I ever got in my life. I don't know how it came to me, just in a flash. I was sitting home tonight and I thought to myself, My God, what a picture it would make! *Invasion of Earth by Mars.* So what I got to do? I got to find an adviser for the film. So I climbed in my car and found you and here we are. Drink up! Here's to your health and our future. *Skoal!*"

"But—" said Ettil.

"Now, I know, you'll want money. Well, we got plenty of that. Besides, I got a li'l black book full of peaches I can lend you."

"I don't like most of your Earth fruit and—"

"You're a card, mac, really. Well, here's how I get the picture in my mind—listen." He leaned forward excitedly. "We got a flash scene of the Martians at a big powwow, drummin' drums, gettin' stewed on Mars. In the background are huge silver cities—"

"But that's not the way Martian cities are—"

"We got to have color, kid. Color. Let your pappy fix this. Anyway, there are all the Martians doing a dance around a fire—"

"We don't dance around fires—"

"In *this* film you got a fire and you dance," declared Van Plank, eyes shut, proud of his certainty. He nodded, dreaming it over on his tongue. "Then we got a beautiful Martian woman, tall and blond."

"Martian women are dark—"

"Look, I don't see how we're going to be happy, E.V. By the way, son, you ought to change your name. What was it again?"

"Ettil."

"That's a woman's name. I'll give you a better one. Call you Joe. Okay, Joe. As I was saying, our Martian women are gonna be blond, because, see, just because. Or else your poppa won't be happy. You got any suggestions?"

"I thought that—"

"And another thing we gotta have is a scene, very tear-

ful, where the Martian woman saves the whole ship of Martian men from dying when a meteor or something hits the
ship. That'll make a whackeroo of a scene. You know, I'm
glad I found you, Joe. You're going to have a good deal with
us, I tell you."

Ettil reached out and held the man's wrist tight. "Just a
minute. There's something I want to ask you."

"Sure, Joe, shoot."

"Why are you being so nice to us? We invade your
planet, and you welcome us—everybody—like long-lost children. Why?"

"They sure grow 'em green on Mars, don't they? You're
a naïve-type guy—I can see from way over here. Mac, look
at it this way. We're all Little People, ain't we?" He waved a
small tan hand garnished with emeralds.

"We're all common as dirt, ain't we? Well, here on Earth,
we're proud of that. This is the century of the Common Man,
Bill, and we're proud we're small. Billy, you're looking at a
planet full of Saroyans. Yes, sir. A great big fat family of
friendly Saroyans—everybody loving everybody. We understand you Martians, Joe, and we know why you invaded
Earth. We know how lonely you were up on that little cold
planet Mars, how you envied us our cities—"

"Our civilization is much older than yours—"

"Please, Joe, you make me unhappy when you interrupt.
Let me finish my theory and then you talk all you want. As
I was saying, you was lonely up there, and down you came
to see our cities and our women and all, and we welcomed
you in, because you're our brothers, Common Men like all
of us.

"And then, as a kind of side incident, Roscoe, there's a
certain little small profit to be had from this invasion. I mean

for instance this picture I plan, which will net us, neat, a billion dollars, I bet. Next week we start putting out a special Martian doll at thirty bucks a throw. Think of the millions there. I also got a contact to make a Martian game to sell for five bucks. There's all sorts of angles."

"I see," said Ettil, drawing back.

"And then of course there's that whole nice new market. Think of all the depilatories and gum and shoeshine we can sell to you Martians."

"Wait. Another question."

"Shoot."

"What's your first name? What's the R. R. stand for?"

"Richard Robert."

Ettil looked at the ceiling. "Do they sometimes, perhaps, on occasion, once in a while, by accident, call you—Rick?"

"How'd you guess, mac? Rick, sure."

Ettil sighed and began to laugh and laugh. He put out his hand. "So you're Rick? Rick! So you're Rick!"

"What's the joke, laughing boy? Let Poppa in!"

"You wouldn't understand—a private joke. Ha, ha!" Tears ran down his cheeks and into his open mouth. He pounded the table again and again. "So you're Rick. Oh, how different, how funny. No bulging muscles, no lean jaw, no gun. Only a wallet full of money and an emerald ring and a big middle!"

"Hey, watch the language! I may not be no Apollo, but—"

"Shake hands, Rick. I've wanted to meet you. You're the man who'll conquer Mars, with cocktail shakers and foot arches and poker chips and riding crops and leather boots and checkered caps and rum collinses."

"I'm only a humble businessman," said Van Plank, eyes slyly down. "I do my work and take my humble little piece of money pie. But, as I was saying, Mort, I been thinking of the market on Mars for Uncle Wiggily games and Dick Tracy comics, all new. A big wide field never even heard of cartoons, right? Right! So we just toss a great big bunch of stuff on the Martians' heads. They'll fight for it, kid, fight! Who wouldn't, for perfumes and Paris dresses and Oshkosh overalls, eh? And nice new shoes—"

"We don't wear shoes."

"What have I got here?" R. R. asked of the ceiling. "A planet full of Okies? Look, Joe, we'll take care of that. We'll shame everyone into wearing shoes. Then we sell them the polish!"

"Oh."

He slapped Ettil's arm. "Is it a deal? Will you be technical director on my film? You'll get two hundred a week to start, a five-hundred top. What you say?"

"I'm sick," said Ettil. He had drunk the manhattan and was now turning blue.

"Say, I'm sorry. I didn't know it would do that to you. Let's get some fresh air."

In the open air Ettil felt better. He swayed. "So that's why Earth took us in?"

"Sure, son. Any time an Earthman can turn an honest dollar, watch him steam. The customer is always right. No hard feelings. Here's my card. Be at the studio in Hollywood tomorrow morning at nine o'clock. They'll show you your office. I'll arrive at eleven and see you then. Be sure you get there at nine o'clock It's a strict rule."

"Why?"

"Gallagher, you're a queer oyster, but I love you. Good night. Happy Invasion!"

The car drove off.

Ettil blinked after it, incredulous. Then, rubbing his brow with the palm of his hand, he walked slowly along the street toward the rocket port.

"Well, what are you going to do?" he asked himself, aloud.

The rockets lay gleaming in the moonlight, silent. From the city came the sounds of distant revelry. In the medical compound an extreme case of nervous breakdown was being tended to: a young Martian who, by his screams, had seen too much, drunk too much, heard too many songs on the little red-and-yellow boxes in the drinking places, and had been chased around innumerable tables by a large elephant-like woman. He kept murmuring:

"Can't breathe . . . crushed, trapped."

The sobbing faded. Ettil came out of the shadows and moved on across a wide avenue toward the ships. Far over, he could see the guards lying about drunkenly. He listened. From the vast city came the faint sounds of cars and music and sirens. And he imagined other sounds too: the insidious whir of malt machines stirring malts to fatten the warriors and make them lazy and forgetful, the narcotic voices of the cinema caverns lulling and lulling the Martians fast, fast into a slumber through which, all of their remaining lives, they would sleepwalk.

A year from now, how many Martians dead of cirrhosis of the liver, bad kidneys, high blood pressure, suicide?

He stood in the middle of the empty avenue. Two blocks away a car was rushing toward him.

He had a choice: stay here, take the studio job, report for work each morning as adviser on a picture, and, in time, come to agree with the producer that, yes indeed, there were massacres on Mars; yes, the women were tall and blond; yes, there were tribal dances and sacrifices; yes, yes, yes. Or he could walk over and get into a rocket ship and, alone, return to Mars.

"But what about next year?" he said.

The Blue Canal Night Club brought to Mars. The Ancient City Gambling Casino, Built Right Inside. Yes, Right Inside a Real Martian Ancient City! Neons, racing forms blowing in the old cities, picnic lunches in the ancestral graveyards—all of it, all of it.

But not quite yet. In a few days he could be home. Tylla would be waiting with their son, and then for the last few years of gentle life he might sit with his wife in the blowing weather on the edge of the canal reading his good, gentle books, sipping a rare and light wine, talking and living out their short time until the neon bewilderment fell from the sky.

And then perhaps he and Tylla might move into the blue mountains and hide for another year or two until the tourists came to snap their cameras and say how quaint things were.

He knew just what he would say to Tylla. "War is a bad thing, but peace can be a living horror."

He stood in the middle of the wide avenue.

Turning, it was with no surprise that he saw a car bearing down upon him, a car full of screaming children. These boys and girls, none older than sixteen, were swerving and ricocheting their open-top car down the avenue. He saw them point at him and yell. He heard the motor roar louder. The car sped forward at sixty miles an hour.

He began to run.

Yes, yes, he thought tiredly, with the car upon him, how strange, how sad. It sounds so much like . . . a concrete mixer.

Marionettes, Inc.

They walked slowly down the street at about ten in the evening, talking calmly. They were both about thirty-five, both eminently sober.

"But why so early?" said Smith.

"Because," said Braling.

"Your first night out in years and you go home at ten o'clock."

"Nerves, I suppose."

"What I wonder is how you ever managed it. I've been trying to get you out for ten years for a quiet drink. And now, on the one night, you insist on turning in early."

"Mustn't crowd my luck," said Braling.

"What did you do, put sleeping powder in your wife's coffee?"

"No, that would be unethical. You'll see soon enough."

They turned a corner. "Honestly, Braling, I hate to say this, but you _have_ been patient with her. You may not admit it to me, but marriage has been awful for you, hasn't it?"

"I wouldn't say that."

"It's got around, anyway, here and there, how she got you to marry her. That time back in 1979 when you were going to Rio—"

"Dear Rio. I never *did* see it after all my plans."

"And how she tore her clothes and rumpled her hair and threatened to call the police unless you married her."

"She always was nervous, Smith, understand."

"It was more than unfair. You didn't love her. You told her as much, didn't you?"

"I recall that I was quite firm on the subject."

"But you married her anyhow."

"I had my business to think of, as well as my mother and father. A thing like that would have killed them."

"And it's been ten years."

"Yes," said Braling, his gray eyes steady. "But I think perhaps it might change now. I think what I've waited for has come about. Look here."

He drew forth a long blue ticket.

"Why, it's a ticket for Rio on the Thursday rocket!"

"Yes, I'm finally going to make it."

"But how wonderful! You *do* deserve it! But won't *she* object? Cause trouble?"

Braling smiled nervously. "She won't know I'm gone. I'll be back in a month and no one the wiser, except you."

Smith sighed. "I wish I were going with you."

"Poor Smith, *your* marriage hasn't exactly been roses, has it?"

"Not exactly, married to a woman who overdoes it. I mean, after all, when you've been married ten years, you don't expect a woman to sit on your lap for two hours every evening, call you at work twelve times a day and talk baby talk. And it seems to me that in the last month she's gotten worse. I wonder if perhaps she isn't a little simpleminded?"

"Ah, Smith, always the conservative. Well, here's my house. Now, would you like to know my secret? How I made it out this evening?"

"Will you really tell?"

"Look up, there!" said Braling.

They both stared up through the dark air.

In the window above them, on the second floor, a shade was raised. A man about thirty-five years old, with a touch of gray at either temple, sad gray eyes, and a small thin mustache looked down at them.

"Why, that's *you!*" cried Smith.

"Sh-h-h, not so loud!" Braling waved upward. The man in the window gestured significantly and vanished.

"I must be insane," said Smith.

"Hold on a moment."

They waited.

The street door of the apartment opened and the tall spare gentleman with the mustache and the grieved eyes came out to meet them.

"Hello, Braling," he said.

"Hello, Braling," said Braling.

They were identical.

Smith stared. "Is this your twin brother? I never knew—"

"No, no," said Braling quietly. "Bend close. Put your ear to Braling Two's chest."

Smith hesitated and then leaned forward to place his head against the uncomplaining ribs.

Tick-tick-tick-tick-tick-tick-tick-tick.

"Oh no! It *can't* be!"

"It is."

"Let me listen again."

Tick-tick-tick-tick-tick-tick-tick-tick.

Smith staggered back and fluttered his eyelids, appalled. He reached out and touched the warm hands and the cheeks of the thing.

"Where'd you get him?"

"Isn't he excellently fashioned?"

"Incredible. Where?"

"Give the man your card, Braling Two."

Braling Two did a magic trick and produced a white card:

MARIONETTES, INC.
Duplicate self or friends; new humanoid plastic 1990 models, guaranteed against all physical wear. From $7,600 to our $15,000 de luxe model.

"No," said Smith.

"Yes," said Braling.

"Naturally," said Braling Two.

"How long has this gone on?"

"I've had him for a month. I keep him in the cellar in a toolbox. My wife never goes downstairs, and I have the only lock and key to that box. Tonight I said I wished to take a walk to buy a cigar. I went down to the cellar and took Braling Two out of his box and sent him back up to sit with my wife while I came on out to see you, Smith."

"Wonderful! He even *smells* like you: Bond Street and Melachrinos!"

"It may be splitting hairs, but I think it highly ethical. After all, what my wife wants most of all is *me*. This marionette *is* me to the hairiest detail. I've been home all evening. I shall be home with her for the next month. In the meantime another gentleman will be in Rio after ten years of waiting. When I return from Rio, Braling Two here will go back in his box."

Smith thought that over a minute or two. "Will he walk around without sustenance for a month?" he finally asked.

"For six months if necessary. And he's built to do everything—eat, sleep, perspire—everything, natural as natural is. You'll take good care of my wife, won't you, Braling Two?"

"Your wife is rather nice," said Braling Two. "I've grown rather fond of her."

Smith was beginning to tremble. "How long has Marionettes, Inc., been in business?"

"Secretly, for two years."

"Could I—I mean, is there a possibility—" Smith took his friend's elbow earnestly. "Can you tell me where I can get one, a robot, a marionette, for myself? You *will* give me the address, won't you?"

"Here you are."

Smith took the card and turned it round and round. "Thank you," he said. "You don't know what this means. Just a little respite. A night or so, once a month even. My wife loves me so much she can't bear to have me gone an hour. I love her dearly, you know, but remember the old poem: 'Love will fly if held too lightly, love will die if held too tightly.' I just want her to relax her grip a little bit."

"You're lucky, at least, that your wife loves you. Hate's my problem. Not so easy."

"Oh, Nettie loves me madly. It will be my task to make her love me comfortably."

"Good luck to you, Smith. Do drop around while I'm in Rio. It will seem strange, if you suddenly stop calling by, to my wife. You're to treat Braling Two, here, just like me."

"Right! Good-by. And thank you."

Smith went smiling down the street. Braling and Braling Two turned and walked into the apartment hall.

On the crosstown bus Smith whistled softly, turning the white card in his fingers:

> Clients must be pledged to secrecy, for while an act is pending in Congress to legalize Marionettes, Inc., it is still a felony, if caught, to use one.

"Well," said Smith.

> Clients must have a mold made of their body and a color index check of their eyes, lips, hair, skin, etc. Clients must expect to wait for two months until their model is finished.

Not so long, thought Smith. Two months from now my ribs will have a chance to mend from the crushing they've taken. Two months from now my hand will heal from being so constantly held. Two months from now my bruised underlip will begin to reshape itself. I don't mean to sound *ungrateful* . . . He flipped the card over.

Marionettes, Inc., is two years old and has a fine
record of satisfied customers behind it. Our motto is
"No Strings Attached." Address: 43 South Wesley
Drive.

The bus pulled to his stop; he alighted, and while humming up the stairs he thought, Nettie and I have fifteen thousand in our joint bank account. I'll just slip eight thousand
out as a business venture, you might say. The marionette will
probably pay back my money, with interest, in many ways.
Nettie needn't know. He unlocked the door and in a minute
was in the bedroom. There lay Nettie, pale, huge, and pi-
ously asleep.

"Dear Nettie." He was almost overwhelmed with remorse
at her innocent face there in the semidarkness. "If you were
awake you would smother me with kisses and coo in my ear.
Really, you make me feel like a criminal. You have been such
a good, loving wife. Sometimes it is impossible for me to
believe you married me instead of that Bud Chapman you
once liked. It seems that in the last month you have loved
me more wildly than *ever* before."

Tears came to his eyes. Suddenly he wished to kiss her,
confess his love, tear up the card, forget the whole business.
But as he moved to do this, his hand ached and his ribs
cracked and groaned. He stopped, with a pained look in his
eyes, and turned away. He moved out into the hall and
through the dark rooms. Humming, he opened the kidney
desk in the library and filched the bankbook. "Just take eight
thousand dollars is all," he said. "No more than that." He
stopped. "Wait a minute."

He rechecked the bankbook frantically. "Hold on here!"

he cried. "Ten thousand dollars is missing!" He leaped up. "There's only five thousand left! What's she done? What's Nettie done with it? More hats, more clothes, more perfume! Or, wait—I know! She bought that little house on the Hudson she's been talking about for months, without so much as a by your leave!"

He stormed into the bedroom, righteous and indignant. What did she mean, taking their money like this? He bent over her. "Nettie!" he shouted. "Nettie, wake up!"

She did not stir. "What've you done with my money!" he bellowed.

She stirred fitfully. The light from the street flushed over her beautiful cheeks.

There was something about her. His heart throbbed violently. His tongue dried. He shivered. His knees suddenly turned to water. He collapsed. "Nettie, Nettie!" he cried. "What've you done with my money!"

And then, the horrid thought. And then the terror and the loneliness engulfed him. And then the fever and disillusionment. For, without desiring to do so, he bent forward and yet forward again until his fevered ear was resting firmly and irrevocably upon her round pink bosom. "Nettie!" he cried.

Tick, tick, tick, tick, tick, tick, tick, tick, tick, tick, tick.

As Smith walked away down the avenue in the night, Braling and Braling Two turned in at the door to the apartment. "I'm glad he'll be happy too," said Braling.

"Yes," said Braling Two abstractedly.

"Well, it's the cellar box for you, B-Two." Braling guided the other creature's elbow down the stairs to the cellar.

"That's what I want to talk to you about," said Braling Two, as they reached the concrete floor and walked across it. "The cellar. I don't like it. I don't like that toolbox."

"I'll try and fix up something more comfortable."

"Marionettes are made to move, not lie still. How would you like to lie in a box most of the time?"

"Well—"

"You wouldn't like it at all. I keep running. There's no way to shut me off. I'm perfectly alive and I have feelings."

"It'll only be a few days now. I'll be off to Rio and you won't have to stay in the box. You can live upstairs."

Braling Two gestured irritably. "And when you come back from having a good time, back in the box I go."

Braling said, "They didn't tell me at the marionette shop that I'd get a difficult specimen."

"There's a lot they don't know about us," said Braling Two. "We're pretty new. And we're sensitive. I hate the idea of you going off and laughing and lying in the sun in Rio while we're stuck here in the cold."

"But I've wanted that trip all my life," said Braling quietly.

He squinted his eyes and could see the sea and the mountains and the yellow sand. The sound of the waves was good to his inward mind. The sun was fine on his bared shoulders. The wine was most excellent.

"I'll never get to go to Rio," said the other man. "Have you thought of that?"

"No, I—"

"And another thing. Your wife."

"What about her?" asked Braling, beginning to edge toward the door.

"I've grown quite fond of her."

"I'm glad you're enjoying your employment." Braling licked his lips nervously.

"I'm afraid you don't understand. I think—I'm in love with her."

Braling took another step and froze. "You're *what*?"

"And I've been thinking," said Braling Two, "how nice it is in Rio and how I'll never get there, and I've thought about your wife and—I think we could be very happy."

"T-that's nice." Braling strolled as casually as he could to the cellar door. "You won't mind waiting a moment, will you? I have to make a phone call."

"To whom?" Braling Two frowned.

"No one important."

"To Marionettes, Incorporated? To tell them to come get me?"

"No, no—nothing like that!" He tried to rush out the door.

A metal-firm grip seized his wrists. "Don't run!"

"Take your hands off!"

"No."

"Did my wife put you up to this?"

"No."

"Did she guess? Did she talk to you? Does she know? Is *that* it?" He screamed. A hand clapped over his mouth.

"You'll never know, will you?" Braling Two smiled delicately. "You'll never know."

Braling struggled. "She *must* have guessed; she *must* have affected you!"

Braling Two said, "I'm going to put you in the box, lock

it, and lose the key. Then I'll buy another Rio ticket for your wife."

"Now, now, wait a minute. Hold on. Don't be rash. Let's talk this over!"

"Good-by, Braling."

Braling stiffened. "What do you mean, 'good-by'?"

Ten minutes later Mrs. Braling awoke. She put her hand to her cheek. Someone had just kissed it. She shivered and looked up. "Why—you haven't done that in years," she murmured.

"We'll see what we can do about that," someone said.

The City

The city waited twenty thousand years.

The planet moved through space and the flowers of the fields grew up and fell away, and still the city waited; and the rivers of the planet rose and waned and turned to dust. Still the city waited. The winds that had been young and wild grew old and serene, and the clouds of the sky that had been ripped and torn were left alone to drift in idle whitenesses. Still the city waited.

The city waited with its windows and its black obsidian walls and its sky towers and its unpennanted turrets, with its untrod streets and its untouched doorknobs, with not a scrap of paper or a fingerprint upon it. The city waited while the planet arced in space, following its orbit about a blue-white sun, and the seasons passed from ice to fire and back to ice and then to green fields and yellow summer meadows.

It was on a summer afternoon in the middle of the twenty thousandth year that the city ceased waiting.

In the sky a rocket appeared.

The rocket soared over, turned, came back, and landed in the shale meadow fifty yards from the obsidian wall.

There were booted footsteps in the thin grass and calling voices from men within the rocket to men without.

"Ready?"

"All right, men. Careful! Into the city. Jensen, you and Hutchinson patrol ahead. Keep a sharp eye."

The city opened secret nostrils in its black walls and a steady suction vent deep in the body of the city drew storms of air back through channels, through thistle filters and dust collectors, to a fine and tremblingly delicate series of coils and webs which glowed with silver light. Again and again the immense suctions occurred; again and again the odors from the meadow were borne upon warm winds into the city.

"Fire odor, the scent of a fallen meteor, hot metal. A ship has come from another world. The brass smell, the dusty fire smell of burned powder, sulphur, and rocket brimstone."

This information, stamped on tapes which sprocketed into slots, slid down through yellow cogs into further machines.

Click-chakk-chakk-chakk.

A calculator made the sound of a metronome. Five, six, seven, eight, nine. Nine men! An instantaneous typewriter inked this message on tape which slithered and vanished.

Clickety-click-chakk-chakk.

The city awaited the soft tread of their rubberoid boots.

The great city nostrils dilated again.

The smell of butter. In the city air, from the stalking men, faintly, the aura which wafted to the great Nose broke down into memories of milk, cheese, ice cream, butter, the effluvium of a dairy economy.

Click-click.

"Careful, men!"

"Jones, get your gun out. Don't be a fool!"

"The city's dead; why worry?"

"You can't tell."

Now, at the barking talk, the Ears awoke. After centuries of listening to winds that blew small and faint, of hearing leaves strip from trees and grass grow softly in the time of melting snows, now the Ears oiled themselves in a self-lubrication, drew taut, great drums upon which the heartbeat of the invaders might pummel and thud delicately as the tremor of a gnat's wing. The Ears listened and the Nose siphoned up great chambers of odor.

The perspiration of frightened men arose. There were islands of sweat under their arms, and sweat in their hands as they held their guns.

The Nose sifted and worried this air, like a connoisseur busy with an ancient vintage.

Chikk-chikk-chakk-click.

Information rotated down on parallel check tapes. Perspiration; chlorides such and such percent; sulphates so-and-so; urea nitrogen, ammonia nitrogen, *thus:* creatinine, sugar, lactic acid, *there!*

Bells rang. Small totals jumped up.

The Nose whispered, expelling the tested air. The great Ears listened:

"I think we should go back to the rocket, Captain."

"I give the orders, Mr. Smith!"

"Yes, sir."

"You, up there! Patrol! See anything?"

"Nothing, sir. Looks like it's been dead for a long time!"

"You see, Smith? Nothing to fear."

"I don't like it. I don't know why. You ever feel you've seen a place before? Well, this city's too familiar."

"Nonsense. This planetary system's billions of miles from Earth; we couldn't possibly've been here ever before. Ours is the only light-year rocket in existence."

"That's how I feel, anyway, sir. I think we should get out."

The footsteps faltered. There was only the sound of the intruder's breath on the still air.

The Ear heard and quickened. Rotors glided, liquids glittered in small creeks through valves and blowers. A formula and a concoction—one followed another. Moments later, responding to the summons of the Ear and Nose, through giant holes in the city walls a fresh vapor blew out over the invaders.

"Smell *that*, Smith? Ahh. Green grass. Ever smell anything better? By God, I just like to stand here and smell it."

Invisible chlorophyll blew among the standing men.

"Ahh!"

The footsteps continued.

"Nothing wrong with *that*, eh, Smith? Come on!"

The Ear and Nose relaxed a billionth of a fraction. The countermove had succeeded. The pawns were proceeding forward.

Now the cloudy Eyes of the city moved out of fog and mist.

"Captain, the windows!"

"What?"

"Those house windows, there! I saw them move!"

"*I* didn't see it."

"They shifted. They changed color. From dark to light."

"Look like ordinary square windows to me."

Blurred objects focused. In the mechanical ravines of the city oiled shafts plunged, balance wheels dipped over into green oil pools. The window frames flexed. The windows gleamed.

Below, in the street, walked two men, a patrol, followed, at a safe interval, by seven more. Their uniforms were white, their faces as pink as if they had been slapped; their eyes were blue. They walked upright, upon hind legs, carrying metal weapons. Their feet were booted. They were males, with eyes, ears, mouths, noses.

The windows trembled. The windows thinned. They dilated imperceptibly, like the irises of numberless eyes.

"I tell you, Captain, it's the windows!"

"Get along."

"I'm going back, sir."

"What?"

"I'm going back to the rocket."

"Mr. Smith!"

"I'm not falling into any trap!"

"Afraid of an empty city?"

The others laughed, uneasily.

"Go on, laugh!"

The street was stone-cobbled, each stone three inches wide, six inches long. With a move unrecognizable as such, the street settled. It weighed the invaders.

In a machine cellar a red wand touched a numeral: 178 pounds . . . 210, 154, 201, 198—each man weighed, registered and the record spooled down into a correlative darkness.

Now the city was fully awake!

Now the vents sucked and blew air, the tobacco odor

from the invaders' mouths, the green soap scent from their hands. Even their eyeballs had a delicate odor. The city detected it, and this information formed totals which scurried down to total other totals. The crystal windows glittered, the Ear tautened and skinned the drum of its hearing tight, tighter—all of the senses of the city swarming like a fall of unseen snow, counting the respiration and the dim hidden heartbeats of the men, listening, watching, tasting.

For the streets were like tongues, and where the men passed, the taste of their heels ebbed down through stone pores to be calculated on litmus. This chemical totality, so subtly collected, was appended to the now increasing sums waiting the final calculation among the whirling wheels and whispering spokes.

Footsteps. Running.

"Come back! Smith!"

"No, blast you!"

"Get him, men!"

Footsteps rushing.

A final test. The city, having listened, watched, tasted, felt, weighed, and balanced, must perform a final task.

A trap flung wide in the street. The captain, unseen to the others, running, vanished.

Hung by his feet, a razor drawn across his throat, another down his chest, his carcass instantly emptied of its entrails, exposed upon a table under the street, in a hidden cell, the captain died. Great crystal microscopes stared at the red twines of muscle; bodiless fingers probed the still pulsing heart. The flaps of his sliced skin were pinned to the table while hands shifted parts of his body like a quick and curious player of chess, using the red pawns and the red pieces.

Above on the street the men ran. Smith ran, men

shouted. Smith shouted, and below in this curious room blood flowed into capsules, was shaken, spun, shoved on smear slides under further microscopes, counts made, temperatures taken, heart cut in seventeen sections, liver and kidneys expertly halved. Brain was drilled and scooped from bone socket, nerves pulled forth like the dead wires of a switchboard, muscles plucked for elasticity, while in the electric subterrene of the city the Mind at last totaled out its grandest total and all of the machinery ground to a monstrous and momentary halt.

The total.

These *are* men. These *are* men from a far world, a *certain* planet, and they have certain eyes, certain ears, and they walk upon legs in a specified way and carry weapons and think and fight, and they have particular hearts and all such organs as are recorded from long ago.

Above, men ran down the street toward the rocket.

Smith ran.

The total.

These are our enemies. These are the ones we have waited for twenty thousand years to see again. These are the men upon whom we waited to visit revenge. Everything totals. These are the men of a planet called Earth, who declared war upon Taollan twenty thousand years ago, who kept us in slavery and ruined us and destroyed us with a great disease. Then they went off to live in another galaxy to escape that disease which they visited upon us after ransacking our world. They have forgotten that war and that time, and they have forgotten us. But we have not forgotten them. These are our enemies. This is certain. Our waiting is done.

"Smith, come back!"

Quickly. Upon the red table, with the spread-eagled

captain's body empty, new hands began a fight of motion. Into the wet interior were placed organs of copper, brass. silver, aluminum, rubber and silk; spiders spun gold web which was stung into the skin; a heart was attached, and into the skull case was fitted a platinum brain which hummed and fluttered small sparkles of blue fire, and the wires led down through the body to the arms and legs. In a moment the body was sewn tight, the incisions waxed, healed at neck and throat and about the skull—perfect, fresh, new.

The captain sat up and flexed his arms.

"Stop!"

On the street the captain reappeared, raised his gun and fired.

Smith fell, a bullet in his heart.

The other men turned.

The captain ran to them.

"That fool! Afraid of a city!"

They look at the body of Smith at their feet.

They looked at their captain, and their eyes widened and narrowed.

"Listen to me," said the captain. "I have something important to tell you."

Now the city, which had weighed and tasted and smelled them, which had used all its powers save one, prepared to use its final ability, the power of speech. It did not speak with the rage and hostility of its massed walls or towers, nor with the bulk of its cobbled avenues and fortresses of machinery. It spoke with the quiet voice of one man.

"I am no longer your captain," he said. "Nor am I a man."

The men moved back.

"I am the city," he said, and smiled.

"I've waited two hundred centuries," he said. "I've waited for the sons of the sons of the sons to return."

"Captain, sir!"

"Let me continue. Who built me? The city. The men who died built me. The old race who once lived here. The people whom the Earthmen left to die of a terrible disease, a form of leprosy with no cure. And the men of that old race, dreaming of the day when Earthmen might return, built this city, and the name of this city was and is Revenge, upon the planet of Darkness, near the shore of the Sea of Centuries, by the Mountains of the Dead; all very poetic. This city was to be a balancing machine, a litmus, an antenna to test all future space travelers. In twenty thousand years only two other rockets landed here. One from a distant galaxy called Ennt, and the inhabitants of that craft were tested, weighed, found wanting, and let free, unscathed, from the city. As were the visitors in the second ship. But today! At long last, you've come! The revenge will be carried out to the last detail. Those men have been dead two hundred centuries, but they left a city here to welcome you."

"Captain, sir, you're not feeling well. Perhaps you'd better come back to the ship, sir."

The city trembled.

The pavements opened and the men fell, screaming. Falling, they saw bright razors flash to meet them!

Time passed. Soon came the call:

"Smith?"

"Here!"

"Jensen?"

"Here!"

"Jones, Hutchinson, Springer?"

"Here, here, here!"

They stood by the door of the rocket.

"We return to Earth immediately."

"Yes, sir!"

The incisions on their necks were invisible, as were their hidden brass hearts and silver organs and the fine golden wire of their nerves. There was a faint electric hum from their heads.

"On the double!"

Nine men hurried the golden bombs of disease culture into the rocket.

"These are to be dropped on Earth."

"Right, sir!"

The rocket valve slammed. The rocket jumped into the sky.

As the thunder faded, the city lay upon the summer meadow. Its glass eyes were dulled over. The Ear relaxed, the great nostril vents stopped, the streets no longer weighed or balanced, and the hidden machinery paused in its bath of oil.

In the sky the rocket dwindled.

Slowly, pleasurably, the city enjoyed the luxury of dying.

Zero Hour

Oh, it was to be so jolly! What a game! Such excitement they hadn't known in years. The children catapulted this way and that across the green lawns, shouting at each other, holding hands, flying in circles, climbing trees, laughing. Overhead the rockets flew, and beetle cars whispered by on the streets, but the children played on. Such fun, such tremulous joy, such tumbling and hearty screaming.

Mink ran into the house, all dirt and sweat. For her seven years she was loud and strong and definite. Her mother, Mrs. Morris, hardly saw her as she yanked out drawers and rattled pans and tools into a large sack.

"Heavens, Mink, what's going on?"

"The most exciting game ever!" gasped Mink, pink-faced.

"Stop and get your breath," said the mother.

"No, I'm all right," gasped Mink. "Okay I take these things, Mom?"

"But don't dent them," said Mrs. Morris.

"Thank you, thank you!" cried Mink, and boom! she was gone, like a rocket.

Mrs. Morris surveyed the fleeing tot. "What's the name of the game?"

"Invasion!" said Mink. The door slammed.

In every yard on the street children brought out knives and forks and pokers and old stovepipes and can openers.

It was an interesting fact that this fury and bustle occurred only among the younger children. The older ones, those ten years and more, disdained the affair and marched scornfully off on hikes or played a more dignified version of hide-and-seek on their own.

Meanwhile, parents came and went in chromium beetles. Repairmen came to repair the vacuum elevators in houses, to fix fluttering television sets or hammer upon stubborn food-delivery tubes. The adult civilization passed and repassed the busy youngsters, jealous of the fierce energy of the wild tots, tolerantly amused at their flourishings, longing to join in themselves.

"This and this and *this*," said Mink, instructing the others with their assorted spoons and wrenches. "Do that, and bring *that* over here. No! *Here*, ninny! Right. Now, get back while I fix this." Tongue in teeth, face wrinkled in thought. "Like that. See?"

"Yayyyy!" shouted the kids.

Twelve-year-old Joseph Connors ran up.

"Go away," said Mink straight at him.

"I wanna play," said Joseph.

"Can't!" said Mink.

"Why not?"

"You'd just make fun of us."

"Honest. I wouldn't."

"No. We know you. Go away or we'll kick you."

Another twelve-year-old boy whirred by on little motor skates. "Hey, Joe! Come on! Let them sissies play!"

Joseph showed reluctance and a certain wistfulness. "I want to play," he said.

"You're old," said Mink firmly.

"Not *that* old," said Joe sensibly.

"You'd only laugh and spoil the Invasion."

The boy on the motor skates made a rude lip noise. "Come on, Joe! Them and their fairies! Nuts!"

Joseph walked off slowly. He kept looking back, all down the block.

Mink was already busy again. She made a kind of apparatus with her gathered equipment. She had appointed another little girl with a pad and pencil to take down notes in painful slow scribbles. Their voices rose and fell in the warm sunlight.

All around them the city hummed. The streets were lined with good green and peaceful trees. Only the wind made a conflict across the city, across the country, across the continent. In a thousand other cities there were trees and children and avenues, businessmen in their quiet offices taping their voices or watching televisors. Rockets hovered like darning needles in the blue sky. There was the universal, quiet conceit and easiness of men accustomed to peace, quite certain there would never be trouble again. Arm in arm, men all over earth were a united front. The perfect weapons were held in equal trust by all nations. A situation of incredibly beautiful balance had been brought about. There were no traitors among men. No unhappy ones, no disgruntled ones; therefore the world was based upon a stable ground. Sunlight illumined half the world and the trees drowsed in a tide of warm air.

Mink's mother, from her upstairs window, gazed down.

The children. She looked upon them and shook her head. Well, they'd eat well, sleep well, and be in school on Monday. Bless their vigorous little bodies. She listened.

Mink talked earnestly to someone near the rose bush— though there was no one there.

These odd children. And the little girl, what was her name? Anna? Anna took notes on a pad. First, Mink asked the rosebush a question, then called the answer to Anna.

"Triangle," said Mink.

"What's a tri," said Anna with difficulty, "angle?"

"Never mind," said Mink.

"How you spell it?" asked Anna.

"T-r-i—" spelled Mink slowly, then snapped, "Oh, spell it yourself!" She went on to other words. "Beam," she said.

"I haven't got tri," said Anna, "angle down yet!"

"Well, hurry, hurry!" cried Mink.

Mink's mother leaned out the upstairs window. "A-n-g-l-e," she spelled down at Anna.

"Oh, thanks, Mrs. Morris," said Anna.

"Certainly," said Mink's mother and withdrew, laughing, to dust the hall with an electro-duster magnet.

The voices wavered on the shimmery air. "Beam," said Anna. Fading.

"Four-nine-seven-A-and-B-and-X," said Mink, far away, seriously. "And a fork and a string and a—hex-hex-agony— hexagonal!"

At lunch Mink gulped milk at one toss and was at the door. Her mother slapped the table.

"You sit right back down," commanded Mrs. Morris. "Hot soup in a minute." She poked a red button on the kitchen butler, and ten seconds later something landed with a bump in the rubber receiver. Mrs. Morris opened it, took out a can with a pair of aluminum holders, unsealed it with a flick, and poured hot soup into a bowl.

During all this Mink fidgeted. "Hurry, Mom! This is a matter of life and death! Aw—"

"I was the same way at your age. Always life and death. I know."

Mink banged away at the soup.

"Slow down," said Mom.

"Can't," said Mink. "Drill's waiting for me."

"Who's Drill? What a peculiar name," said Mom.

"You don't know him," said Mink.

"A new boy in the neighborhood?" asked Mom.

"He's new all right," said Mink. She started on her second bowl.

"Which one is Drill?" asked Mom.

"He's around," said Mink evasively. "You'll make fun. Everybody pokes fun. Gee, darn."

"Is Drill shy?"

"Yes. No. In a way. Gosh, Mom, I got to run if we want to have the Invasion!"

"Who's invading what?"

"Martians invading Earth. Well, not exactly Martians. They're—I don't know. From up." She pointed with her spoon.

"And *inside*," said Mom, touching Mink's feverish brow.

Mink rebelled. "You're laughing! You'll kill Drill and *every*body."

"I didn't mean to," said Mom. "Drill's a Martian?"

"No. He's—well—maybe from Jupiter or Saturn or Venus. Anyway, he's had a hard time."

"I imagine." Mrs. Morris hid her mouth behind her hand.

"They couldn't figure a way to attack Earth."

"We're impregnable." said Mom in mock seriousness.

"That's the word Drill used! Impreg—That was the word, Mom."

"My, my, Drill's a brilliant little boy. Two-bit words."

"They couldn't figure a way to attack. Mom. Drill says—he says in order to make a good fight you got to have a new way of surprising people. That way you win. And he says also you got to have help from your enemy."

"A fifth column," said Mom.

"Yeah. That's what Drill said. And they couldn't figure a way to surprise Earth or get help."

"No wonder. We're pretty darn strong," Mom laughed, cleaning up. Mink sat there, staring at the table, seeing what she was talking about.

"Until, one day," whispered Mink melodramatically, "they thought of children!"

"*Well!*" said Mrs. Morris brightly.

"And they thought of how grownups are so busy they never look under rosebushes or on lawns!"

"Only for snails and fungus."

"And then there's something about dim-dims."

"Dim-dims?"

"Dimens-shuns."

"Dimensions?"

"Four of 'em! And there's something about kids under nine and imagination. It's real funny to hear Drill talk."

Mrs. Morris was tired. "Well, it must be funny. You're keeping Drill waiting now. It's getting late in the day and, if you want to have your Invasion before your supper bath, you'd better jump."

"Do I have to take a bath?" growled Mink.

"You do. Why is it children hate water? No matter what age you live in children hate water behind the ears!"

"Drill says I won't have to take baths," said Mink.

"Oh, he does, does he?"

"He told all the kids that. No more baths. And we can stay up till ten o'clock and go to two televisor shows on Saturday 'stead of one!"

"Well, Mr. Drill better mind his p's and q's. I'll call up his mother and—"

Mink went to the door. "We're having trouble with guys like Pete Britz and Dale Jerrick. They're growing up. They make fun. They're worse than parents. They just won't believe in Drill. They're so snooty, 'cause they're growing up. You'd think they'd know better. They were little only a coupla years ago. I hate them worst. We'll kill them *first*."

"Your father and I last?"

"Drill says you're dangerous. Know why? 'Cause you don't believe in Martians! They're going to let *us* run the world. Well, not just us, but the kids over in the next block, too. I might be queen." She opened the door.

"Mom?"

"Yes?"

"What's lodge-ick?"

"Logic? Why, dear, logic is knowing what things are true and not true."

"He *mentioned* that," said Mink. "And what's im-pres-sion-able?" It took her a minute to say it.

"Why, it means—" Her mother looked at the floor, laughing gently. "It means—to be a child, dear."

"Thanks for lunch!" Mink ran out, then stuck her head back in. "Mom, I'll be sure you won't be hurt much, really!"

"Well, thanks," said Mom.

Slam went the door.

At four o'clock the audio-visor buzzed. Mrs. Morris flipped the tab. "Hello, Helen!" she said in welcome.

"Hello, Mary. How are things in New York?"

"Fine. How are things in Scranton? You look tired."

"So do you. The children. Underfoot," said Helen.

Mrs. Morris sighed. "My Mink too. The super-Invasion."

Helen laughed. "Are your kids playing that game too?"

"Lord, yes. Tomorrow it'll be geometrical jacks and motorized hopscotch. Were we this bad when we were kids in '48?"

"Worse. Japs and Nazis. Don't know how my parents put up with me. Tomboy."

"Parents learn to shut their ears."

A silence.

"What's wrong, Mary?" asked Helen.

Mrs. Morris's eyes were half closed, her tongue slid slowly, thoughtfully, over her lower lip. "Eh?" She jerked. "Oh, nothing. Just thought about *that*. Shutting ears and such. Never mind. Where were we?"

"My boy Tim's got a crush on some guy named—*Drill*, I think it was."

"Must be a new password. Mink likes him too."

"Didn't know it had got as far as New York. Word of mouth, I imagine. Looks like a scrap drive. I talked to Josephine and she said her kids—that's in Boston—are wild on this new game. It's sweeping the country."

At this moment Mink trotted into the kitchen to gulp a glass of water. Mrs. Morris turned. "How're things going?"

"Almost finished," said Mink.

"Swell," said Mrs. Morris. "What's *that*?"

"A yo-yo," said Mink. "Watch."

She flung the yo-yo down its string. Reaching the end it—It vanished.

"See?" said Mink. "Ope!" Dibbling her finger, she made the yo-yo reappear and zip up the string.

"Do that again," said her mother.

"Can't. Zero hour's five o'clock! 'By." Mink exited, zipping her yo-yo.

On the audio-visor, Helen laughed. "Tim brought one of those yo-yos in this morning, but when I got curious he said he wouldn't show it to me, and when I tried to work it, finally, it wouldn't work."

"You're not *impressionable*," said Mrs. Morris.

"What?"

"Never mind. Something I thought of. Can I help you, Helen?"

"I wanted to get that black-and-white cake recipe—"

The hour drowsed by. The day waned. The sun lowered in the peaceful blue sky. Shadows lengthened on the green lawns. The laughter and excitement continued. One little girl ran away, crying. Mrs. Morris came out the front door.

"Mink, was that Peggy Ann crying?"

Mink was bent over in the yard, near the rosebush. "Yeah. She's a scarebaby. We won't let her play, now. She's getting too old to play. I guess she grew up all of a sudden."

"Is that why she cried? Nonsense. Give me a civil answer, young lady, or inside you come!"

Mink whirled in consternation, mixed with irritation. "I can't quit now. It's almost time. I'll be good. I'm sorry."

"Did you hit Peggy Ann?"

"No, honest. You ask her. It was something—well, she's just a scaredy pants."

The ring of children drew in around Mink where she scowled at her work with spoons and a kind of square-shaped arrangement of hammers and pipes. "There and there," murmured Mink.

"What's wrong?" said Mrs. Morris.

"Drill's stuck. Halfway. If we could only get him all the way through, it'd be easier. Then all the others could come through after him."

"Can I help?"

"No'm, thanks. I'll fix it."

"All right. I'll call you for your bath in half an hour. I'm tired of watching you."

She went in and sat in the electric relaxing chair, sipping a little beer from a half-empty glass. The chair massaged her back. Children, children. Children and love and hate, side by side. Sometimes children loved you, hated you—all in half a second. Strange children, did they ever forget or forgive the whippings and the harsh, strict words of command? She wondered. How can you ever forget or forgive those over and above you, those tall and silly dictators?

Time passed. A curious, waiting silence came upon the street, deepening.

Five o'clock. A clock sang softly somewhere in the house in a quiet, musical voice: "Five o'clock—five o'clock. Time's a-wasting. Five o'clock," and purred away into silence.

Zero hour.

Mrs. Morris chuckled in her throat. Zero hour.

A beetle car hummed into the driveway. Mr. Morris. Mrs. Morris smiled. Mr. Morris got out of the beetle, locked it, and called hello to Mink at her work. Mink ignored him. He laughed and stood for a moment watching the children. Then he walked up the front steps.

"Hello, darling."

"Hello, Henry."

She strained forward on the edge of the chair, listening. The children were silent. Too silent.

He emptied his pipe, refilled it. "Swell day. Makes you glad to be alive."

Buzz.

"What's that?" asked Henry.

"I don't know." She got up suddenly, her eyes widening. She was going to say something. She stopped it. Ridiculous. Her nerves jumped. "Those children haven't anything dangerous out there, have they?" she said.

"Nothing but pipes and hammers. Why?"

"Nothing electrical?"

"Heck, no," said Henry. "I looked."

She walked to the kitchen. The buzzing continued. "Just the same, you'd better go tell them to quit. It's after five. Tell them—" Her eyes widened and narrowed. "Tell them to put off their Invasion until tomorrow." She laughed, nervously.

The buzzing grew louder.

"What are they up to? I'd better go look, all right."

The explosion!

The house shook with dull sound. There were other explosions in other yards on other streets.

Involuntarily, Mrs. Morris screamed. "Up this way!" she cried senselessly, knowing no sense, no reason. Perhaps she saw something from the corners of her eyes; perhaps she smelled a new odor or heard a new noise. There was no time to argue with Henry to convince him. Let him think her insane. Yes, insane! Shrieking, she ran upstairs. He ran after her to see what she was up to. "In the attic!" she screamed. "That's where it is!" It was only a poor excuse to get him in the attic in time. Oh, God—in time!

Another explosion outside. The children screamed with delight, as if at a great fireworks display.

"It's not in the attic!" cried Henry. "It's outside!"

"No, no!" Wheezing, gasping, she fumbled at the attic door. "I'll show you. Hurry! I'll show you!"

They tumbled into the attic. She slammed the door, locked it, took the key, threw it into a far, cluttered corner. She was babbling wild stuff now. It came out of her. All the subconscious suspicion and fear that had gathered secretly all afternoon and fermented like a wine in her. All the little revelations and knowledges and sense that had bothered her all day and which she had logically and carefully and sensibly rejected and censored. Now it exploded in her and shook her to bits.

"There, there," she said, sobbing against the door. "We're safe until tonight. Maybe we can sneak out. Maybe we can escape!"

Henry blew up too, but for another reason. "Are you crazy? Why'd you throw that key away? Damn it, honey!"

"Yes, yes, I'm crazy, if it helps, but stay here with me!"

"I don't know how in hell I *can* get out!"

"Quiet. They'll hear us. Oh, God, they'll find us soon enough—"

Below them, Mink's voice. The husband stopped. There was a great universal humming and sizzling, a screaming and giggling. Downstairs the audio-televisor buzzed and buzzed insistently, alarmingly, violently. *Is that Helen calling?* thought Mrs. Morris. *And is she calling about what I think she's calling about?*

Footsteps came into the house. Heavy footsteps.

"Who's coming in my house?" demanded Henry angrily. "Who's tramping around down there?"

Heavy feet. Twenty, thirty, forty, fifty of them. Fifty persons crowding into the house. The humming. The giggling of the children. "This way!" cried Mink, below.

"Who's downstairs?" roared Henry. "Who's there!"

"Hush. Oh, nononononono!" said his wife weakly, holding him. "Please, be quiet. They might go away."

"Mom?" called Mink. "Dad?" A pause. "Where are you?"

Heavy footsteps, heavy, heavy, *very heavy* footsteps, came up the stairs. Mink leading them.

"Mom?" A hesitation. "Dad?" A waiting, a silence.

Humming. Footsteps toward the attic. Mink's first.

They trembled together in silence in the attic, Mr. and Mrs. Morris. For some reason the electric humming, the queer cold light suddenly visible under the door crack, the strange odor and the alien sound of eagerness in Mink's voice finally got through to Henry Morris too. He stood, shivering, in the dark silence, his wife beside him.

"Mom! Dad!"

Footsteps. A little humming sound. The attic lock melted. The door opened. Mink peered inside, tall blue shadows behind her.

"Peekaboo," said Mink.

The Rocket

Many nights Fiorello Bodoni would awaken to hear the rockets sighing in the dark sky. He would tiptoe from bed, certain that his kind wife was dreaming, to let himself out into the night air. For a few moments he would be free of the smells of old food in the small house by the river. For a silent moment he would let his heart soar alone into space, following the rockets.

Now, this very night, he stood half naked in the darkness, watching the fire fountains murmuring in the air. The rockets on their long wild way to Mars and Saturn and Venus!

"Well, well, Bodoni."

Bodoni started.

On a milk crate, by the silent river, sat an old man who also watched the rockets through the midnight hush.

"Oh, it's you, Bramante!"

"Do you come out every night, Bodoni?"

"Only for the air."

"So? I prefer the rockets myself," said old Bramante. "I

was a boy when they started. Eighty years ago, and I've never been on one yet."

"I will ride up in one someday," said Bodoni.

"Fool!" cried Bramante. "You'll never go. This is a rich man's world." He shook his gray head, remembering. "When I was young they wrote it in fiery letters: THE WORLD OF THE FUTURE! Science, Comfort, and New Things for All! Ha! Eighty years. The Future becomes Now! Do we fly rockets? No! We live in shacks like our ancestors before us."

"Perhaps my *sons*—" said Bodoni.

"No, nor *their* sons!" the old man shouted. "It's the rich who have dreams and rockets!"

Bodoni hesitated. "Old man, I've saved three thousand dollars. It took me six years to save it. For my business, to invest in machinery. But every night for a month now I've been awake. I hear the rockets. I think. And tonight I've made up my mind. One of us will fly to Mars!" His eyes were shining and dark.

"Idiot," snapped Bramante. "How will you choose? Who will go? If you go, your wife will hate you, for you will be just a bit nearer God, in space. When you tell your amazing trip to her, over the years, won't bitterness gnaw at her?"

"No, no!"

"Yes! And your children? Will their lives be filled with the memory of Papa, who flew to Mars while they stayed here? What a senseless task you will set your boys. They will think of the rocket all their lives. They will lie awake. They will be sick with wanting it. Just as you are sick now. They will want to die if they cannot go. Don't set that goal, I warn you. Let them be content with being poor. Turn their eyes down to their hands and to your junk yard, not up to the stars."

"But—"

"Suppose your wife went? How would you feel, knowing she had *seen* and you had not? She would become holy. You would think of throwing her in the river. No, Bodoni, buy a new wrecking machine, which you need, and pull your dreams apart with it, and smash them to pieces."

The old man subsided, gazing at the river in which, drowned, images of rockets burned down the sky.

"Good night," said Bodoni.

"Sleep well," said the other.

When the toast jumped from its silver box, Bodoni almost screamed. The night had been sleepless. Among his nervous children, beside his mountainous wife, Bodoni had twisted and stared at nothing. Bramante was right. Better to invest the money. Why save it when only one of the family could ride the rocket, while the others remained to melt in frustration?

"Fiorello, eat your toast," said his wife, Maria.

"My throat is shriveled," said Bodoni.

The children rushed in, the three boys fighting over a toy rocket, the two girls carrying dolls which duplicated the inhabitants of Mars, Venus, and Neptune, green mannequins with three yellow eyes and twelve fingers.

"I saw the Venus rocket!" cried Paolo.

"It took off, *whoosh!*" hissed Antonello.

"Children!" shouted Bodoni, hands to his ears.

They stared at him. He seldom shouted.

Bodoni arose. "Listen, all of you," he said. "I have enough money to take one of us on the Mars rocket."

Everyone yelled.

"You understand?" he asked. "Only *one* of us. Who?"

"Me, me, me!" cried the children.

"You," said Maria.

"You," said Bodoni to her.

They all fell silent.

The children reconsidered. "Let Lorenzo go—he's oldest."

"Let Miriamne go—she's a girl!"

"Think what you would see," said Bodoni's wife to him. But her eyes were strange. Her voice shook. "The meteors, like fish. The universe. The Moon. Someone should go who could tell it well on returning. You have a way with words."

"Nonsense. So have you," he objected.

Everyone trembled.

"Here," said Bodoni unhappily. From a broom he broke straws of various lengths. "The short straw wins." He held out his tight fist. "Choose."

Solemnly each took his turn.

"Long straw."

"Long straw."

Another.

"Long straw."

The children finished. The room was quiet.

Two straws remained. Bodoni felt his heart ache in him. "Now," he whispered. "Maria."

She drew.

"The short straw," she said.

"Ah," sighed Lorenzo, half happy, half sad. "Mama goes to Mars."

Bodoni tried to smile. "Congratulations. I will buy your ticket today."

"Wait, Fiorello—"

"You can leave next week," he murmured.

She saw the sad eyes of her children upon her, with the smiles beneath their straight, large noses. She returned the straw slowly to her husband. "I cannot go to Mars."

"But why not?"

"I will be busy with another child."

"What!"

She would not look at him. "It wouldn't do for me to travel in my condition."

He took her elbow. "Is this the truth?"

"Draw again. Start over."

"Why didn't you tell me before?" he said incredulously.

"I didn't remember."

"Maria, Maria," he whispered, patting her face. He turned to the children. "Draw again."

Paolo immediately drew the short straw.

"I go to Mars!" He danced wildly. "Thank you, Father!"

The other children edged away. "That's swell, Paolo."

Paolo stopped smiling to examine his parents and his brothers and sisters. "I *can* go, can't I?" he asked uncertainly.

"Yes."

"And you'll *like* me when I come back?"

"Of course."

Paolo studied the precious broomstraw on his trembling hand and shook his head. He threw it away. "I forgot. School starts. I can't go. Draw again."

But none would draw. A full sadness lay on them.

"None of us will go," said Lorenzo.

"That's best," said Maria.

"Bramante was right," said Bodoni.

With his breakfast curdled within him, Fiorello Bodoni worked in his junk yard, ripping metal, melting it, pouring out usable ingots. His equipment flaked apart; competition had kept him on the insane edge of poverty for twenty years. It was a very bad morning.

In the afternoon a man entered the junk yard and called up to Bodoni on his wrecking machine. "Hey, Bodoni, I got some metal for you!"

"What is it, Mr. Mathews?" asked Bodoni, listlessly.

"A rocket ship. What's wrong? Don't you want it?"

"Yes, yes!" He seized the man's arm, and stopped, bewildered.

"Of course," said Mathews, "it's only a mockup. *You* know. When they plan a rocket they build a full-scale model first, of aluminum. You might make a small profit boiling her down. Let you have her for two thousand—"

Bodoni dropped his hand. "I haven't the money."

"Sorry. Thought I'd help you. Last time we talked you said how everyone outbid you on junk. Thought I'd slip this to you on the q.t. Well—"

"I need new equipment. I saved money for that."

"I understand."

"If I bought your rocket, I wouldn't even be able to melt it down. My aluminum furnace broke down last week—"

"Sure."

"I couldn't possibly use the rocket if I bought it from you."

"I know."

Bodoni blinked and shut his eyes. He opened them and looked at Mr. Mathews. "But I am a great fool. I will take my money from the bank and give it to you."

"But if you can't melt the rocket down—"

"Deliver it," said Bodoni.

"All right, if you say so. Tonight?"

"Tonight," said Bodoni, "would be fine. Yes, I would like to have a rocket ship tonight."

There was a moon. The rocket was white and big in the junk yard. It held the whiteness of the moon and the blueness of the stars. Bodoni looked at it and loved all of it. He wanted to pet it and lie against it, pressing it with his cheek, telling it all the secret wants of his heart.

He stared up at it. "You are all mine," he said. "Even if you never move or spit fire, and just sit there and rust for fifty years, you are mine."

The rocket smelled of time and distance. It was like walking into a clock. It was finished with Swiss delicacy. One might wear it on one's watch fob. "I might even sleep here tonight," Bodoni whispered excitedly.

He sat in the pilot's seat.

He touched a lever.

He hummed in his shut mouth, his eyes closed.

The humming grew louder, louder, higher, higher, wilder, stranger, more exhilarating, trembling in him and leaning him forward and pulling him and the ship in a roaring silence and in a kind of metal screaming, while his fists flew over the controls, and his shut eyes quivered, and the sound grew and grew until it was a fire, a strength, a lifting and a pushing of power that threatened to tear him in half. He gasped. He hummed again and again, and did not stop, for it could not be stopped, it could only go on, his eyes tighter, his heart furious. "Taking off!" he screamed. *The jolting concussion! The thunder!* "The Moon!" he cried, eyes blind, tight. "The meteors!" *The silent rush in volcanic light.* "Mars. Oh, God, Mars! Mars!"

He fell back, exhausted and panting. His shaking hands

came loose of the controls and his head tilted back wildly. He sat for a long time, breathing out and in, his heart slowing.

Slowly, slowly, he opened his eyes.

The junk yard was still there.

He sat motionless. He looked at the heaped piles of metal for a minute, his eyes never leaving them. Then, leaping up, he kicked the levers. "Take off, damn you!"

The ship was silent.

"I'll show you!" he cried.

Out in the night air, stumbling, he started the fierce motor of his terrible wrecking machine and advanced upon the rocket. He maneuvered the massive weights into the moonlit sky. He readied his trembling hands to plunge the weights, to smash, to rip apart this insolently false dream, this silly thing for which he had paid his money, which would not move, which would not do his bidding. "I'll teach you!" he shouted.

But his hand stayed.

The silver rocket lay in the light of the moon. And beyond the rocket stood the yellow lights of his home, a block away, burning warmly. He heard the family radio playing some distant music. He sat for half an hour considering the rocket and the house lights, and his eyes narrowed and grew wide. He stepped down from the wrecking machine and began to walk, and as he walked he began to laugh, and when he reached the back door of his house he took a deep breath and called, "Maria, Maria, start packing. We're going to Mars!"

"Oh!"

"Ah!"

"I can't *believe* it!"

"You will, you will."

The children balanced in the windy yard, under the glowing rocket, not touching it yet. They started to cry.

Maria looked at her husband. "What have you done?" she said. "Taken our money for this? It will never fly."

"It will fly," he said, looking at it.

"Rocket ships cost millions. Have you millions?"

"It will fly," he repeated steadily. "Now, go to the house, all of you. I have phone calls to make, work to do. Tomorrow we leave! Tell no one, understand? It is a secret."

The children edged off from the rocket, stumbling. He saw their small, feverish faces in the house windows, far away.

Maria had not moved. "You have ruined us," she said. "Our money used for this—this thing. When it should have been spent on equipment."

"You will see," he said.

Without a word she turned away.

"God help me," he whispered, and started to work.

Through the midnight hours trucks arrived, packages were delivered, and Bodoni, smiling, exhausted his bank account. With blowtorch and metal stripping he assaulted the rocket, added, took away, worked fiery magics and secret insults upon it. He bolted nine ancient automobile motors into the rocket's empty engine room. Then he welded the engine room shut, so none could see his hidden labor.

At dawn he entered the kitchen. "Maria," he said, "I'm ready for breakfast."

She would not speak to him.

*   *   *

At sunset he called to the children. "We're ready! Come on!" The house was silent.

"I've locked them in the closet," said Maria.

"What do you mean?" he demanded.

"You'll be killed in that rocket," she said. "What kind of rocket can you buy for two thousand dollars? A bad one!"

"Listen to me, Maria."

"It will blow up. Anyway, you are no pilot."

"Nevertheless. I can fly *this* ship. I have fixed it."

"You have gone mad," she said.

"Where is the key to the closet?"

"I have it here."

He put out his hand. "Give it to me."

She handed it to him. "You will kill them."

"No, no."

"Yes, you will. I *feel* it."

He stood before her. "You won't come along?"

"I'll stay here," she said.

"You will understand; you will see then," he said, and smiled. He unlocked the closet. "Come, children. Follow your father."

"Good-by, good-by, Mama!"

She stayed in the kitchen window, looking out at them, very straight and silent.

At the door of the rocket the father said, "Children, we will be gone a week. You must come back to school, and I to my business." He took each of their hands in turn. "Listen. This rocket is very old and will fly only *one* more journey. It will not fly again. This will be the one trip of your life. Keep your eyes wide."

"Yes, Papa."

"Listen, keep your ears clean. Smell the smells of a

rocket. *Feel. Remember.* So when you return you will talk of it all the rest of your lives."

"Yes, Papa."

The ship was quiet as a stopped clock. The airlock hissed shut behind them. He strapped them all, like tiny mummies, into rubber hammocks. "Ready?" he called.

"Ready!" all replied.

"Take-off!" He jerked ten switches. The rocket thundered and leaped. The children danced in their hammock, screaming.

"Here comes the Moon!"

The moon dreamed by. Meteors broke into fireworks. Time flowed away in a serpentine of gas. The children shouted. Released from their hammocks, hours later, they peered from the ports. "There's Earth!" "There's Mars!"

The rocket dropped pink petals of fire while the hour dials spun; the child eyes dropped shut. At last they hung like drunken moths in their cocoon hammocks.

"Good," whispered Bodoni, alone.

He tiptoed from the control room to stand for a long moment, fearful, at the airlock door.

He pressed a button. The airlock door swung wide. He stepped out. Into space? Into inky tides of meteor and gaseous torch? Into swift mileages and infinite dimensions?

No. Bodoni smiled.

All about the quivering rocket lay the junk yard.

Rusting, unchanged, there stood the padlocked junkyard gate, the little silent house by the river, the kitchen window lighted, and the river going down to the same sea. And in the center of the junk yard, manufacturing a magic dream, lay the quivering, purring rocket. Shaking and roaring, bouncing the netted children like flies in a web.

Maria stood in the kitchen window.

He waved to her and smiled.

He could not see if she waved or not. A small wave, perhaps. A small smile.

The sun was rising.

Bodoni withdrew hastily into the rocket. Silence. All still slept. He breathed easily. Tying himself into a hammock, he closed his eyes. To himself he prayed, Oh, let nothing happen to the illusion in the next six days. Let all of space come and go, and red Mars come up under our ship, and the moons of Mars, and let there be no flaws in the color film. Let there be three dimensions; let nothing go wrong with the hidden mirrors and screens that mold the fine illusion. Let time pass without crisis.

He awoke.

Red Mars floated near the rocket.

"Papa!" The children thrashed to be free.

Bodoni looked and saw red Mars and it was good and there was no flaw in it and he was very happy.

At sunset on the seventh day the rocket stopped shuddering.

"We are home." said Bodoni.

They walked across the junk yard from the open door of the rocket, their blood singing, their faces glowing.

"I have ham and eggs for all of you," said Maria, at the kitchen door.

"Mama, Mama, you should have come, to see it, to see Mars, Mama, and meteors, and everything!"

"Yes," she said.

At bedtime the children gathered before Bodoni. "We want to thank you, Papa."

"It was nothing."

"We will remember it for always, Papa. We will never forget."

Very late in the night Bodoni opened his eyes. He sensed that his wife was lying beside him, watching him. She did not move for a very long time, and then suddenly she kissed his cheeks and his forehead. "What's this?" he cried.

"You're the best father in the world," she whispered.

"Why?"

"Now I see," she said. "I understand."

She lay back and closed her eyes, holding his hand. "Is it a very lovely journey?" she asked.

"Yes," he said.

"Perhaps," she said, "perhaps, some night, you might take me on just a little trip, do you think?"

"Just a little one, perhaps," he said.

"Thank you," she said. "Good night."

"Good night," said Fiorello Bodoni.

The Illustrated Man

"Hey, the Illustrated Man!"

A calliope screamed, and Mr. William Philippus Phelps stood, arms folded, high on the summer-night platform, a crowd unto himself.

He was an entire civilization. In the Main Country, his chest, the Vasties lived—nipple-eyed dragons swirling over his fleshpot, his almost feminine breasts. His navel was the mouth of a slit-eyed monster—an obscene, in-sucked mouth, toothless as a witch. And there were secret caves where Darklings lurked, his armpits, adrip with slow subterranean liquors, where the Darklings, eyes jealously ablaze, peered out through rank creeper and hanging vine.

Mr. William Philippus Phelps leered down from his freak platform with a thousand peacock eyes. Across the sawdust meadow he saw his wife, Lisabeth, far away, ripping tickets in half, staring at the silver belt buckles of passing men.

Mr. William Philippus Phelps' hands were tattooed roses. At the sight of his wife's interest, the roses shriveled, as with the passing of sunlight.

A year before, when he had led Lisabeth to the marriage bureau to watch her work her name in ink, slowly, on the form, his skin had been pure and white and clean. He glanced down at himself in sudden horror. Now he was like a great painted canvas, shaken in the night wind! How had it happened? Where had it all begun?

It had started with the arguments, and then the flesh, and then the pictures. They had fought deep into the summer nights, she like a brass trumpet forever blaring at him. And he had gone out to eat five thousand steaming hot dogs, ten million hamburgers, and a forest of green onions, and to drink vast red seas of orange juice. Peppermint candy formed his brontosaur bones, the hamburgers shaped his balloon flesh, and strawberry pop pumped in and out of his heart valves sickeningly, until he weighed three hundred pounds.

"William Philippus Phelps," Lisabeth said to him in the eleventh month of their marriage, "you're dumb and fat."

That was the day the carnival boss handed him the blue envelope. "Sorry, Phelps. You're no good to me with all that gut on you."

"Wasn't I always your best tent man, boss?"

"Once. Not anymore. Now you sit, you don't get the work out."

"Let me be your Fat Man."

"I got a Fat Man. Dime a dozen." The boss eyed him up and down. "Tell you what, though. We ain't had a Tattooed Man since Gallery Smith died last year. . . ."

That had been a month ago. Four short weeks. From someone, he had learned of a tattoo artist far out in the rolling Wisconsin country, an old woman, they said, who knew her trade. If he took the dirt road and turned right at the river and then left . . .

He had walked out across a yellow meadow, which was crisp from the sun. Red flowers blew and bent in the wind as he walked, and he came to the old shack, which looked as if it had stood in a million rains.

Inside the door was a silent, bare room, and in the center of the bare room sat an ancient woman.

Her eyes were stitched with red resin-thread. Her nose was sealed with black wax-twine. Her ears were sewn, too, as if a darning-needle dragonfly had stitched all her senses shut. She sat, not moving, in the vacant room. Dust lay in a yellow flour all about, unfootprinted in many weeks; if she had moved it would have shown, but she had not moved. Her hands touched each other like thin, rusted instruments. Her feet were naked and obscene as rain rubbers, and near them sat vials of tattoo milk—red, lightning-blue, brown, cat-yellow. She was a thing sewn tight into whispers and silence.

Only her mouth moved, unsewn: "Come in. Sit down. I'm lonely here."

He did not obey.

"You came for the pictures," she said in a high voice. "I have a picture to show you first."

She tapped a blind finger to her thrust-out palm. "See!" she cried.

It was a tattoo-portrait of William Philippus Phelps.

"Me!" he said.

Her cry stopped him at the door. "Don't run."

He held to the edges of the door, his back to her. "That's me, that's me on your hand!"

"It's been there fifty years." She stroked it like a cat, over and over.

He turned. "It's an *old* tattoo." He drew slowly nearer. He edged forward and bent to blink at it. He put out a

trembling finger to brush the picture. "Old. That's impossible!
You don't know *me*. I don't know *you*. Your eyes, all sewed
shut."

"I've been waiting for you." she said. "And many people."
She displayed her arms and legs, like the spindles of an an-
tique chair. "I have pictures on me of people who have already come here to see me. And there are other pictures of
other people who are coming to see me in the next one
hundred years. And you, you have come."

"How do you know it's me? You can't see!"

"You *feel* like the lions, the elephants, and the tigers to
me. Unbutton your shirt. You need me. Don't be afraid. My
needles are as clean as a doctor's fingers. When I'm finished
with illustrating you, I'll wait for someone else to walk along
out here and find me. And someday, a hundred summers from
now, perhaps, I'll just go lie down in the forest under some
white mushrooms, and in the spring you won't find anything
but a small blue cornflower. . . ."

He began to unbutton his sleeves.

"I know the Deep Past and the Clear Present and the
even Deeper Future," she whispered, eyes knotted into blindness, face lifted to this unseen man. "It is on my flesh. I will
paint it on yours, too. You will be the only *real* illustrated
Man in the universe. I'll give you special pictures you will
never forget. Pictures of the Future on your skin."

She pricked him with a needle.

He ran back to the carnival that night in a drunken
terror and elation. Oh, how quickly the old dust-witch had
stitched him with color and design. At the end of a long
afternoon of being bitten by a silver snake, his body was
alive with portraiture. He looked as if he had dropped and

been crushed between the steel rollers of a print press, and come out like an incredible rotogravure. He was clothed in a garment of trolls and scarlet dinosaurs.

"Look!" he cried to Lisabeth. She glanced up from her cosmetic table as he tore his shirt away. He stood in the naked bulb-light of their car-trailer, expanding his impossible chest. Here, the Tremblies, half-maiden, half-goat, leaping when his biceps flexed. Here, the Country of Lost Souls, his chins. In so many accordion pleats of fat, numerous small scorpions, beetles, and mice were crushed, held, hid, darting into view, vanishing, as he raised or lowered his chins.

"My God," said Lisabeth. "My husband's a freak."

She ran from the trailer and he was left alone to pose before the mirror. Why had he done it? To have a job, yes, but, most of all, to cover the fat that had larded itself impossibly over his bones. To hide the fat under a layer of color and fantasy, to hide it from his wife, but most of all from himself.

He thought of the old woman's last words. She had needled him two *special* tattoos, one on his chest, another for his back, which she would not let him see. She covered each with cloth and adhesive.

"You are not to look at these two," she had said.

"Why?"

"Later, you may look. The Future is in these pictures. You can't look now or it may spoil them. They are not quite finished. I put ink on your flesh, and the sweat of you forms the rest of the picture, the Future—your sweat and your thought." Her empty mouth grinned. "Next Saturday night, you may advertise! The Big Unveiling! Come see the Illustrated Man unveil his picture! You can make money in that way. You can charge admission to the Unveiling, like to an art gallery. Tell them you have a picture that even *you* never have seen, that *nobody* has seen yet. The most unusual picture ever painted. Almost alive. And it tells the Future. Roll the drums and blow the trumpets. And you can stand there and unveil at the Big Unveiling."

"That's a good idea," he said.

"But only unveil the picture on your chest," she said. "That is first. You must save the picture on your back, under the adhesive, for the following week. Understand?"

"How much do I owe you?"

"Nothing," she said. "If you walk with these pictures on you, I will be repaid with my own satisfaction. I will sit here for the next two weeks and think how clever my pictures are, for I make them fit each man himself and what is inside him. Now, walk out of this house and never come back. Good-by."

"Hey! The Big Unveiling!"

The red signs blew in the night wind: NO ORDINARY TATTOOED MAN! THIS ONE IS "ILLUSTRATED"! GREATER THAN MICHELANGELO! TONIGHT! ADMISSION 10 CENTS!

Now the hour had come. Saturday night, the crowd stirring their animal feet in the hot sawdust.

"In one minute—" the carny boss pointed his cardboard megaphone—"in the tent immediately to my rear, we will unveil the Mysterious Portrait upon the Illustrated Man's chest! Next Saturday night, the same hour, same location, we'll unveil the Picture upon the Illustrated Man's *back!* Bring your friends!"

There was a stuttering roll of drums.

Mr. William Philippus Phelps jumped back and vanished; the crowd poured into the tent, and, once inside, found him re-established upon another platform, the band brassing out a jig-time melody.

He looked for his wife and saw her, lost in the crowd, like a stranger, come to watch a freakish thing, a look of contemptuous curiosity upon her face. For, after all, he was her husband, this was a thing she didn't know about him herself. It gave him a feeling of great height and warmness and light to find himself the center of the jangling universe, the carnival world, for one night. Even the other freaks—the Skeleton, the Seal Boy, the Yoga, the Magician, and the Balloon—were scattered through the crowd.

"Ladies and gentlemen, the great moment!"

A trumpet flourish, a hum of drumsticks on tight cowhide.

Mr. William Philippus Phelps let his cape fall. Dinosaurs, trolls, and half-women-half-snakes writhed on his skin in the stark light.

Ah, murmured the crowd, for surely there had never been a tattooed man like this! The beast eyes seemed to take red fire and blue fire, blinking and twisting. The roses on his fingers seemed to expel a sweet pink bouquet. The Tyrannosaurus rex reared up along his leg, and the sound of the brass trumpet in the hot tent heavens was a prehistoric cry from the red monster throat. Mr. William Philippus Phelps was a museum jolted to life. Fish swam in seas of electric-blue ink. Fountains sparkled under yellow suns. Ancient buildings stood in meadows of harvest wheat. Rockets burned across spaces of muscle and flesh. The slightest inhalation of his breath threatened to make chaos of the entire printed universe. He seemed afire, the creatures flinching from the flame, drawing back from the great heat of his pride, as he expanded under the audience's rapt contemplation.

The carny boss laid his fingers to the adhesive. The audience rushed forward, silent in the oven vastness of the night tent.

"You ain't seen nothing yet!" cried the carny boss.

The adhesive ripped free.

There was an instant in which nothing happened. An instant in which the Illustrated Man thought that the Unveiling was a terrible and irrevocable failure.

But then the audience gave a low moan.

The carny boss drew back, his eyes fixed.

Far out at the edge of the crowd, a woman, after a moment, began to cry, began to sob, and did not stop.

Slowly, the Illustrated Man looked down at his naked chest and stomach.

The thing that he saw made the roses on his hands discolor and die. All of his creatures seemed to wither, turn inward, shrivel with the arctic coldness that pumped from his heart outward to freeze and destroy them. He stood trembling. His hands floated up to touch that incredible picture, which lived, moved and shivered with life. It was like gazing into a small room, seeing a thing of someone else's life so intimate, so impossible that one could not believe and one could not long stand to watch without turning away.

It was a picture of his wife, Lisabeth, and himself.

And he was killing her.

Before the eyes of a thousand people in a dark tent in the center of a black-forested Wisconsin land, he was killing his wife.

His great flowered hands were upon her throat, and her face was turning dark and he killed her and he killed her and did not ever in the next minute stop killing her. It was real. While the crowd watched, she died, and he turned very sick.

He was about to fall straight down into the crowd. The tent whirled like a monster bat wing, flapping grotesquely. The last thing he heard was a woman, sobbing, far out on the shore of the silent crowd.

And the crying woman was Lisabeth, his wife.

In the night, his bed was moist with perspiration. The carnival sounds had melted away, and his wife, in her own bed, was quiet now, too. He fumbled with his chest. The adhesive was smooth. They had made him put it back.

He had fainted. When he revived, the carny boss had yelled at him, "Why didn't you *say* what the picture was like?"

"I didn't know, I didn't," said the Illustrated Man.

"Good God!" said the boss. "Scare hell outa everyone. Scared hell outa Lizzie, scared hell outa me. Christ, where'd you *get* that damn tattoo?" He shuddered. "Apologize to Lizzie, now."

His wife stood over him.

"I'm sorry, Lisabeth," he said, weakly, his eyes closed. "I didn't know."

"You did it on purpose," she said. "To scare me."

"I'm sorry."

"Either it goes or I go," she said.

"Lisabeth."

"You heard me. That picture comes off or I quit this show."

"Yeah, Phil," said the boss. "That's how it is."

"Did you lose money? Did the crowd demand refunds?"

"It ain't the money, Phil. For that matter, once the word got around, hundreds of people wanted in. But I'm runnin' a clean show. That tattoo comes off! Was this your idea of a practical joke, Phil?"

He turned in the warm bed. No, not a joke. Not a joke

at all. He had been as terrified as anyone. Not a joke. That little old dust-witch, what had she *done* to him and how had she done it? Had she put the picture there? No; she had said that the picture was unfinished, and that he himself, with his thoughts and perspiration, would finish it. Well, he had done the job all right.

But what, if anything, was the significance? He didn't want to kill anyone. He didn't want to kill Lisabeth. Why should such a silly picture burn here on his flesh in the dark?

He crawled his fingers softly, cautiously down to touch the quivering place where the hidden portrait lay. He pressed tight, and the temperature of that spot was enormous. He could almost feel that little evil picture killing and killing and killing all through the night.

I don't wish to kill her, he thought, insistently, looking over at her bed. And then, five minutes later, he whispered aloud: "Or *do* I?"

"What?" she cried, awake.

"Nothing," he said, after a pause, "Go to sleep."

The man bent forward, a buzzing instrument in his hand. "This costs five bucks an inch. Costs more to peel tattoos off than put 'em on. Okay, jerk the adhesive."

The Illustrated Man obeyed.

The skin man sat back. "Christ! No wonder you want that off! That's ghastly. *I* don't even want to look at it." He flicked his machine. "Ready? This won't hurt."

The carny boss stood in the tent flap, watching. After five minutes, the skin man changed the instrument head, cursing. Ten minutes later he scraped his chair back and scratched his head. Half an hour passed and he got up, told Mr. William Philippus Phelps to dress, and packed his kit.

"Wait a minute," said the carny boss. "You ain't done the job."

"And I ain't going to," said the skin man.

"I'm paying good money. What's wrong?"

"Nothing, except that damn picture just won't come off. Damn thing must go right down to the bone."

"You're crazy."

"Mister, I'm in business thirty years and never seen a tattoo like this. An inch deep, if it's anything."

"But I've got to get it off!" cried the Illustrated Man.

The skin man shook his head. "Only one way to get rid of that."

"How?"

"Take a knife and cut off your chest. You won't live long, but the picture'll be gone."

"Come back here!"

But the skin man walked away.

They could hear the big Sunday-night crowd, waiting.

"That's a big crowd," said the Illustrated Man.

"But they ain't going to see what they came to see," said the carny boss. "You ain't going out there, except with the adhesive. Hold still now, I'm curious about this *other* picture, on your back. We might be able to give 'em an Unveiling on this one instead."

"She said it wouldn't be ready for a week or so. The old woman said it would take time to set, make a pattern."

There was a soft ripping as the carny boss pulled aside a flap of white tape on the Illustrated Man's spine.

"What do you see?" gasped Mr. Phelps, bent over.

The carny boss replaced the tape. "Buster, as a Tattooed

Man, you're a washout, ain't you? Why'd you let that old dame fix you up this way?"

"I didn't know who she was."

"She sure cheated you on this one. No design to it. Nothing. No picture at all."

"It'll come clear. You wait and see."

The boss laughed. "Okay. Come on. We'll show the crowd part of you, anyway."

They walked out into an explosion of brassy music.

He stood monstrous in the middle of the night, putting out his hands like a blind man to balance himself in a world now tilted, now rushing, now threatening to spin him over and down into the mirror before which he raised his hands. Upon the flat, dimly lighted table top were peroxide, acids, silver razors, and squares of sandpaper. He took each of them in turn. He soaked the vicious tattoo upon his chest, he scraped at it. He worked steadily for an hour.

He was aware, suddenly, that someone stood in the trailer door behind him. It was three in the morning. There was a faint odor of beer. She had come home from town. He heard her slow breathing. He did not turn. "Lisabeth?" he said.

"You'd better get rid of it," she said, watching his hands move the sandpaper. She stepped into the trailer.

"I didn't want the picture this way," he said.

"You did," she said. "You planned it."

"I didn't."

"I know you," she said. "Oh, I know you hate me. Well, that's nothing. I hate you. I've hated you a long time now. Good God, when you started putting on the fat, you think anyone could love you then? I could teach you some things about hate. Why don't you ask me?"

"Leave me alone," he said.

"In front of that crowd, making a spectacle out of me!"

"I didn't know what was under the tape."

She walked around the table, hands fitted to her hips, talking to the beds, the walls, the table, talking it all out of her. And he thought: *Or did I know? Who made this picture, me or the witch? Who formed it? How? Do I really want her dead? No! And yet.* . . . He watched his wife draw nearer, nearer, he saw the ropy strings of her throat vibrate to her shouting. This and this and *this* was wrong with him! That and that and *that* was unspeakable about him! He was a liar, a schemer, a fat, lazy, ugly man, a child. Did he think he could compete with the carny boss or the tentpeggers? Did he think he was sylphine and graceful, did he think he was a framed El Greco? DaVinci, huh! Michelangelo, my eye! She brayed. She showed her teeth. "Well, you can't scare me into staying with someone I don't want touching me with their slobby paws!" she finished, triumphantly.

"Lisabeth," he said.

"Don't Lisabeth me!" she shrieked. "I know your plan. You had that picture put on to scare me. You thought I wouldn't *dare* leave you. Well!"

"Next Saturday night, the Second Unveiling," he said. "You'll be proud of me."

"Proud! You're silly and pitiful. God, you're like a whale. You ever see a beached whale? I saw one when I was a kid. There it was, and they came and shot it. Some lifeguards shot it. Jesus, a whale!"

"Lisabeth."

"I'm leaving, that's all, and getting a divorce."

"Don't."

"And I'm marrying a man, not a fat woman—that's what you are, so much fat on you there ain't no sex!"

"You can't leave me," he said.

"Just watch!"

"I love you," he said.

"Oh," she said. "Go look at your pictures."

He reached out.

"Keep your hands off," she said.

"Lisabeth."

"Don't come near. You turn my stomach."

"Lisabeth."

All the eyes of his body seemed to fire, all the snakes to move, all the monsters to seethe, all the mouths to widen and rage. He moved toward her—not like a man, but a crowd.

He felt the great blooded reservoir of orangeade pump through him now, the sluice of cola and rich lemon pop pulse in sickening sweet anger through his wrists, his legs, his heart. All of it, the oceans of mustard and relish and all the million drinks he had drowned himself in in the last year were aboil; his face was the color of a steamed beef. And the pink roses of his hands became those hungry, carnivorous flowers kept long years in tepid jungle and now let free to find their way on the night air before him.

He gathered her to him, like a great beast gathering in a struggling animal. It was a frantic gesture of love, quickening and demanding, which, as she struggled, hardened to another thing. She beat and clawed at the picture on his chest.

"You've got to love me, Lisabeth."

"Let go!" she screamed. She beat at the picture that

burned under her fists. She slashed at it with her finger-nails.

"Oh, Lisabeth," he said, his hands moving up her arms.

"I'll scream," she said, seeing his eyes.

"Lisabeth." The hands moved up to her shoulders, to her neck. "Don't go away."

"Help!" she screamed. The blood ran from the picture on his chest.

He put his fingers about her neck and squeezed.

She was a calliope cut in mid-shriek.

Outside, the grass rustled. There was the sound of running feet.

Mr. William Philippus Phelps opened the trailer door and stepped out.

They were waiting for him. Skeleton, Midget, Balloon, Yoga, Electra, Popeye, Seal Boy. The freaks, waiting in the middle of the night, in the dry grass.

He walked toward them. He moved with a feeling that he must get away; these people would understand nothing, they were not thinking people. And because he did not flee, because he only walked, balanced, stunned, between the tents, slowly, the freaks moved to let him pass. They watched him, because their watching guaranteed that he would not escape. He walked out across the black meadow, moths fluttering in his face. He walked steadily as long as he was visible, not knowing where he was going. They watched him go, and then they turned and all of them shuffled to the silent car-trailer together and pushed the door slowly wide. . . .

The Illustrated Man walked steadily in the dry meadows beyond the town.

"He went that way!" a faint voice cried. Flashlights bobbled over the hills. There were dim shapes, running.

Mr. William Philippus Phelps waved to them. He was tired. He wanted only to be found now. He was tired of running away. He waved again.

"There he is!" The flashlights changed direction. "Come on! We'll get the bastard!"

When it was time, the Illustrated Man ran again. He was careful to run slowly. He deliberately fell down twice. Looking back, he saw the tent stakes they held in their hands.

He ran toward a far crossroads lantern, where all the summer night seemed to gather: merry-go-rounds of fireflies whirling, crickets moving their song toward that light, everything rushing, as if by some midnight attraction, toward that one high-hung lantern—the Illustrated Man first, the others close at his heels.

As he reached the light and passed a few yards under and beyond it, he did not need to look back. On the road ahead, in silhouette, he saw the upraised tent stakes sweep violently up, up, and then *down!*

A minute passed.

In the country ravines, the crickets sang. The freaks stood over the sprawled Illustrated Man, holding their tent stakes loosely.

Finally they rolled him over on his stomach. Blood ran from his mouth.

They ripped the adhesive from his back. They stared down for a long moment at the freshly revealed picture. Someone whispered. Someone else swore, softly. The Thin Man pushed back and walked away and was sick. Another and another of the freaks stared, their mouths trembling, and moved away, leaving the Illustrated Man on the deserted road, the blood running from his mouth.

In the dim light, the unveiled Illustration was easily seen.

It showed a crowd of freaks bending over a dying fat man on a dark and lonely road, looking at a tattoo on his back which illustrated a crowd of freaks bending over a dying fat man on a . . .

Epilogue

It was almost midnight. The moon was high in the sky now. The Illustrated Man lay motionless. I had seen what there was to see. The stories were told; they were over and done.

There remained only that empty space upon the Illustrated Man's back, that area of jumbled colors and shapes. Now, as I watched, the vague patch began to assemble itself, in slow dissolvings from one shape to another and still another. And at last a face formed itself there, a face that gazed out at me from the colored flesh, a face with a familiar nose and mouth, familiar eyes.

It was very hazy. I saw only enough of the Illustration to make me leap up. I stood there in the moonlight, afraid that the wind or the stars might move and wake the monstrous gallery at my feet. But he slept on, quietly.

The picture on his back showed the Illustrated Man himself, with his fingers about my neck, choking me to death. I didn't wait for it to become clear and sharp and a definite picture.

I ran down the road in the moonlight. I didn't look back. A small town lay ahead, dark and asleep. I knew that, long before morning, I would reach the town. . . .